BLACKSTONE AND THE NEW WORLD

Recent Titles by Sally Spencer from Severn House

THE BUTCHER BEYOND
DANGEROUS GAMES
THE DARK LADY
DEAD ON CUE
DEATH OF A CAVE DWELLER
DEATH OF AN INNOCENT
A DEATH LEFT HANGING
DEATH WATCH
DYING IN THE DARK
A DYING FALL
THE ENEMY WITHIN
FATAL QUEST
GOLDEN MILE TO MURDER
A LONG TIME DEAD
MURDER AT SWANN'S LAKE
THE PARADISE JOB
THE RED HERRING
THE SALTON KILLINGS
SINS OF THE FATHERS
STONE KILLER
THE WITCH MAKER

The Inspector Sam Blackstone Series

RENDEZVOUS WITH DEATH
BLACKSTONE AND THE TIGER
BLACKSTONE AND THE GOLDEN EGG
BLACKSTONE AND THE FIRE BUG
BLACKSTONE AND THE BALLOOON OF DEATH
BLACKSTONE AND THE HEART OF DARKNESS

BLACKSTONE AND THE NEW WORLD

An Inspector Blackstone Mystery

Sally Spencer

This first world edition published 2009
in Great Britain and in the USA by
SEVERN HOUSE PUBLISHERS LTD of
9–15 High Street, Sutton, Surrey, England, SM1 1DF.
Trade paperback edition published
in Great Britain and the USA 2009 by
SEVERN HOUSE PUBLISHERS LTD

British Library Cataloguing in Publication Data

Rustage, Alan
   Blackstone and the new world
   1. Blackstone, Sam (Fictitious character) - Fiction
   2. Police - New York (State) - New York - Fiction 3. New
   York (N.Y.) - Social life and customs - 20th century -
   Fiction 4. Detective and mystery stories
   I. Title
      823.9'14 [F]

   ISBN-13: 978-0-7278-6754-4   (cased)
   ISBN-13: 978-1-84751-121-8   (trade paper)

All Severn House titles are printed on acid-free paper.

Typeset by Palimpsest Book Production Ltd.,
Grangemouth, Stirlingshire, Scotland.
Printed and bound in Great Britain by
MPG Books Ltd., Bodmin, Cornwall.

For Martin Chambers, with thanks

PROLOGUE

New York City, 23rd August 1900

The beer hall's sole purpose was to make the burly men in lederhosen forget that they had left their home country for ever, and in this it was a great success.

They sat, squeezed tightly together, at the long wooden tables. Some rubbed shoulders with lifelong friends, some with casual acquaintances and some with men they had only just met. None of that mattered, because they were all Bavarians, and when one spoke of the mountains and lakes he had once known, they all pictured it in their minds.

They drank foaming beer from stone steins, and nibbled at large German sausages. They swayed – gently and in unison – to the syrupy music which was being pumped out by the two accordionists on the small stage. Occasionally, one of them would sing, and even if his voice was not particularly strong, the others would beat out the time on the table in a gesture of solidarity – for though they all led separate lives on the outside, in here they were a single entity.

But there was one man – alone at the bar counter – who stood out as different. It was not simply his clothing which distinguished him, though his sober suit certainly *looked* out of place. Nor was it the fact that he was not German–American. What truly set him apart was the fact that he was clearly not having a good time.

Inspector Patrick O'Brien took a listless sip of his beer and checked his pocket watch for perhaps the fifth or sixth time.

He felt a bubbling in his stomach – like Irish stew boiling over – and accepted, with some reluctance, that he was nervous. It was a new experience for him. He had spent the previous seven years investigating police corruption, and in that time there had been death threats – and even one actual assassination attempt – yet his nerve had held throughout it all. But this was different. This was more important. His fate – and the fate of others – was being held in the balance.

He checked his watch again.

His contact was late.

Very late.

A tuba player had now joined the accordionists on the stage, and the music, while not losing any of its sentimentality, had become more strident.

O'Brien fought the temptation to glance at his watch again, knowing that – at most – a minute had passed since he'd last looked at it.

'*Noch einer?*' asked the barman.

'I beg your pardon?'

'Would you like another beer?'

O'Brien looked down at his stein, and saw that it was nearly empty.

'No, I . . . no, thank you, I've had enough.'

The barman gave him a look which said that a real man would be on his third or fourth drink by now, then turned away dismissively.

It had seemed like a good idea to arrange the rendezvous somewhere he was not known himself, but which was familiar territory to his contact, O'Brien thought. But now – as he saw that at least one of the drinkers was casting curious glances in his direction – he was beginning to think it had been a mistake.

And that was not the *only* mistake he had made.

It had been a mistake to go and see Senator Plunkitt – a sign of weakness that, even after this matter was resolved, a devious man like Plunkitt might be able to use against him.

His fingers instinctively reached for the chain which held his pocket watch, and it was only with considerable mental effort that he forced them to withdraw again.

Perhaps he should tell the barman that he wanted another beer after all, he thought, for though he was not normally much of a drinker, it might do him good to get really rolling drunk just this once.

'Fool!' he snapped at himself. 'Coward!'

And it was only when the barman turned around and looked at him enquiringly that he realized he must not only have said the words aloud, but also rather loudly.

It was more to save an explanation, rather than for any other reason, that O'Brien turned and walked towards the frosted-glass door which led out of the beer hall.

It wasn't a retreat, he told himself as he reached for the door handle. It wasn't even a tactical withdrawal. He was simply leaving the place because there was no point in staying there any longer.

It was his natural caution, he had long been convinced, which had kept him alive for so long, and, once outside, O'Brien quickly checked the street.

There was not a great deal to see. The shops had closed, so both the shoppers and traders who had been so much in evidence when he'd entered the beer hall had now completely vanished. Nor was there any sign of any other foot traffic – those men set on drinking in a saloon had already reached their destination, and those men intending to leave a saloon and go home were certainly not planning to make any such move yet.

It was perhaps *because* the street was so tranquil that he was alarmed when, from the corner of his eye, he detected a sudden movement.

He turned quickly. From out of the shadows beyond the nearest street light, a figure had emerged, and was running towards him. His first instinct was to reach for his revolver, but then he let his hand fall to his side again.

The runner was only a boy – probably fourteen or fifteen at the most – and a very *poor* boy, judging by his threadbare jacket and shabby pants.

And was he – *a police inspector* – to take out his weapon to defend himself against a mere child?

Of course not!

Yet the closer the boy got to him, the more concerned Patrick O'Brien became.

In part, this was due to the *way* the boy was running – zigzagging as if he expected to come under fire at any moment.

In part, it was because, though it was a pleasantly warm evening, the boy had his cap pulled down over his eyes and had covered the lower half of his face with a muffler.

The boy was no more than a few yards away when he reached into his jacket pocket and pulled out a pistol.

Cursing his own stupidity – his own complacency – O'Brien went for his revolver, this time in earnest. He did not *want* to kill a child, but since the child was clearly intending to kill him, he had very little choice in the matter.

His fingers had only just made contact with the handle of

his Colt when he felt something slam heavily into his chest, and realized he had left it too late.

He staggered backwards, and was still trying to pull his weapon clear when the second jolt came, followed rapidly by a third.

His legs would no longer support him, and he fell heavily to the ground. He noted, with some surprise, that the fall seemed to have caused him more pain than the bullets.

So perhaps he was not badly wounded after all.

Perhaps he would survive.

But even if he lived, his recovery would take months, his fevered brain reminded him – and he did not *have* months, because what he needed to do, he needed to do *now*.

Maybe they're nothing more than flesh wounds, he thought desperately. Maybe I'll be back on my feet in a day or two.

But he knew that he had been hit three times – squarely in the chest. And he knew that the pain now coursing round his body was greater than any pain he had ever experienced before.

He heard the sound of fast footfalls as his assassin ran away.

And then he died.

ONE

Since the moment they had both embarked on the ship at Liverpool, Hiram Johnson had been fascinated by the brown-suited Englishman.

The suit itself had been the starting point of this fascination. It was, to be frank (and Johnson valued frankness as a thoroughly American virtue), not quite 'the thing'. It might once, in its heyday, have been classified as a *good* suit, but those days of glory were far behind it now, and while such apparel might have gone unnoticed in the steerage section of the ship, it stood out like a sore thumb within the universe that was the second-class deck.

So why would a man who could afford to pay the forty dollars passage money not buy himself another, smarter suit? Johnson asked himself.

The man inside the suit was also worthy of further study.

He was rather tall for an Englishman – over six foot – and as thin as a rail. Yet he seemed to exude great physical strength, and in a fight between him and one of the beefy bully-boys who swaggered around the Bowery, Johnson had no doubt which of the two *he* would put his money on.

Then there was the man's general attitude. From the moment the ship had pulled away from the dock, the rest of the passengers had seemed positively desperate to mingle. They had attended the tea dances, dined at each other's tables and had swapped their life stories with the reckless abandon of people who know they are never likely to meet again.

The man in the brown suit, in contrast, had kept himself very much aloof. From the very start of the journey, he had eaten alone, strolled around the deck by himself, and merely shaken his head – in a firm, though not unfriendly manner – when asked if he wished to join in any of the deck games.

Yet, for all that, it seemed to Hiram Johnson, the man in the brown suit had missed nothing – *for all that,* he had probably learned a great deal more about his fellow passengers than they (despite their loquaciousness) had learned about each other.

And so it had continued for the six days, one hour and seventeen minutes they had been on the ship. Now, as they were sailing towards the dock, the man in the brown suit stood on the deck, looking out over – and apparently absorbed by – the Manhattan skyline, and it seemed to Johnson that if he were ever to crack through the man's shell, this was not only his *last* chance, but also the *best* one which had been presented so far.

He sidled up to the rail, coughed discreetly, and when the Englishman noticed him, held out his hand and said, 'Hiram Johnson.'

He would only have been slightly surprised if the other man had turned away at that point, but instead the Englishman took the proffered hand and said, 'Sam Blackstone.'

The man had a powerful grip, Johnson thought, but it was a natural power, rather than one designed to intimidate.

'Could I ask you if this is your first visit to my country, Mr Blackstone?' the American said.

'Yes, it is.'

'And what do you think of it?'

'I'm impressed,' Blackstone said.

Johnson felt a surge of satisfaction course through his veins.

'And what, particularly, is it that you find impressive, Mr Blackstone?' he asked.

'Those very tall buildings, beyond the port. We don't have anything like them back in London.'

Johnson nodded. He supposed it would have to have been that. It was the tall buildings just beyond the port which impressed *everyone*.

'Over here, we call them skyscrapers,' he said. 'It's a term that was originally applied to tall sails on ships, you know.'

'Yes, I did know that,' Blackstone replied, though without any hint of superiority in his voice.

'They look like they've been here for ever, don't they?' Johnson continued. 'As much a part of the natural landscape as your own baronial castles back in England?'

'Well, perhaps not *quite* as much as the castles,' Blackstone said, in polite disagreement.

'No, perhaps not,' Johnson conceded. 'And, in fact, they haven't been there very long *at all*. The first one was completed in '89.'

'Only eleven years ago,' Blackstone said reflectively.

'Only eleven years ago,' Johnson echoed. 'And that particular building has quite a story attached to it, if you'd care to hear it.'

'I would,' Blackstone agreed.

'It all started when a smart young silk merchant by the name of Stearns bought a vacant lot at 50 Broadway. He planned to put up a building that he could rent out as offices, but the problem was that the frontage was only twenty-one and a half feet wide, and if he built it out of stone – which is what all buildings of that nature *were* built of at the time – the walls would be so thick there wouldn't be enough space inside to turn a profit.' Johnson chuckled. 'And we Americans, you know, always want to turn a profit.'

'So I've heard,' Blackstone said.

'Well, sir, Stearns pondered on the problem mightily, and then the solution came to him in a flash. Why not build it on a steel skeleton framework, a bit like a bridge – although in this case, the bridge would be standing on its end, rather than spanning a gap? If he did it that way, he argued, the walls would only have to be twelve inches thick, and need bear no weight at all.'

'Very clever,' Blackstone said.

'Not everybody thought so. When the newspapers got to hear of it, they soon started calling it the Idiotic Building.'

Blackstone's lips twitched, forming a slight smile. 'That does sound rather unkind of them,' he said.

'Yes, it was rather unkind,' Johnson agreed. 'But you could see their point, because apart from Stearns and his architect – a guy called Gilbert – there wasn't a soul in New York who didn't believe that it would blow over in the first strong wind. Then, one Sunday morning in '89 – when all thirteen floors had been finished and there was only the roof left to be put on – there was one God Almighty storm, with the winds reaching up to eighty miles an hour. Stearns and Gilbert rushed straight to their building, as you'd imagine they would, and by the time they arrived, there was already a crowd there – just waiting for it to come toppling down. And do you know what Gilbert did next?'

'No, I don't,' Blackstone said.

'He grabbed a plumb line and began to climb a ladder up the side of the building. The people who'd come to watch began screaming at him, telling him not to be such a reckless fool and to come down before he was killed. But he didn't pay them no mind.'

'A determined man.'

'A very determined man. He climbed right to the top of that thirteen-floor building, and once he was there, he crawled on his hands and knees along the scaffolding, until he reached the very edge of the structure.'

'This would be where the plumb line comes in,' Blackstone suggested.

'You've heard the story before, Mr Blackstone,' Johnson said, sounding a little disappointed.

'No, I promise you that I haven't,' Blackstone replied. 'Do please go on, Mr Johnson.'

Well, Gilbert got the plumb line out of his pocket, held one end, and let the other – the one with the lead weight on it – fall towards the street. And there it was – hanging taut. Which meant, as I'm sure you'll appreciate, that the building wasn't vibrating at all. And that day, sir,' Hiram Johnson said, with an impressive swelling to his voice which indicated he was reaching the grand finale of his story, 'was the day that changed the history of New York City.'

'Is that the place?' Blackstone asked, pointing at a domed building in the distance.

'Why, no sir, that's the Pulitzer Building. It's named after its owner, Joseph Pulitzer, the publisher of the *New York World* newspaper, and that's got a story of its own.'

The ship had almost reached the dock, and already there was a flurry of activity, as stevedores prepared to unload the cargo, and customs offices stood waiting to come on board. Within half an hour or so, he would be on American soil for the first time in his life, Blackstone thought.

'I said, the Pulitzer Building's got a story of its own,' Johnson repeated. 'Would you care to hear that, too?'

Blackstone smiled again. 'Why not?'

'Pulitzer's a Hungarian by birth,' Johnson said. He paused. 'I guess that's *somewhere* in Europe.'

'Yes, it is,' Blackstone confirmed.

'Joe came here in the Fifties, and when the Civil War broke out in '61, he already felt patriotic enough about his new home to join the Union Army as a cavalryman. Well, one day, when he was on a short leave in New York City, he went into French's Hotel in search of some refreshment, but the management was worried his frayed uniform might offend some of their fancier guests, so they refused to serve him.'

'Bastards,' said Blackstone, who had been a soldier himself, and knew all about frayed uniforms.

'Joe survived the war, and started his newspaper, which became a big success, and when he'd made enough money, he bought French's Hotel outright, had it razed to the ground, and put the Pulitzer Building there in its place.'

'So the story had a happy ending,' Blackstone said.

'Yes, it did,' Johnson said, though that was not the point of *his* story at all. 'But do you know why he built it so tall?'

'Because he needed a great deal of space to run his newspaper properly?' Blackstone guessed.

'That's part of the answer, but *only* part of it. You see, the *World*'s two biggest rivals, the *Sun* and the *Herald*, have their offices nearby, and Joe wanted his building to dwarf theirs. The popular tale is that he said he wanted a building in which his editors only had to go to the window in order to spit on the *Sun*, but I believe – if you'll excuse the crudity – that what he actually said was that they only had to go to the window in order to *piss* on it.'

'That sounds more like a Hungarian,' Blackstone said in a tone which left the American unsure whether he was joking or not.

'So that's the building he wanted, and that's what he *got*,' Hiram Johnson continued. 'It's three hundred and nine feet tall, which makes it the *tallest* building in the whole wide world.'

'But from what I've already learned about you Americans, I don't think it will be the tallest building in the world for long.'

'I do believe you're right, sir,' Johnson agreed.

'And this Joe Pulitzer bloke started out with nothing,' Blackstone said thoughtfully.

'And he started out with nothing,' Johnson confirmed.

'So it would seem that this really *is* the land of opportunity.'

'It is, sir. We pride ourselves on the fact.'

The ship had docked, and no sooner had the gangplank been lowered than a stream of people poured down it. There were men, women and children, all poorly dressed (though not a great deal more poorly than Blackstone himself), and they carried their possessions in a variety of carpet bags, sacks and small steamer trunks. The dockside police had been waiting for them, and shepherded them towards a number of moored barges.

'Where are they going?' Blackstone asked.

'Ellis Island,' Hiram Johnson told him. 'It's out in the bay. It's where they'll be processed.'

'And will you and I be going out to this Ellis Island, too?' Blackstone wondered aloud.

'No, sir, we will not. It's only the steerage passengers who are taken to the island. We'll be processed on board the ship.'

'So despite this being the land of opportunity, there's still one law for the rich and another for the poor?'

Johnson chuckled. 'Now you're catching on,' he said. 'The preamble to our Declaration of Independence says, "We hold these truths to be self-evident, that all men are created equal." However, if you read between the lines, it *also* says, "But if you think the rich will get the same treatment as the poor, you must be crazy".'

He paused, as if suddenly concerned that having held his

country up as a shining example, he had now said something
which might tarnish it in Blackstone's eyes.

'Of course, with the numbers involved, we've no choice in the
matter,' he continued hastily. 'Why, last year alone, a million and
a half people passed through Ellis Island. There simply wouldn't
be the space to process that many people anywhere else.'

'You're probably right,' Blackstone agreed non-committally.

A new thought came into Johnson's mind. It had been his
mission to find out more about the other man, and in that he
had failed miserably. Where he should have been asking shrewd
questions, he had fallen into the trap of instead boosting his
home country. Where he should have been analysing responses,
he had instead provided responses to be analysed.

Well, there were still a few minutes left, and he was
determined to make the best of them.

'So, tell me, Mr Blackstone, what brings you to the United
States of America?' he asked. 'Business?'

'I suppose you could say it was business, in a way,' the
other man replied enigmatically.

'You're a salesman perhaps?' Johnson suggested, though
Blackstone's shabby suit seemed to argue against that possibility. 'That's my own particular line of work, you know.'

'I'd never have guessed that,' Blackstone said, and once again
the American was not sure whether he was joking or not.

'Yes, I represent Buffalo Pharmaceuticals,' Johnson continued.
'We started out small, but we're growing bigger every day, and
now we even have a European office, which is why I happen
to be . . .' He paused, conscious of the fact that he had allowed
himself to drift away from his intended aim again. 'So *are* you
a salesman?' he asked, getting back on course.

'No,' Blackstone said, 'I'm not.'

'Then perhaps you're an engineer of some kind?' Johnson
said doggedly. 'A railway engineer? We're very big on railways
in America.'

'No, not that, either,' Blackstone replied. For a moment he
said no more, then – perhaps deciding it would be rude to
supply no details at all – he added, 'I'm here to pick up a
man, and escort him back to England.'

'Then you're kinda like the Pinkertons?' Johnson exclaimed.

'I beg your pardon?'

'They're a big detective agency, but most of their work doesn't involve *detecting* at all. Their main business comes from providing protection. I suppose you'd call them bodyguards.'

'Ah!' Blackstone said.

If that was Blackstone's line of work, it would certainly explain his innate hardness and aloofness, Hiram Johnson thought. It would *even* explain why he felt under no compulsion to be more smartly kitted out. Because if you were willing to entrust your life to a man – and he was good at his job – you wouldn't give a damn how he dressed.

Blackstone had still neither denied nor confirmed that this *was* his line of work.

'So you're a bodyguard of some sort?' Johnson repeated.

'In a way, I suppose I am,' Blackstone conceded, smiling again, but very thinly this time. 'It is my job to see that nothing untoward happens to the man who I'm picking up until he's safely back in London.'

What a very strange way to phrase it, Johnson thought.

'And will something "untoward" happen to him once he *is* back in London?' he asked jovially.

'That would depend on your point of view,' Blackstone said. 'I wouldn't regard it as untoward at all. In fact, I would see it as a very satisfactory conclusion to the whole affair. But I suspect the man I'm escorting won't see it in quite the same way.'

'Why? What *will* happen to him?' Johnson asked, with an eagerness to know which almost made his question a demand.

'Once back in London, his accommodation will be provided for him. So will his food, and though, for the most part it will be pretty plain fare, he will be allowed to order whatever he wishes on his last night in that accommodation.'

'Oh,' Johnson said, disappointed at the mundane nature of the answer. And then something in the back of his brain picked up on the last few words and decided they were important.

'On his last night there?' he repeated.

'Before he goes on his short journey,' Blackstone explained.

But that was no explanation at all, Johnson thought.

'The man will be going on a short journey, will he?' he asked.

'A very short one,' Blackstone agreed. 'It can't be more than twelve yards from the condemned cell to the gallows.'

TWO

The first-class passengers, whose carriages were already waiting in attendance on the dockside, were the first to disembark. They did so at a slow, stately pace (as suited their exalted position), and were seemingly unaware of the inconvenience this caused the second-class passengers who, once *they* had finally disembarked themselves, would be forced to rush towards the cab rank in order to secure one of the waiting vehicles.

Blackstone did not mind the delay. He had spent six days at sea, in a cabin which, while it would no doubt have horrified the people who were used to plush staterooms, had seemed perfectly adequate to him. He had enjoyed his food and the sea air, and – even more importantly – he had enjoyed the leisure.

Six days of doing nothing! He couldn't remember when he had last spent six whole days doing nothing, because he was too good a copper to rest while crimes were being committed – and crimes were *always* being committed.

He had, he now admitted to himself, even been half-expecting that there would be a murder on the ship in the mid-Atlantic, because it somehow didn't seem quite *right* that he should be allowed this treat. But there had been no murder, and now he felt more rested and relaxed than he had in years.

He chuckled softly to himself, as his mind drifted back to that morning, only a week earlier, when Sir Roderick Todd had summarily called him to his office.

It had been some time since Blackstone had been commanded to appear before Todd, and he hadn't minded that one iota.

He didn't like the man. Todd was both a complete idiot and an opium addict, though the inspector was not sure which of those had come first. He was, moreover, a terrible snob, who would almost rather have had cases go unsolved than have the solution come from an ex-army sergeant who had been brought up in an orphanage – and who clearly did not think, as he was supposed to, that the sun shone out of the assistant commissioner's backside.

'Do you remember a villain called James Duffy?' Todd demanded, by way of greeting.

Blackstone grimaced at Todd's use of the word 'villain'. The AC had used it to show that he was a hard-nosed copper who lived and breathed the London underworld, whereas the truth was that the closest he got to it was the occasional view from his carriage window.

'Yes, I remember him, sir,' Blackstone said. 'Ran a brothel in the East End, and just to keep his girls in line, he'd cut off one of their heads now and again. I arrested him, and he was sentenced to hang, but then some silly bugger in Pentonville slipped up, and he managed to escape.'

'I have long believed that he fled to America, and now I appear to have been proved right,' Todd said.

Long believed, Blackstone repeated silently to himself. Proved right!

The assistant commissioner, Blackstone suspected, had never even heard Duffy's name until that morning, and now he was trying to create the impression that if the man had been tracked down, it was entirely due to his own efforts.

'Yes, it appears the police department in New York City has detained a man who might well be Duffy,' Todd continued. 'But there is a problem.'

How he liked to pad it out, Blackstone thought. How much the assistant commissioner loved the sound of his own voice.

'A problem, sir?' he said.

'That is correct. They are not prepared to extradite the man until they're sure he really is Duffy.'

'Then we should send them a set of his fingerprints, sir.'

'We're talking about colonials, here,' Todd said, a sneer entering his voice. 'We're talking of people who speak English – just about – but are otherwise completely backward.'

It was clear that Todd had never read Mark Twain, Nathaniel Hawthorne or Herman Melville, Blackstone told himself.

'Is that right, sir?' he asked. 'Backward?'

'Indeed. And a prime example of this is that the American so-called police forces don't use fingerprinting.'

'In that case, sir, I don't see how we'll ever be able to prove whether it's Duffy or not.'

'Of course you don't,' Todd agreed. 'But, you see, I do. I
know how to use my brain, Inspector – which is why I'm
sitting behind this desk and you're standing in front of it.'

'I knew there had to be some reason for it, sir,' Blackstone
said. 'Thank you for explaining it to me.'

Todd looked at him suspiciously. 'Are you being insolent,
Inspector? Or, perhaps, in the interest of strictest accuracy,
I should say, are you being insolent again?'

'Of course not, sir,' Blackstone assured him.

'Good,' Todd said. 'Would you now like to hear how I've
solved this problem to which you see no solution?'

'If you wouldn't mind, sir.'

'The New York Police have agreed that if one Scotland Yard
officer can personally identify the man as Duffy, that will be
sufficient cause to extradite him. And that officer, Inspector
Blackstone, will be you.'

'You want me to go to America, sir?'

'Good Lord, but you do catch on quickly,' Todd said
sarcastically. 'You sail from Liverpool the day after tomorrow.'

'First class, I take it,' Blackstone said, before he could stop
himself.

Todd glared at him. 'You'll be travelling second class,' he
said. 'And you can thank your lucky stars you're even doing
that, because, if it wasn't for the need to uphold the dignity of
Scotland Yard in the eyes of the travelling public, I'd have booked
you into steerage, with the rest of the riff-raff.' He glanced up
at the clock on the wall. 'I assume you have no questions.'

'Well, sir, I was wondering—'

'Good, because I'm a busy man, and I've already spent more
than enough time on this minor matter. You can go, Inspector.'

'Thank you, sir,' Blackstone said.

He had almost reached the door when he heard Todd say,
'Actually, there's one question I'd like to ask you.'

Blackstone turned around again. 'Yes, sir?'

'Are you a good sailor, Inspector?' the assistant commissioner
asked.

'I'm afraid not,' Blackstone replied. 'I think I must have been
at the back of the queue when they were handing out sea legs.'

Todd permitted himself one of his rare smiles. 'Excellent,' he
said.

Blackstone had lied about the sea legs, of course, but it had been a lie with a purpose. Because if Todd had even suspected that he would enjoy the trip, the assistant commissioner would have done his damnedest to make sure somebody else – *anybody else* – was sent instead.

It was as Blackstone was walking down the gangplank that he first noticed the man standing directly in his path. He was a young man, not more than twenty-five or twenty-six. He had a straw boater on his head and was dressed in a white linen suit, which matched his white bow tie. In his hands, he held a large piece of cardboard, on which he had written – in impeccable script – the words 'Inspector Blackstone, New Scotland Yard'.

The last three words seemed a little unnecessary to Blackstone, but since this was clearly his reception committee of one, he walked over to the young man and said, 'I'm Blackstone.'

His words had an instantaneous effect. The young man immediately let the card fall, and before it had even had time to reach the ground, he was already holding out his hand.

'Gosh, this is a real honour, sir,' he said, as he pumped Blackstone's hand up and down.

'Is it always this hot here?' Blackstone asked, loosening his tie with his free hand.

'Hot?' the young man repeated, as if, in his bubbling enthusiasm, he had not even noticed the temperature. 'Oh, hot! Yeah, this is New York City in July, and it *is* always hot.' He continued pumping away at Blackstone's hand. 'I have to tell you, sir, you have absolutely no idea how long I've been waiting to finally meet a real police detective.'

'Oh?' Blackstone replied, mystified. 'I shouldn't have thought it would have been difficult to meet one in a city this size. The police force must have hundreds of detectives on its strength.'

'It does, and I'm one of them,' the young man said, finally releasing his grip. 'I'm Detective Sergeant Alexander Meade.'

'Then I don't see what you meant,' Blackstone confessed. 'If *you're* a police detective . . .'

'I said a *real* police detective, sir,' Meade said. 'Not just a man who carries a badge, but one who solves *real* crimes.'

'But don't the—?'

'Oh, things are a little better since the Lexow Committee

completed its investigation,' Meade interrupted, 'but not *that* much better. The problem is Tammany Hall, you see. Always was. And until we can get rid of it, there'll never be a *major* improvement.'

'Is that right?' Blackstone asked, and he was thinking that while they were undoubtedly talking the same language, the young sergeant might as well have been speaking Hindustani for all the sense he was making.

Blackstone had always thought the traffic on London's streets was bad enough. But compared to Manhattan, those streets were country lanes. Carriage fought against carriage to gain the advantage. Long, single-decker horse-drawn buses – which Meade informed him were called 'streetcars' in New York – moved at a ponderous pace most of the time, yet seemed to put on a malicious burst of speed when they saw the opportunity of blocking the progress of other vehicles. Electric taxi cabs hooted their horns in frustration as the drivers fretted that their batteries would be drained before they reached their destination. And, overhead, the elevated railway – the 'El', Meade called it – thundered along, pushing clouds of smoke into the sky and filling the air beneath it with small, glowing cinders.

'You have an *underground* railway in London, don't you?' Meade asked, across the carriage which was taking the two of them to the Mulberry Street police headquarters.

'Yes, we do,' Blackstone agreed.

'A *well-established* underground railway.'

'It's certainly been around for quite some time.'

'We could have had one for "quite some time", too,' Meade said gloomily. 'The mayor was talking about building one *twelve years* ago. But Tammany Hall didn't like the idea, you see, because most of the guys who work for Tammany have got shares in the streetcars and the El.'

'That's the second time you've mentioned Tammany Hall,' Blackstone pointed out. 'What exactly is it?'

'It's complicated,' Meade said, in a tone which suggested that he really didn't want to talk about it. 'And, hell, I didn't volunteer for this assignment in order to tell you about New York's problems. I want to hear what it's like to work in the famous Scotland Yard, so give me some of the juice.'

It was *complicated* to talk about the workings of the

Metropolitan Police, too, but Blackstone did his best, and all the time he was speaking, Meade listened with rapt attention.

'It's like I always imagined,' Meade said, almost dreamily, when Blackstone had finished. '*You* don't rely almost entirely on the words of crooked informers to make your cases. *You* don't beat a confession out of the nearest available suspect. *You* conduct investigations. *You* follow clues.'

'Well, yes, I suppose we do,' Blackstone admitted. 'But then, don't all police forces—?'

'Gee, I'd love to work with you,' Meade interrupted him. 'I'd learn so much from the experience.'

Was Meade doing no more than serving up a dish of gently warmed flattery seasoned with faux-admiration? Blackstone wondered.

Or was it merely that he hated his own job so much that he simply refused to see any of the virtues of the New York Police Department?

Whichever it was, the young man's attitude was making him feel distinctly uncomfortable.

'I'm sure your own police department is, in its own way, just as good, *and* just as bad, as the Met,' he said.

Meade's face darkened, and, as it did, the expression of youthful enthusiasm it had been displaying quite melted away.

'The police in New York City have two functions – and two functions only,' he said.

'And what are they?' Blackstone asked.

'To protect the rich, and to line their own pockets,' Meade replied. The carriage came to a sudden, juddering halt. 'We're here,' the sergeant continued. 'This is 300 Mulberry Street. Our headquarters – the very heart of stinking police corruption.'

THREE

The Mulberry Street police headquarters was five storeys high (including the basement) and was sandwiched between a slightly shorter building to its left and a slightly taller one to its right. Each floor had ten windows looking out on to the street. Its architectural style was decidedly Georgian

– though Blackstone doubted that a country which had fought
two wars against King George would ever have used that term
to describe it. It was a pleasant, solid-enough building, though
it was nothing like as impressive as New Scotland Yard.

'There are plans afoot to build a new headquarters,' Meade
said, almost as if he'd read Blackstone's mind. 'It's going
to be neoclassical. We just *love* neoclassical, here in the
States.'

And why wouldn't you? Blackstone asked himself, continuing
his earlier train of thought. After all, the ancient Greeks never
tried to tax your tea, and it certainly wasn't the Romans who
burned down your White House.

The Mulberry Street desk sergeant sat at his desk. A pile of
white forms were close to his left hand and a stack of blue ones
were close to his right, but he did not appear to be showing
much enthusiasm for either set of documents. He had, Blackstone
decided, the same air of weariness and cynicism about him as
seemed to be the lot of every desk sergeant, everywhere.

'This is Inspector Blackstone of New Scotland Yard,
London, England,' Alex Meade announced, with considerable
gravity. 'He has come here to identify his suspect.'

The desk sergeant looked up with a blank expression in his
eyes. Then enlightenment dawned.

'Oh, yeah, the Limey cop,' he said.

'The Limey *inspector*,' Meade said, somewhat rebuking.

'Sure,' the sergeant agreed easily. 'We got your guy down
in the cells. Wanna see him?'

'If you wouldn't mind,' Blackstone said.

'Why *would* I mind?' the sergeant replied. 'He's down in
the basement. Go see him.'

'I expect that the inspector would appreciate an escort down
to the cells,' Meade said.

'For what?' the sergeant wondered. 'He wants to know what
direction to go in, he can ask. An' he should recognize the
prisoner when he sees him, 'cos he's the one on the wrong
side of the bars.'

A look of concern and uncertainty was spreading across
Alexander Meade's face.

He was embarrassed by the way his guest was being treated
by the desk sergeant, Blackstone thought, but he was still

unsure whether saying anything further would make the situation better, or if it would simply make it worse.

The phone rang on the sergeant's desk, and the sergeant picked up the earpiece.

'The Limey cop, sir?' he asked, once he'd listened to the man on the other end of the line for a moment. 'Yes, sir, he's . . .'

The sergeant's expression suddenly grew more alert – and perhaps a little troubled.

'Yes, sir, Inspector Blackstone, that's who I meant . . .' he continued. 'No, I . . . I'll get right on to it, sir.'

He hung the earpiece up, and turned to Blackstone.

'Would you mind waiting here for a few minutes, while we make the necessary arrangements, sir?' he asked, in a voice which was now unashamedly ingratiating.

'What arrangements?' Meade enquired.

'The arrangements that need to be arranged,' said the desk sergeant, whose instructions to be pleasant clearly had not extended to being pleasant to Sergeant Meade.

It was the desk sergeant himself who, ten minutes later, escorted Blackstone down the steps to the basement cells.

Though there were several such cells there, only one of them was occupied, and the inspector immediately recognized the man staring at him through the bars as James Duffy.

Blackstone turned on his heel, and began to walk back towards the stairs.

'Hold on,' the desk sergeant said, taking him by the arm.

'Yes?' Blackstone replied.

'Is that *it*? You ain't even talked to the guy.'

'There's no need to talk to him,' Blackstone said. 'That's James Duffy. There's no doubt about it.'

'Yeah, but I think you should still *talk* to him,' the sergeant, said, beginning to sound a little desperate.

'Why?'

'Well, 'cos . . .'cos . . .'

'Yes?'

''Cos the commissioner don't want no mistakes.'

'There is no mistake.'

'Talk to the prisoner, can't you?' the desk sergeant asked, wheedling.

'Why should I?'

'Do it as a favour to me.'

'As a favour to you?' Blackstone said. 'Why should I do *you* a favour? Ah, now I see. Since we're already such good pals . . .'

'OK, I admit that I was bit rough on you when you came in,' the desk sergeant conceded. 'But I was busy!'

'Yes, it must have been hard work staring at all those forms,' Blackstone agreed.

'An' if you want anything at all while you're in New York,' the sergeant said, 'booze, a girl . . . a boy even . . .'

'I'll talk to the prisoner,' Blackstone said quickly, before the offers could get any worse.

'Thanks,' the desk sergeant said, turning on his *own* heel and almost rushing for the stairs.

'Wait a minute,' Blackstone called after him. 'Don't you want to be here when I question the suspect?'

'Hell, no,' the sergeant said over his shoulder. as he mounted the first step.

Blackstone walked towards the cell. He remembered James Duffy as a vicious brute, and it was clear from the way he looked now that his time in America had not changed him.

Yet Duffy himself seemed quite pleased to see his visitor, and even gave him a crooked smile as he said, 'Hello, Mr Blackstone.'

'What's been happening to you in the last ten minutes?' the inspector demanded.

'Happening to me?' Duffy asked, mystified.

'The sergeant said I could see you straight away, then he got a phone call, and suddenly I couldn't see you at all until arrangements had been made. So what were those arrangements?'

'Oh, that,' Duffy said. 'They moved me, didn't they?'

'From where to where?'

'From the cell on the end of the row to the one that I'm in now.'

Blackstone walked to the end of the row and inspected the other cell. It seemed identical, in every way, to the one Duffy was currently occupying.

Which was strange.

'So, how are you, Jimmy?' he asked the prisoner.

'On top of the world, Mr Blackstone,' Duffy replied. 'Best fing I ever did, coming to America.'

'Why's that?'

'It's a land of opportunity, ain't it? If yer've got a bit of go about yer, yer can make a fortune.'

'And have you made a fortune?'

Duffy smirked. 'I've done all right. Even in prison, yer looked after if yer've got the dosh to pay for special treatment – which I have.'

'Then it should be some consolation to you to know that when you hang, you'll hang as a rich man,' Blackstone said.

'Fing is, Inspector, I don't 'ave to 'ang at all, when you fink about it,' Duffy said.

'No?'

'No! The Yanks won't send me back unless you say I'm the man yer looking for.'

'True,' Blackstone agreed.

'And for five 'undred dollars, most men I know would be willin' to say almost anyfing.'

Blackstone smiled. 'But there are some men who wouldn't settle for less than a thousand,' he pointed out.

Duffy grinned back at him. 'Yer drive an 'ard bargain, don't yer, Mr Blackstone?' he said. 'But since you seem to be 'olding all the cards, let's call it a fousand.'

'And just what makes you think that you *can* bribe me, Jimmy?' Blackstone asked.

The other man shrugged. 'Every man 'as 'is price, Mr Blackstone. That's somefink they understand over 'ere. Why do you fink the desk sergeant left when he did?'

'I don't know. You tell me.'

'So we could get on wiv our negotiation in peace an' quiet. Course, 'e'll demand 'is cut, which is fair enough – but if I was you, I wouldn't give him more than ten per cent.'

'I intend to give him *fifty* per cent,' Blackstone said.

'That's up to you, but I wouldn't . . .'

'Or even a *hundred* per cent! Because a hundred per cent of nothing is still nothing.'

'Yer what?' Duffy asked.

'I've seen what you did to one of your victims,' Blackstone told him. 'Her name was Maggie Blair, and you cut her head off with a saw. At what stage in that grisly process did she die?'

Duffy shrugged. ''Ard to say. But it wasn't my fault that it 'appened, Mr Blackstone.'

'Then whose fault was it?'

'Maggie's. She was asking for it. The little slut simply wouldn't do as she was told.'

'And having seen her,' Blackstone continued, 'there's no amount of money in the world that would compensate me for missing the sight of you dangling at the end of a rope.'

'All right, all right, two fousand, then,' Duffy said.

'Not if you were to offer me a million,' Blackstone told him.

'Four fousand,' Duffy said desperately. 'That's all the money I've got. I swear it.'

'If they calculate the drop right, then when the trapdoor opens, the fall breaks your neck, you know,' Blackstone said, conversationally. 'They say it's an instant death, but it isn't.'

'I just ain't got more than four fousand, Mr Blackstone,' Duffy whined.

'There are still what the doctors call "vital signs of life" for at least half an hour after that,' Blackstone continued. 'It's widely believed that since you're unconscious for that time, you don't feel a thing, but who knows whether that's true or not?'

'I . . . I . . .' Duffy gasped.

'*You'll* know, Jimmy,' Blackstone said. 'Hanging there, soaked in your own shit – because your bowels will open, like they always do – you'll know. But the pity of it is, you'll never be able to tell me.'

There was the sound of trickling water, and looking down at the leg of Duffy's prison uniform, Blackstone saw that the man had wet himself.

He nodded his head, with satisfaction at a job well done.

'If it feels like that now, just imagine how it will feel when they're actually putting the rope around your neck,' he said.

Then, without another word, he turned and walked towards the steps.

When Blackstone appeared at the head of the stairs, the first thing the desk sergeant did was to look up at the wall clock.

'You were talkin' to him for six minutes,' he said. 'Maybe six and a half minutes.'

'And was that long enough?' Blackstone asked.

'Long enough for what?' the sergeant countered, a shifty, evasive look coming into his eye.

'Long enough to satisfy whoever it was told you to get me talking to Duffy in the first place.'

'I have no idea what you mean,' the sergeant said.

'So if you have no idea, you – and whoever put you up to it – won't be expecting a cut of the bribe, then?' Blackstone asked.

The sergeant paled. 'Don't tell me . . . don't tell me you took a bribe. Not with the . . .'

'Not with the what?' Blackstone asked.

'Well, if you did take one, it don't have nothin' to do with me,' the sergeant said, ignoring the question.

'Not with the *what*?' Blackstone persisted.

'I swear before God that my slate is clean, an' I'm innocent on all counts,' the sergeant said, as if he was already addressing the court.

This was beginning to sound like a conversation between a dog and duck, Blackstone decided – because not only was it *not* going anywhere, but it seemed increasing unlikely that it ever *would* go anywhere.

'Do you know if the police department has booked me into some sort of lodgings?' he asked.

He certainly *hoped* it had, because the weather had been unpleasantly warm even when he'd landed, and as the morning had progressed it had grown even hotter. Now, with his shirt stuck to his back and small rivers of sweat cascading down his neck, what he wanted – more than anything else in the whole world – was a good cold bath.

'Lodgings?' the sergeant repeated. 'Oh, yeah, you got a room booked for you at –' he rifled through the stack of paper to his left – 'the Mayfair Hotel.'

'Is that far from here?'

'Maybe five minutes.'

'Then if you'll give me instructions on how to find it, I'd like to go there now.'

'There ain't time,' the desk sergeant said. 'Sergeant Meade's expectin' to take you out to lunch at twelve.'

Blackstone glanced up at the wall clock.

'It's only just after ten thirty now,' he said. 'If my lodgings *are* only five minutes away . . .'

'An' before that, we've got your meeting,' the sergeant said.

'My meeting?' Blackstone repeated. 'What meeting is that?'

'The one with Commissioner Comstock,' the sergeant told him.

FOUR

Assistant Commissioner Todd of New Scotland Yard would have stayed firmly seated when Blackstone entered his office, but Commissioner Comstock of the New York Police Department was on his feet before the Englishman had even crossed the threshold.

Blackstone's initial impression was of a scholarly, slightly built man, who wore a pair of pince-nez spectacles on the end of his nose, and looked as if he would have been far more at home on a small university campus than he could ever be in a large police department. But before there was time for further speculation, the inspector found his thoughts shifting away from the commissioner – and on to his own particular circumstances at that moment.

There was something wrong with the whole situation, he thought, as he crossed the office.

More than *one* thing, he told himself, as he shook the commissioner's hand.

A whole *series* of things, he decided, as he accepted the commissioner's invitation to take a seat.

The *first* thing that was wrong was that he was there in Comstock's office *at all*. He was a relatively unimportant officer from Scotland Yard – fairly low on the totem pole, as the Americans might say – and yet he had been taken to meet one of the four police commissioners in charge of New York City.

The second – and more important – thing was the way in which Comstock himself was acting. He was doing his best to appear to be the patrician host welcoming his foreign visitor – but all he was actually *succeeding* in doing was looking unhappy.

Or nervous.

Or unsure of what to do or say next.

Or a combination of all of these.

The third thing . . .

'It is certainly a pleasure to meet you, Inspector,' Comstock said in a low fussy voice which pushed the third thing Blackstone had been wondering about to the back of his mind.

'And it's a pleasure – and an honour – to meet you, too, sir,' Blackstone countered.

Comstock unconvincingly shuffled some papers about on his desk for a few moments, then said, 'I take it, Inspector, that there is no doubt at all in your mind that the man who you were sent to New York to identify is the one we are actually holding in our cells.'

'No doubt at all, sir. As per the instructions *you* gave to your desk sergeant, I spent some time talking to him – even though, for identification purposes, there was no need to.'

He was taking a shot in the dark by assuming that the man who'd rung the sergeant had been the commissioner himself, but the look on Comstock's face quickly confirmed that the shot had found its target.

'Yes . . . er . . . as per my instructions. Quite,' Comstock said. He glanced down, once more, at the pieces of paper on his desk. 'Did this man Duffy by any chance attempt to *bribe* you?' he asked, without looking up.

'Bribe me?' Blackstone repeated.

'Bribe you.'

'Why should you ask that?'

'Just idle curiosity,' Comstock said, unconvincingly. 'After all, it's not every man who would turn down the chance of earning four thou . . .'

The commissioner clamped his mouth tightly shut, but the damage had already been done.

Duffy had been moved from one cell to another for one specific reason, Blackstone thought. And that reason had been that while there were no hidden microphones in his first cell, there undoubtedly were in his second.

But why should the commissioner have even *wanted* to listen in on the conversation?

Could it be because he had intended to skim off a portion of the bribe for himself?

Possibly.

But, thinking about it, it *did* seem highly unlikely that a police commissioner for New York City – even if he were corrupt – would wish to be become involved in such a thing. For Blackstone himself, four thousand dollars was a great deal of money, but for the commissioner it must seem like very petty graft indeed.

And even if that *were* his intention, he would now know
that though a bribe had been offered by Duffy, it had certainly
not been accepted by Blackstone.

While these thoughts had been running through Blackstone's
mind, Comstock had clearly been working out how to cover
his gaffe.

'You were planning to sail back to England as soon as possible,
weren't you?' he asked, apparently having decided that his best
course would be to pretend the gaffe had never happened.

Were planning?

'I still *am* planning to sail as soon as possible, sir,'
Blackstone said emphatically. 'I've got what I came here for,
and the sooner my prisoner is hanging at the end of a rope,
the happier I'll be.'

'Perhaps so,' Comstock said. 'Certainly so. The guilty must
be punished as speedily as possible. I agree with you on that.'
He paused. 'And, indeed, passage has been booked for you
on the first available ship, which sets sail in four days' time.
But, as regards the other matter I just mentioned . . .'

'I wasn't aware you *had* mentioned another matter, sir.'

'Weren't you? Then perhaps I didn't make myself clear. At
any rate, during the course of last night, and then again this
morning, I exchanged a number of telegrams with Assistant
Commissioner Todd on the subject of when you will, in fact,
return to England yourself.'

When you don't know which way a conversation is going,
the quickest way to find out is to shut your trap and just listen,
Blackstone thought – and then followed his own advice.

'Yes, Assistant Commissioner Todd,' Comstock repeated.
'Even from his telegrams, he struck me as a fine man who I
am sure is a credit to his force.'

There were many things Blackstone *could have* said at that
moment – but he said nothing.

'And . . . er . . . between us we have decided that one of my
men will be given the task of escorting Duffy back to England
instead, and that you, for your part, will remain with us for
a while.'

'What would be the point of that?' Blackstone asked.

'I . . . er . . . felt – and your assistant commissioner agreed
with me – that this visit of yours presented us with the ideal
opportunity to give you the chance to learn how we do things

over here, while one of my men would learn how you do things over there.'

It made sense in a way, Blackstone thought, but it still didn't quite add up – particularly given Todd's attitude to American policing methods.

'I see,' he said, non-committally.

'And I further thought that the best way for you to profit from the experience would be to work on an actual case that we have pending at the moment – specifically, a murder case, in which field, I'm led to believe by Mr Todd, you yourself are something of an expert.'

'I'm not sure—' Blackstone began.

'Nor is it any *ordinary* murder investigation,' Comstock interrupted him. 'The victim, in this case, was Inspector O'Brien, a very bright young man whose promising future was sadly curtailed by an assassin's bullet.'

Now, finally, a few of the pieces of the puzzle were starting to click into place, Blackstone thought.

The murder of one of its own was a traumatic event for any police force to have to deal with, and that would certainly explain Comstock's nervousness and hesitation – though it didn't *quite* yet explain why he himself had been drawn into the process.

'I'll be glad to help you in any way I can, sir,' he said, 'but I'm sure that the team you already have investigating the case won't need – and probably wouldn't appreciate – any guidance from a—'

'The investigation will be headed by Detective Sergeant Meade, who I believe you have already met,' Comstock said, interrupting for a second time, 'and you will serve as his assistant, though, strictly speaking, you outrank him.'

'A detective sergeant?' Blackstone repeated incredulously. 'You're going to put a mere *detective sergeant* in charge of an investigation into the murder of an inspector?'

'That is correct.'

'In London, we would never even consider—'

'This isn't London,' Commissioner Comstock said. 'This is New York – and we do things differently here.'

He had overstepped the mark, Blackstone realized.

'Of course, sir,' he said apologetically. 'It was not my intention to criticize your procedures.'

'I'm sure it wasn't,' Comstock said generously.

'How many men are you planning to assign to Sergeant Meade's team, sir?' Blackstone asked.

Commissioner Comstock sniffed uneasily. 'As I thought I'd already made clear to you, Inspector Blackstone, there will be Detective Sergeant Meade, and there will be yourself.'

'Just the *two* of us?' Blackstone exclaimed, convinced that he must have somehow misheard.

'Yes, just the two of you,' Commissioner Comstock confirmed.

'Nobody else at all?'

'Nobody else at all.'

Insane, Blackstone thought. Completely bloody insane!

Sergeant Meade took the astounding news that he was to be placed in charge of a serious investigation – and that Blackstone was to be his one and only assistant – in his stride.

'The moment I heard that Commissioner Comstock wanted to see you, I knew it had to be connected with the investigation, though I rather thought that *you* would be in charge and *I* would be your assistant,' he said.

Blackstone took a close look at the other man.

A few hours earlier, when Meade had met him off the boat, the sergeant had seemed as fresh-faced and unsure as a youth at his first dance, as overenthusiastic as a playful puppy let loose in the wool basket. Now the lines on his face had hardened considerably, and there was a crispness to both his words and his bearing which had been entirely missing before.

So what had brought about the sudden change – the virtual metamorphosis – in him, Blackstone wondered.

'The last time we were together, I still hadn't heard about Inspector O'Brien's murder,' Meade said, reading his mind again.

'He was your friend, was he?' Blackstone asked, sympathetically.

'He was more than my friend – he was my hero!'

'And you're really not in the least surprised to have been put in charge of investigating the murder?' Blackstone asked.

'No, I'm not.'

'You don't think, perhaps, that someone with more experience in that kind of work would have a better chance of bringing your friend's killer to justice?' Blackstone asked tactfully.

'I do not. And if you knew this city like I do, neither would you,' Meade said, with bitterness in his voice.

'In that case, I think it's perhaps time that I *learned* a little bit more about this city,' Blackstone said.

'So do I,' Meade agreed. 'We'll talk about it over lunch.'

FIVE

Meade had decided to take Blackstone to lunch at Delmonico's Restaurant on Beaver Street.

'Delmonico's is the oldest restaurant in New York City,' the sergeant said, as they approached the place. 'And some parts of it are older than others. See those marble pillars around the door?'

'Yes.'

'They were brought all the way from Pompeii, Italy.'

Blackstone grinned. 'As you told me earlier, Americans just *love* neoclassical,' he said.

'And *real* classical – gen-u-ine classical – is even better,' Meade said, smiling back.

They entered the restaurant, and Blackstone quickly glanced around the interior. Even from the outside, it had been plain to him that this was not the kind of restaurant he could ever afford to patronize himself, and the splendour he was now confronted with only confirmed the impression.

'Is the police department paying for this?' he asked, trying not to sound nervous.

'No,' Meade told him. 'I am.'

They ordered two of Delmonico's special steaks, which Meade promised were the finest steaks in the world, and when the waiter had left them, the sergeant began his lesson.

'This city runs on two things,' he began. 'Power and money.'

'That's what all big cities run on,' Blackstone said.

'Maybe they do,' Meade agreed. 'But not like here.' He paused to take a sip of water. 'I have to start with Tammany Hall, because that's where everything *does* start.'

'All right,' Blackstone said.

'The Tammany Society was named after Tamanend, who

was an Indian chief. It started out as a social organization,
but about sixty years ago, it began getting political. The key
to its power is its ability not only to get the voters out on
polling day, but to get them to vote Democrat.'

'How do they manage that?'

'They have a political machine that would take your breath
away. They started out by mobilizing the Irish vote – most of
the Tammany leaders are Irish – but as there were successive
waves of new immigrants – German Jews, Italians, Central
Europeans, Russian Jews – they began working with them,
too. You have to put yourself in the shoes of those immigrants,
Inspector Blackstone . . .'

'Call me Sam.'

'And you call me Alex. You have to put yourself in their
shoes. They've left their homelands behind them, and they're
in a new country where they don't even speak the language.
America is so very different, and they simply don't understand how things work. So they go to their ward leader, who's
a Tammany man.'

'And what does he do?'

'He *makes* things work for them. If they need a pedlar's
licence, he gets them one. If they want to apply for citizen-
ship, he goes through the forms with them. If they want a job,
he usually finds them one. If they're behind on their rent, he
pays it. When they can't afford fuel in winter, he sees to it
that some is delivered to them. And all he asks in return is
that they vote on a straight Democratic ticket.'

'Which means that the people from Tammany Hall get
elected?' Blackstone guessed.

'No, some of them *do* stand for public office, but more
often than not, they don't want to be elected themselves.'

'Then what *do* they want?'

'They want to be the people who *choose* the people who
are elected.'

'People who will forever be in their debt,' Blackstone said.

'Now you're catching on, Sam,' Meade said. 'Tammany
controls the people who have their hands on the purse strings
of New York City, and it uses that fact to its own advantage.
And both because Tammany Hall is corrupt, and because its
web stretches everywhere, every public body in the city is
corrupt, too.'

'Including the police,' Blackstone said, starting to see where Meade was going.

Meade nodded. 'Six years back, a special committee headed by State Senator Lexow looked into municipal corruption. The report it produced was 10,500 pages long, and 9,500 of those pages were concerned with corruption in the police department. The police commissioner admitted to the committee that eighty-five per cent of the men joining the police were accepted on the recommendation of Tammany Hall, and in the previous five years, he'd only promoted two men based on merit alone.'

Blackstone whistled softly. 'That's bad,' he said.

'It gets worse,' Meade told him. 'What the commissioner didn't admit – though everybody knew – was that Tammany had to be bribed to make those recommendations. It would cost a man $300 to be accepted as a patrolman. If he wanted to be promoted to sergeant, that would cost him $2,500. A captaincy was anything between $10,000 and $15,000, even though captains only earned $2,750 a year, and if you wanted to be an inspector, that could be anything up to $20,000. And there were always plenty of men willing to pay those bribes – because they knew just how much *they* could make through bribery and extortion once they were in their new positions.'

'But, surely, once the report was published, the whole rotten system was cleaned up, wasn't it?' Blackstone asked.

'You'd have thought so, wouldn't you?' Meade said. 'It started promisingly enough. The mayor, who, for once, wasn't a Tammany nominee, sacked the four commissioners and brought in new ones, including Teddy Roosevelt.' Meade paused, as if expecting Blackstone to say something, and when the Englishman remained silent, he continued, almost incredulously, 'You haven't heard of Teddy Roosevelt?'

'Can't say I have,' Blackstone admitted.

'He's a famous man in this country,' Meade said. 'Teddy likes to think of himself as a cowboy, even though he's a native New Yorker. And I guess you could say he's done just about everything – though none of it for very long. He worked for the Civil Service Commission, he was Assistant Secretary of the Navy – a position he used to start a war with Spain over Cuba—'

'On his own?' Blackstone interrupted.

Meade grinned. 'No, he had some help from the Hearst and Pulitzer newspapers, but a lot of it was down to him. When war was declared, he raised his own regiment to fight in it, and after the war, when he was discharged from the Army, he became governor of New York State. Now he's President McKinley's running mate in the November election, which means – God help us – that he's only a bullet away from being president himself.' Meade paused. 'That last bit's a joke.'

'But not a very funny one,' Blackstone said.

Meade shook his head. 'Maybe you have to be American to understand it,' he said. 'Anyway, the Mayor brought him in to sweep the stable clean, and he tackled that job like he's tackled most of the others he's been given – with a lot of energy and enthusiasm, and only the occasional pause for effective thought and planning. Do you know that while the other three commissioners walked down Mulberry Street to their new jobs, Teddy *ran*?'

'I see,' Blackstone said.

'He did do some good things,' Meade admitted. 'He fired some of the worst policemen. He insisted on promotion based on merit – and that worked for a while. But he acted as if he was running a one-man show, and the other commissioners grew to hate him. And he enforced old laws that banned soda fountains, florists, delicatessens, boot blacks and ice dealers from working on a Sunday – so pretty soon the public hated him, too. He left the job less than two years after he'd been sworn in.'

'And nothing much had changed,' Blackstone guessed.

'And nothing much had changed,' Meade agreed. 'As a result of the Lexow Report, seventy policemen, including two former commissioners, four inspectors and twenty-four captains, were charged with criminal offences. And despite the fact that they were appearing before Tammany-appointed judges, some of them were actually *convicted*. But then most of those convictions were reversed by other Tammany judges in the higher courts. So not only did the guilty men get off free and clear, but some of them were even given their old jobs back.'

'I see,' Blackstone said again, sounding more troubled this time.

'You're wondering how I ever got to be a sergeant, aren't

you, Sam?' Meade asked. 'You're wondering if I'm up to my elbows in filth and corruption like almost everybody else.'

'It had crossed my mind,' Blackstone admitted.

'I used influence,' Meade said. 'Not money, but influence.'

'I see,' Blackstone said for a third time.

'No, you don't,' Meade contradicted him. 'My father's a state senator, but he's also a lawyer – a very good one, and a very rich one – and when I was studying at Harvard, it was always assumed I'd join the family firm. I assumed it myself – and then I met Patrick O'Brien.'

'The dead inspector,' Blackstone said.

'The dead inspector,' Meade confirmed. 'He was a captain then, and he addressed a debating club I belonged to. What he said was that New York City, and the police department in particular, was a cesspit, and was likely to *stay* a cesspit as long as people like us simply walked past it holding our noses. And I knew immediately that he was right, and that it was up to people like me – people from the patrician class, if you like – to do something about it. So I used my father's influence to join the police – but only so I could do good.'

'Good afternoon, Alexander,' said a female voice.

Meade looked up, then *stood* up so quickly that he almost knocked the table over.

'Good afternoon, Clarissa,' he said, almost with a gasp.

The young woman who had so quickly reduced him to this state was perhaps a year or two younger than he was. It would have been stretching the truth somewhat to say that she was a pretty girl, but even the least charitable of men could scarcely have avoided describing her as 'sweet'.

'This is Miss Clarissa Bonneville,' Meade said to Blackstone. 'Clarissa, may I introduce you to Inspector Sam Blackstone, a famous detective from England.'

'Charmed, Mr Blackstone,' the girl said, holding out her hand for him.

'My pleasure,' Blackstone replied, wondering if that was the correct etiquette in America.

'We seem to see so little of you, these days,' the girl said to Meade.

'That's true,' Meade agreed. 'Perhaps we could . . .'

Another woman had suddenly appeared at the table. She was older and stockier than Clarissa, and her face was pure vinegar.

'You are keeping our guests waiting, Clarissa,' she said sternly.

'I only wanted a few words with Alex, Mama,' the girl protested.

'I am sure that Mr Meade understands that your guests must take priority over other social acquaintances,' Mrs Bonneville said. She turned her sour face on Alex. 'Isn't that so, Mr Meade?'

'Indeed it is, Mrs Bonneville,' Meade agreed.

'Then let us go, child,' Mrs Bonneville said, almost pushing Clarissa away from the table.

Meade watched the two women depart, then sighed softly to himself.

'There was a time when that dragon would have given her right arm to see me marry her daughter,' he said.

'So what changed?' Blackstone asked.

'I became a policeman, and her attitude towards me altered overnight.'

'What if you left the force and joined your father's firm? Would her attitude alter again?'

'Oh, yes. Then I'd once more be a good catch,' Meade said. 'But I don't really care what she thinks of me.'

'No?'

'Not at all. I love Clarissa, and, in the end, we *will be* married.'

'And does she love you?' Blackstone wondered.

'Of course she does,' Meade said. He grinned, a little sheepishly. 'But perhaps she's not yet quite as aware of it as she might be.'

'Tell me more about Inspector O'Brien,' Blackstone said.

'He was a wonderful man,' Meade said, and as he spoke, his eyes began to mist over. 'Of all the appointments Roosevelt made during his brief tenure, Patrick's was by far the most important. Teddy gave him a roving brief – to root out police corruption wherever he could find it – and though there were plenty of people who would have liked to have stripped him of that power once Roosevelt went, nobody's ever had the guts to do it. It was Patrick's mission to cleanse the department or die trying.' The sergeant shuddered. 'And die trying is just what he did.'

'You know what you're implying, don't you?' Blackstone

said carefully. 'You're implying that O'Brien was killed by a fellow officer.'

'Yes, that is what I believe,' Meade agreed. 'And I'm not the only one.'

'Who else believes it?'

'Commissioner Comstock.'

'Are you sure of that?'

'Of course. Why do you think he arranged for you to be part of this investigation? It's because he knows he can trust you.'

Especially after he listened in on my conversation with James Duffy, Blackstone thought.

'And why did he pick me, a mere sergeant, to lead it?' Meade continued. 'For the same reason. And why are there only two of us involved in the investigation? Because with the whole of the New York Police Department at his disposal, we're the only two people he knows with any certainty that he can have complete faith in.'

SIX

They were surrounded on all sides by things German. There were shops displaying German goods. There were bakeries with German names, which sold German bread and pastries. There were beer gardens which offered only German beer, and where the clients were entertained by brass bands playing only German music. Even the newspaper vendors – looking very Germanic themselves – had nothing to offer but newspapers written in German.

'What did you say that the name of this area was?' Blackstone asked Alex Meade.

'It's called Kleindeutschland,' the sergeant replied. 'That means "Little Germany".'

'And why would they ever have thought of calling it that?' Blackstone said wryly.

'Well, because . . .' Meade began earnestly. Then he stopped himself, and smiled. 'I suppose that would be an example of the English sense of humour, would it?'

'Yes – or what passes for one, anyway,' Blackstone agreed.
'How many Germans are there in New York?'

'There are around three hundred thousand people who are
German or of German extraction.'

'And they all live in this area?'

'They used to – but not any more. They've mostly moved
north to Yorktown, and now the tenements that they formerly
inhabited have been taken over by a new wave of immigrants
– the Eastern European Jews. But even though they no longer
live here, this is where the Germans still come to do most of
their shopping and have a good time.'

'Three hundred thousand,' Blackstone mused. 'That's a hell
of a lot of Germans.'

'That's nothing compared to the number of Irish in the city,'
Meade said dismissively. 'There's maybe one and half million
people living on Manhattan Island, and *eight hundred thousand* of them were either born in Ireland themselves or have
parents or grandparents who were.'

'Big number,' Blackstone said.

'Ain't it, though,' Meade agreed. He smiled again. 'Shows
just how much they must have liked being ruled over by you
English.'

True, Blackstone thought, and wondered if he'd ever see a
solution to the Irish problem in his lifetime.

Blackstone sensed Meade's good humour suddenly evapor-
ate, and looking ahead of him, he thought he understood the
cause.

They were approaching a saloon which called itself the
Bayern Biergarten, and on the sidewalk outside it there was
a rough circle of sawdust.

'Is that where it happened?' Blackstone asked.

'That's where it happened,' Meade confirmed mournfully.
'It was on this very spot that a fine man died last night.'

When they reached the circle of sawdust, they came to a
halt, and Meade brushed some of the sawdust away with his
shoe, revealing the red stain on the sidewalk.

'They just covered it up. They couldn't even be *bothered*
to wash it away,' Meade said angrily. 'And that's how they
want this investigation to go.'

'What do you mean?' Blackstone asked.

'They think all they have to do is cover it up and wait for

it to slowly fade away, so that in the end everybody will simply
have forgotten about it,' Meade said, his rage growing.
'But *I* won't forget. I can promise you that!'

'What *has* the investigation been able to uncover so far?'
Blackstone asked.

'Haven't you even *begun* to understand what's going on
here yet?' Meade demanded, with uncharacteristic rudeness.
'There's *been* no investigation. The owner of the biergarten
called the police, and the police took Inspector O'Brien's body
to the morgue. And that's it! That's all that's been done.'

'You're sure about that?'

'I'm sure. There can't be more than a handful of men on
the force who care whether the murder's solved or not – and
there's probably *at least* a handful who most definitely *don't*
want it solved.'

It bothered Blackstone a great deal that Alex Meade's mind
seemed so closed on the matter.

Because how could you investigate a case properly when
you thought you already had the solution? How could you be
sure you'd not missed any clues when there were only *certain*
clues you were even looking for?

'You *can't* be certain that anyone from the police was
involved,' he cautioned the other man.

'But I *am*,' Meade said firmly. 'There's nobody in this city
who would dare to kill a cop without someone tipping them
the wink that it would be all right. And who else *could* tip
them the wink but another cop?'

They entered the beer hall.

Blackstone looked around him. This wasn't anything like
an English boozer, he thought – not by any stretch of the
imagination.

The pubs at which he drank in London were made up of a
number of rooms, and each of these rooms contained a number
of small tables – little islands around which groups of mates
could congregate. It was true that if the piano was playing, it
would, for a while, become the centre of everyone's attention, but mostly you stuck to your own island, and merely
nodded to the residents of the others.

The Bayern Biergarten operated on an entirely different
philosophy. It was a vast cavern of a place. It had been filled
with long wooden tables, and at each table there were at least

a couple of dozen men in leather shorts and Tyrolean hats, drinking frothy beer from heavy stone mugs and shouting good-naturedly to their friends across the room.

'They're mostly Bavarians – South German Catholics – in here,' Meade said. 'The Prussians, who come from the north of Germany, are Protestant, and have their own beer gardens.'

The bar ran the whole length of one wall, and as they approached it, Meade reached into his pocket for his detective's shield.

The bartender, a broad man in his thirties, followed their progress with interest, but no signs of concern.

Meade showed the man his identification and said, 'We're investigating the shooting that happened last night.'

The barman nodded. 'But why did you take so long?' he asked, in a heavy accent.

'I beg your pardon?' Meade said.

The bartender shrugged. 'In Chermany, we would already have the killer behind bars by now.'

'Were you here in the biergarten when it happened?' Meade asked, ignoring the criticism.

'I was, but I was working, and so I did not see anything.'

Meade gave Blackstone a look which said, ain't that just the way of the world? Whenever there's a shooting – or any other serious incident – nobody's *ever* seen anything.

The sergeant took his notebook out of his pocket. 'I'll need the names of anyone else who you remember seeing here at the time.'

'Of course,' the barman agreed, but instead of beginning to recite a list of names, he reached for a sheet of paper which was lying on one of the shelves behind him, and laid it down on the bar in front of Meade.

The piece of paper had two long columns of words written on it, and the barman pointed his finger at the first column.

'These are the names of the people who were here,' he said.

It was a very long list.

'This is *everyone* who was here?' Meade asked, incredulously.

'Naturally,' the barman replied, as if it were inconceivable to him that anyone who had been there at the time *wouldn't* be on the list. 'And these,' he continued, pointing to the second column, 'are their addresses.'

'What do the stars that you've put against some of the names mean?' Meade asked.

'Ah, those are the men who think that they might have something useful to tell you,' the barman explained.

Meade did his best to suppress a gasp of astonishment, and didn't quite make it.

'Are any of these people here now?' he asked.

The barman looked around. 'Several of them.'

'I'll need a room,' Meade said. 'Somewhere quiet, in which I can talk to them.'

'Of course,' the barman said. 'You may use the manager's office. It has been waiting for you since this morning.'

Meade abandoned any attempt to appear unimpressed.

'You've been very efficient,' he said admiringly.

'Naturally,' the barman agreed. 'I am Cherman.'

'So you saw Inspector O'Brien just before he was killed, Mr Schultz?' Meade asked the fat German who was sitting at the opposite side of the table in the cramped manager's office.

'Yes, I saw him,' Schultz agreed. 'I was waiting for a friend to arrive, so I was watching the door. I noticed O'Brien because he was so different to the other customers.'

'Different in what way?'

Schultz smiled. 'In what way do you think? This is a *German* biergarten. I know most of the people who drink here, and if I do not, I know someone else who knows them. It is like one big club and we are not used to strangers. It is not that we have anything against them – it is simply that we have nothing to say to them, and they have nothing to say to us.'

'I understand,' Meade said.

'The only non-Germans who ever enter this building are policemen. And they only come to pick up their . . . their . . .'

Schultz stopped speaking, and seemed to have developed a sudden fascination for the table top.

'And they only come in to pick up their bribes?' Meade supplied.

'I know nothing of the reason for their visits,' Schultz lied. He raised his head again, but would still not look Meade in the eye. 'But to return to Herr O'Brien,' he continued hastily, 'I found myself wondering what he was doing here.'

'And what *was* he doing here?' Meade asked.

'He went to the bar and bought himself a beer. Then he stood looking at the door, as I had done.'

'You think he was waiting for somebody?'

'He may have been.'

'And how did he seem?'

'Seem?'

'What was the expression on his face? What sort of mood did he appear to be in?'

'Ah, so! He seemed excited. Or perhaps nervous. I do not know which one it was.'

'And what happened next?'

'He sipped his beer very slowly – not in the German way at all – and he kept looking at the door and checking his pocket watch. But no one came to join him, and in the end, looking very disappointed, he left. And it was just after he had stepped outside that I heard the shots.'

'How many of them were there?'

'Two, I think. Or it may have been three.'

'But you didn't see anything?'

'There is frosted glass on the door to the street. Besides, I was not really looking.'

Meade thanked Schultz for his time, and when the German had left, he turned to Blackstone and said, 'The way I see it is that O'Brien was planning to meet someone who could give him information connected with his investigation.'

'Possibly,' Blackstone said cautiously.

'And the *reason* he chose to hold the meeting here was because he knew that both he and his informant were very unlikely to meet anyone they knew in the biergarten.'

The facts, as far as they *had* any facts at all, would easily support Meade's theory, Blackstone thought. But then they would just as easily support any one of half a dozen other theories.

'It's possible that O'Brien was meeting an informant,' he said, 'but it's also possible that—'

'But the sons-of-bitches who he was investigating somehow managed to find out about the meeting. So they dealt with his contact first – which explains why he never turned up – and then they set up an ambush for when Patrick O'Brien left the biergarten.'

'It seems a very public place to have decided to kill him,' Blackstone said dubiously.

'It was late at night. There wouldn't have been many people out on the street,' Meade argued.

'But there was still a chance that there would have been *some*,' Blackstone countered. 'Look, say you were a professional assassin, how would *you* go about your work?'

'Since I'm *not* a professional assassin, Sam, I have no idea,' Meade said stubbornly.

You really don't want to explore this possibility, do you? Blackstone thought. But it has *to be* explored, nevertheless.

'I'll tell you how it works,' he said. 'The killer waits for the right opportunity – for the moment when there is no one in sight but himself and his target. His chance may come down a dark alley. It could be in a park. It could even be in the target's home. But he will wait for that opportunity because he knows it will come *eventually* – even in a big bustling city like New York. The one thing that the professional assassin will *not* do is expose himself to any unnecessary risks. And that's *exactly* what the killer did in this case.'

'So if it's not a professional killing, what *is* your explanation?' Meade demanded, slightly aggressively.

'I don't have one,' Blackstone admitted.

'Well, there you are, then,' Meade said, as if he had conclusively won the argument. 'We go with what we have.'

But it didn't work that way, Blackstone thought.

Three more witnesses confirmed that O'Brien had entered the bar alone – and left alone – and two of them were willing to agree that the inspector had looked either excited or nervous.

But it was with the fifth witness that they really hit pay dirt.

His name was Schiller, and he was a baker.

'I start work very early in the morning,' he said, 'and that is why it is my unhappy lot to go home to my bed while all my friends are still here, enjoying their drinking.'

'So when exactly did you leave?' Meade asked.

'I followed the dead man to the door. I was just behind him when he was shot.'

'You seem very calm about the whole thing,' Meade said, with a hint of suspicion entering his voice.

'I am sorry?'

'You saw a man shot to death in front of you. Most people would still be pretty shaken up by that, even a day later.'

Schiller shrugged. 'When I was a young man, I was in the Bavarian Army. In '66, we fought a war to defend south Germany from Prussian aggression.' He shrugged again. 'But the Prussians won, and only five years later I fought *for* them, against the French.'

'What's your point?' Meade asked.

'I have seen hundreds of men – good men – die in a single day. Last night, only one man died. It was not so much.'

Blackstone nodded, knowing exactly how the man felt.

'What happened once you were out on the pavement, Mr Schiller?' the inspector asked.

'The pavement? What is that?'

'The sidewalk.'

'O'Brien . . . that was his name, was it not?'

'Yes.'

'O'Brien looked up and down the street.'

'As if he was still expecting that his contact would turn up?' Meade asked.

The German shook his head. 'It was more as a soldier would look when he was behind enemy lines – he was checking for danger.'

'So he must have seen his murderer coming towards him?'

'Yes, he saw him.'

'But he didn't draw his revolver?'

'No. I think he was going to, but then he saw that the person running towards him was only a *junge* – a boy.'

'A boy!' Meade exclaimed. 'A damned *boy*!'

Blackstone gave his new partner a questioning look. He had no idea why the sergeant should have suddenly become excited, though it was unquestionable that he had.

'What did this boy look like?' Meade asked.

'I did not see his face,' Schiller replied. 'It was quite dark. Besides, he was wearing a large cap, pulled down over his ears, and had a cloth of some kind covering the lower half of his face.'

'What happened next?'

'The boy stopped running, and took a gun out of his pocket. He fired three times and O'Brien fell to the ground,' Schiller said, almost clinically. 'Then the boy turned, and ran off down the street.'

'Was he making what, when we were in the army, we would have called an "orderly retreat"?' Blackstone asked.

'No,' Schiller said. 'He was running blindly. He was very young, and cannot have killed many men. I think perhaps this was his first.'

'The killer was a member of a gang,' Meade said firmly once Schiller the baker had gone. 'It's most likely that he belongs to the Five Points Gang, though he could have been one of the Eastman crew.'

'What makes you so *sure* that he was a member of a gang?' Blackstone asked.

'His age. This killing has all the signs of being an initiation rite – which gives us the answer to the question you were posing earlier!'

'What question?'

'You wondered why the killer shot Patrick O'Brien right outside a beer hall, when it would have been safer to wait until he got the inspector somewhere more secluded, didn't you?'

'Yes.'

'Well, initiation rites aren't *supposed* to be safe – they're *supposed* to be a test of the potential gang member's nerve. This is just the sort of thing that Paul Kelly – who runs the Five Points Gang – *would* have come up with.'

'Kelly,' Blackstone repeated. 'Is he an Irishman?'

Meade shook his head. 'He's an Italian, and so are most of the members of his gang. His real name's Vaccareli, and he's a truly vicious bastard.'

Why was Alex Meade looking so cheerful, when this new line of thinking would seem to blow his previous theory completely out of the water? Blackstone wondered.

'So if we accept that it was an initiation rite, we must also accept that it had nothing to do with politics or corruption at all,' he said.

'You couldn't be wronger about that,' Meade told him. 'You see, Sam, the Five Points Gang – which, as far as we know, has around six hundred members – works for the Tammany Hall political machine.'

'In what way?'

'In the same way that *everybody else* who works for Tammany does, to a greater or lesser extent. It helps to fix elections.'

'How?'

'In all kinds of ways. It intimidates Republican voters into supporting a straight Democratic ticket. It helps to falsify voter registration lists. It stuffs the ballot boxes with fake papers. Jesus Christ, Sam, in some wards there are more voters than there are actual inhabitants. In some wards, people who've been dead for ten years or more still manage to get down to the polling station to cast their votes. And that's all down to groups of thugs like the Five Points Gang.'

'And what does the gang itself get out of it?' Blackstone asked. 'Money?'

'Oh, sure, it gets paid well enough for its dirty work,' Meade said. 'But more importantly, it earns itself friends in high places. And those friends are more than willing to give it the protection it needs.'

'Protection?' Blackstone repeated. 'Who could an armed gang, which you say has over six hundred members, possibly need protection *from*?'

'From the police!' Meade said, as if the answer were obvious. 'See, in between elections, the gang's involved in prostitution, gambling, robbery, extortion – all kinds of criminal activities. We know *exactly* what they're doing. But we *also* know that if we try to interfere, we'll soon be out of a job. Do you see what I'm getting at, Sam?'

Blackstone nodded. 'Wheels within wheels,' he said.

'Wheels within wheels,' Meade agreed. 'Say there are cops in Mulberry Street who can feel Inspector O'Brien breathing down their necks and are worried that any day now he's going to arrest them. What do they do about it?'

'They go to Tammany Hall and ask for help?' Blackstone guessed.

'Exactly! They go to Tammany Hall and ask for help,' Meade agreed. 'And somebody in Tammany *will* help them. Why?'

'Because he knows that if the cops go down, the chances are they'll be taking him with them?'

'Spot on! So this guy from Tammany contacts Paul Kelly and his Five Points Gang, and says he wants a job doing. And it's done – just like that! And the real beauty of it – at least from their point of view – is that the killer is three removes from the dirty cops who Patrick O'Brien was actually investigating.'

'If that *is* what happened, it makes our job almost impossible,'

Blackstone said darkly. 'Because even if we do manage to track the killer down, it's going to be very difficult to connect him to the people who ordered the murder, since it was all done by proxy.'

Blackstone's words should have had a depressing effect on Meade, but instead, he looked almost relieved.

'You're finally starting to believe me, aren't you, Sam?' the sergeant asked.

'What do you mean?'

'You thought that I'd got a real bee in my bonnet about Tammany Hall and police corruption. You thought there was some other explanation for the murder. But now you're beginning to see – even if you don't want to – that I just might have been right all along.'

Yes, he was, Blackstone admitted to himself. Coming from London, he'd found it hard to accept that any one organization could have a stranglehold on a city the size of New York. Yet every step he took, he found himself tripping over another strand of Tammany Hall's nefarious web. And the more that happened, the harder it became to dismiss Meade as just an inexperienced hothead.

'You do realize that we'll probably *never* solve this case, don't you?' he asked Meade.

'We'll solve it,' Meade said. 'I'm a smart guy . . .'

'I wouldn't dispute that.'

'And you're from New Scotland Yard, which makes you even smarter than I am. If we work together on this investigation, Sam, there's simply no way that we can fail.'

Ah, the optimism of youth, Blackstone thought – and wished he still had a little of it left himself.

SEVEN

'The whole of the police department is rotten through and through, but the Detective Bureau is rotten in its own *special* way,' Alex Meade said, as he and Blackstone walked along Mulberry Street towards police headquarters.

'And what special way is that?' Blackstone asked.

'It pretends it isn't corrupt at all. It *pretends* it's not only as pure as the driven snow, but that it's the best damn detective bureau in the whole world. And it's got a lot of other people – people who should know better – completely buying into that particular story.'

'By "people who should know better" I take it you mean people with some influence – people who *could have* the power to change things if they didn't keep their heads buried in the sand,' Blackstone suggested.

'That's exactly who I mean,' Meade agreed. 'US Congressman McClellan's a good example of that. He's an excellent legislator, and they say he'll be mayor of this city one day. And do you know what this fine man called Thomas Byrnes, who was the first Chief of Detectives? He called him "master psychologist"!'

'And I take it he wasn't.'

'One of the first things that Byrnes did after he was appointed was to have an especially thick carpet laid down on his office floor,' Meade said. 'And can you guess why he did that, Sam?'

'To muffle the noise when he was beating up a suspect?'

'Exactly. He'd have the suspect stand in front of him, manacled between two detectives, and if he didn't like the answers he was getting, he'd proceed to pound the crap out of the man. Now that's what I *call* psychology. But it was *after* he'd beaten the confession out of the suspect that he'd be *really* clever.'

'How so?'

'Say he'd got a guy in the cells who'd confessed to a bank robbery – and who might even have been guilty of it. He'd call a press conference and tell the reporters that the robber was still at large, but that the brilliant investigative team from the Bureau of Detectives was following up a number of clues. He could then confidently promise that an arrest would be made within a few hours. And guess what? Since he already had his man, he was always able to keep his promise – which made the reporters think he was a very smart cop indeed.'

'That really *is* clever,' Blackstone admitted. 'Totally despicable, it's true, but very clever.'

'Were you involved in the Whitechapel hunt for Jack the Ripper, Sam?' Meade asked.

Blackstone shook his head. 'Not really. I'd only just joined the force at that time, so I was on the edges of the investigation, at best.'

'Byrnes gave a press conference in which he told the world how, if he'd been in charge, they'd have caught the man right away. He said he'd have gone to work in a *common sense* way, instead of following mere theories, which was what Scotland Yard seemed to be doing.'

'And just what *was* this "common sense way" of his?' Blackstone asked.

'He said that rather than just wait for the Ripper to seek out new victims, he would have manufactured them for him. Yes, he really did use that word,' Meade continued, with disgust. '*Manufactured!*'

'But what does it mean?' Blackstone asked.

'It means that he would have taken fifty female habitués . . .'

'By which he meant prostitutes?'

'That *is* what he meant. But remember, he was talking to reporters from *family* newspapers, and you can't go using words like "prostitute" in that kind of journal.'

'Although you can go into graphic detail when you're describing the terrible things that happened to the poor women,' Blackstone said.

'Well, exactly. At any rate, Byrnes said he would have taken fifty female habitués of Whitechapel and "covered the ground" with them.'

'Taken them to deserted streets and dumped them?' Blackstone suggested.

'Couldn't have phrased it better myself,' Meade replied. 'Once the women had been abandoned, Byrnes went on, he would have infiltrated the area with his men, and waited for the Ripper to strike. "Even if one of the women fell victim, I should get the murderer," he told the reporters – which is a nice *family newspaper* way of saying that if she got her throat cut and her stomach sliced open, he would have been able to make an arrest.'

'He sounds like a nice man,' Blackstone said.

'A real prince,' Meade replied. 'I could tell you much more about him, but you're probably better hearing it from Sergeant Saddler.'

'Who's Sergeant Saddler?'

'He's Inspector Patrick O'Brien's partner, and he's the next man on our list of people to talk to.'

The desk sergeant looked up at Blackstone with a certain degree of wariness in his eyes, and at Meade with little less than contempt.

It was a neat trick to be able to do both things at the same time, Blackstone thought.

'Have you seen Detective Sergeant Saddler today?' Meade asked.

The desk sergeant shook his head.

'Do you know if he's out on a case?' Meade enquired.

The sergeant shook his head a second time.

Blackstone leant forward, with both his hands resting on the desk. 'Do you know a cure for grazed knuckles?' he asked politely.

The desk sergeant glanced down at his hands. 'Your knuckles *ain't* grazed,' he pointed out.

'No, at the moment, they're not,' Blackstone said. 'But they might be soon, about thirty seconds from now.'

The desk sergeant quickly pushed his chair backwards. 'Is that a threat?' he asked, worriedly.

'Why should I threaten you, of all people?' Blackstone wondered. 'After all, ever since this morning we've been like old pals, haven't we?'

'Look, I don't know where Saddler is,' the desk sergeant said. 'I'd tell you if I did. But just 'cos I ain't seen him don't mean he ain't come in, so why don't you look in his office?'

'Thank you very much, Sergeant,' Blackstone said. 'You really have been most helpful.'

The office that Inspector O'Brien and Sergeant Saddler had shared was at the opposite end of the basement from the cells.

'Is the whole of the Detective Bureau down here?' Blackstone asked Meade, as they walked down the steps.

'Nope, just Patrick's room,' Meade replied. 'The rest of the Bureau wanted to keep him as far away from them as possible, and he always said that was all to the good – because when they began to feel comfortable in his presence, he'd *really* start to worry.'

They had reached the door. Meade knocked, and, when there was no answer after a few seconds, he knocked again.

'I don't think he's in there,' Blackstone said.

'I don't think he is, either,' Meade agreed.

He reached down, and grasped the doorknob. When it turned, he quickly released it again.

'Is there something wrong?' Blackstone asked, and realized that he himself must think there was, since he was whispering.

'Saddler would never leave the door unlocked,' Meade hissed back.

'Do you think there's *someone else* in there?'

Meade drew his .32 revolver from its holster. 'I don't know, but I'm sure as hell going to find out.'

He grasped the revolver in both hands, and signalled with his eyes that the inspector should turn the knob again and push the door slightly.

For a moment Blackstone hesitated, and even thought of counselling caution. But, when all was said and done, Meade was a man – and men made their own decisions.

Blackstone grasped the knob, turned it, and gave it a slight shove.

Meade kicked the door wide open and rushed into the room, his hands swinging his weapon in a wide arc, in search of a target.

But there was no one in the office who *needed* shooting. In fact, there was no one in the office at all.

Blackstone stepped over the threshold behind Meade. The office furniture consisted of two desks and a filing cabinet, he quickly noted. There was a plain calendar on the wall with all the previous days in the month firmly crossed off. In the corner of the room, there was a large blackboard – resting on an easel – which had been wiped clean of chalk. It was all very practical and very utilitarian – the working space of a serious-minded crusader like O'Brien.

There was *one* jarring note, however – a framed poster from the Grand Theatre, Broadway, which proclaimed that Henry Mortimer and Mary Brookes would be appearing in a new production of Macbeth. The picture below the legend showed the two of them, Macbeth-Mortimer and Lady Macbeth-Brookes, gazing nobly and tragically into the near distance.

'Was O'Brien a theatregoer?' Blackstone wondered.

But Meade had his mind on other – more pressing – matters.

He had gone straight to the filing cabinet and opened the top
drawer – and now he was staring mournfully into it.

'Empty!' he cried. 'Completely empty.'

He slid open the second – lower – drawer, and found the
same.

He tried the drawers in both desks, and when he got the
same result, he sat down into what had probably been Inspector
O'Brien's chair and buried his head in his hands.

'How could I have been so damn *stupid*?' he moaned. 'I
should have known that this would happen. I should have
come here the moment that I heard about Patrick's death.'

'Perhaps his sergeant has removed the files for safe-keeping,'
Blackstone suggested.

Meade shook his head despairingly. 'If Sergeant Saddler
had done it himself, he'd only have removed the files that
really mattered. But these thieving bastards didn't know which
of the files mattered and which of them didn't – and that's
why they took *everything*.'

He was right, Blackstone thought. Like burglars – which
was, in fact, exactly what they were – they hadn't dared waste
time sifting through the documents, so they had simply taken
the lot.

'So now we have no way of finding out what case Patrick
was working on when he was killed,' Meade said. 'And since
we don't know that, a second thing we don't know is who
had the strongest motive to have him murdered by the Five
Points Gang.' He paused. 'You do believe I'm right, now, don't
you, Sam? You do believe that it was a policeman who ordered
his execution?'

Blackstone nodded. He didn't *want* to think that any
policeman would have a comrade murdered, but the further
they got into the investigation, the more likely it seemed that
that was the only possible explanation.

'Sergeant Saddler will know what cases Inspector O'Brien
was working on,' he said, in an effort to cheer Meade up. 'If
he's anything like me, all the files will be in his head.'

'Yes, they will, won't they?' Meade agreed bleakly. 'And
you can't take files out of a head like you can take them out
of a filing cabinet, can you? When they're in a man's head,
the only thing you can do is *kill* him.'

'You think he's dead?'

'I don't know. But isn't it likely that he is? They didn't hesitate to kill an inspector. Why would they even think twice about doing the same thing to his sergeant?'

Why indeed? Blackstone agreed silently.

'Wait a minute!' Meade said. 'There's one other person who may have known about the case Patrick was working on. And they won't have dared to kill her, however desperate they were to shut her up – because even sons-of-bitches like them have some standards – even they would baulk at killing a lady.'

'Who are you talking about?'

'Have you ever discussed any of your cases with a woman, Sam?' Meade asked.

'Yes, I have,' Blackstone said, as the memories – most of them painful – came flooding back to him.

He'd discussed his cases with all three women who'd become an important part of his life – Hannah, Agnes and Ellie Carr – and each time it had been a mistake.

'I'd certainly discuss my cases with Clarissa – if I had the opportunity,' Meade said, a little wistfully. 'Do you see what I'm getting at here?'

'You think that Inspector O'Brien might have discussed *his* cases with his wife?'

'I do!' Meade replied, his natural enthusiasm breaking through to the surface again.

'Then it might be a good idea to go and see her,' Blackstone suggested.

'Just what I was thinking,' Meade said.

EIGHT

Pleasant brownstone houses lined the quiet, leafy street. The houses had probably originally been built as private dwellings for single families, Blackstone thought. But that was clearly not the case now – the number of bell-pushes he had observed by every front door suggested to him that while this might still be seen as a desirable area, it was not *quite* as desirable as it had once been.

'One of the few regrets that I ever heard Patrick O'Brien

express was that he could not provide a better life for his family,' Alex Meade said. 'Oh, don't get me wrong, you'll find the apartment pleasant enough – but Mary O'Brien was born into better.'

'So *Mrs* O'Brien comes from a rich family, does she?' Blackstone asked.

'The family has a nice house in the city, a mansion on Long Island, a small army of servants and three or four carriages,' Meade said seriously. 'But that's not *rich* by New York standards.'

'No?'

'Certainly not! New York rich is when you maintain a large ocean-going yacht. New York rich is when you throw a large party and all the men who attend it are offered cigars rolled in hundred dollar bills.'

'New York rich is when you're trapped somewhere between the vulgar and the obscene,' Blackstone said sourly.

'Now you're getting the picture,' Meade said. 'Of course, Mary's family *want* to be rich – they've made that perfectly plain.'

'How?'

'By the way they've gone about expanding their empire. Mary's father is a cigar manufacturer, and her two elder sisters made what I'm sure he would call "good" marriages, which is to say they married not only within their class but also within the cigar industry.'

'Conquest by marriage.'

'Exactly.'

'But I take it that Mary wasn't prepared to follow in her older sisters' footsteps?'

'No, she wasn't. She was a rebel right from the start – someone who wanted to make her *own* mark on the world. So she told her father she was going to train to be an actress, and *he* told *her* if she did, he'd cut her off without a penny. That was meant to bring her to heel, but it didn't. Knowing her as I do, I expect it made her even more determined to follow her dream.'

'So she trained to be an actress, and ended up playing Lady Macbeth on Broadway,' Blackstone said, remembering the poster on the wall of Inspector O'Brien's office.

'How did you know that?' Meade asked, astonished.

Blackstone grinned. 'I'm a detective, remember,' he said. 'A famous *Scotland Yard* detective.'

'I still don't see how you could have . . .'

'So was Mary any good as an actress?' Blackstone asked.

'I'm too young to have ever seen her on the stage myself, but Patrick – who was very proud of her – kept some of her reviews.'

'And what did these reviews say?'

'The only one I remember clearly was on her Lady Macbeth – which I still haven't worked out how you could possibly have known about,' Meade said, studying the other man's face for clues.

Blackstone grinned again. 'A magician never reveals how he does his tricks,' he said. 'So what *did* the reviewer say about her?'

'He said that despite the fact she was actually far too young to play the role, she was stunning in it. And I think she must have been, because even though she's not exactly beautiful – as you'll soon see for yourself – she had scores of admirers, and dozens of marriage proposals, several of them from millionaires.'

'And yet she chose to marry Patrick O'Brien, an honest – and therefore relatively impoverished – policeman.'

'Yes, she did. And you'd have understood the reason for that if you'd ever met him,' Meade said, with a sudden passion. 'Patrick wasn't particularly imposing physically, and you certainly wouldn't have called him handsome, but there was an honesty and integrity about him which could be quite overwhelming at times. It was almost like . . .' He struggled to find the right words. 'It was almost like being in the presence of a column of pure white light.' Meade looked down at his hands, as if he thought he'd embarrassed himself. 'I think I must sound rather foolish to you,' he mumbled.

'Not at all,' Blackstone assured him. 'There's nothing wrong with—'

'We're here,' Meade interrupted, as if eager to leave further discussion on the subject behind him.

He rang the doorbell and it was answered by a woman in her mid-thirties who had a prettiness about her which owed more to character than to anything purely physical.

It could only be Mary O'Brien herself, Blackstone thought.

The woman favoured Meade with a weak smile. 'It was good of you to come, Alex,' she said.

'It was the least I could do, Mary,' Meade replied awkwardly.

'This is Sam Blackstone,' he continued, gesturing towards his companion. 'He's a policeman from England. He just arrived today.'

'I am pleased to meet you, Mr Blackstone,' Mary O'Brien said formally. 'Welcome to America.'

She held out her hand, and Blackstone took it. Her palm felt cold, and though there was some strength to her grip, it was obviously costing her a considerable effort to maintain it.

There was a short, awkward silence, then Meade said stiffly, 'Though the main reason for our call was to offer you our condolences, there is also a secondary purpose.'

Mary nodded, as if she'd been quite expecting him to say something of that nature.

'You're the one who'll be investigating Patrick's murder, aren't you?' she asked.

'Yes,' Meade confirmed.

Mary nodded again. 'I could not have asked for anyone better,' she said. 'Do you wish to ask me some questions?'

'If you can bear it.'

'I can bear anything that *needs* to be borne,' Mary said firmly. 'But we can't talk on the doorstep. You must come inside.'

'It's not necessary.'

'You must come inside,' Mary repeated. 'But since I haven't yet told the children of Patrick's tragic death, I'd be grateful if you did not mention it in their presence.'

She led the two detectives down a pleasant (though modest) hallway into a modest (though pleasant) living room. Then she walked over to the door at the far end of the room and called out, 'Where are you, children? We have visitors who would like to meet you.'

The three children – a boy and two girls – appeared almost immediately. The boy was probably around eight or nine, the younger girl eleven, and the elder thirteen. They were all dressed neatly – if not expensively – and carried themselves with an air of children who had been taught how to behave.

'You already know Mr Meade, but the other gentleman is Mr Blackstone, who is visiting us from England,' Mary O'Brien said. She turned to Blackstone. 'And these are my children, Isobel, my elder daughter, Emily, her sister, and Benjamin, my son.'

The two girls curtsied prettily, but Benjamin (as if he had

already sensed that he was now the man of the house) boldly stepped forward and held out his hand to Blackstone.

'Very nicely done, children,' Mary said approvingly.

'Thank you, Mama,' the three said in quiet unison.

'And now,' Mary continued, 'since we grown-ups wish to talk amongst ourselves, I would be grateful if you would go to your own rooms for a little while.'

'Of course, Mama,' the children said, and dutifully left the room.

'Please be seated,' Mary said, indicating two armchairs, and when Blackstone and Meade had sat down, she continued. 'This is normally a coffee-drinking house, but in honour of Mr Blackstone, we will have tea today.'

'There's no need . . .' Meade began.

But Mary, who had sat down herself, had already picked up the small brass bell which lay on the occasional table and was ringing it.

A girl, dressed in a simple maid's uniform, appeared almost immediately at the door.

'We would like a pot of tea, Jenny,' Mary said. 'You remember how I taught you to make tea, don't you?'

The maid looked down at the floor. 'Yes, ma'am.'

'Good, then see you follow the procedure extremely carefully, because this gentleman – being an Englishman – is something of an expert when it comes to the question of tea.'

She had said it lightly, almost as a joke to put the girl at ease, but Jenny took it deathly seriously.

'I'll do my best, ma'am,' she said. 'I *always* do my best.'

'I know you do,' Mary said, kindly.

The girl couldn't have been more than two or three years older than Isobel O'Brien, Blackstone thought, as he watched the maid leave, but there was a world of difference between them. Isobel, while she clearly knew her place in the order of things, was open and confident. Jenny, on the other hand, had a pinched, haunted face and wore her insecurity like a thick, suffocating blanket.

'You're quite right, Mr Blackstone, she *is* a frightened little thing,' Mary O'Brien said.

'I never meant to . . .' Blackstone began.

'Other people we are acquainted with hire their maids through agencies,' Mary said. 'We take ours from the orphanage, and because my husband is the man he is, he invariably chooses the girls that, for one reason or another, no one else wants to take. They are always difficult at first, but I persevere with them, and train them until they are first-class housemaids. And then Patrick finds them a position in a much grander establishment, and we begin the process all over again.' She gulped. 'I'm talking about him as if he were still alive, aren't I?'

'That's understandable,' Blackstone said.

'And worse than that, I'm talking as if I *disapproved* of what he did, and I *never* meant to suggest that. He was right to help the girls to better themselves – he wanted *everyone* to better themselves.'

'I'm sure he did,' Blackstone said soothingly.

'You really shouldn't be alone in this apartment, you know, Mary,' Meade said.

'But I'm not alone,' Mary replied. 'I have my children and my faithful Jenny with me.'

'But no one whose shoulder you can allow yourself to cry on,' Meade pointed out.

Mary sighed. 'I try to convince myself that I'm waiting for the right moment to tell the children about what happened to their father,' she said. 'But it isn't true. What I am really doing is trying to gather up enough *strength* to tell them. But until I *have* told them, everything must go on as normal, and if the house was suddenly flooded with sobbing relatives and friends, it wouldn't take the children long to work out that something was wrong, now would it?'

'You can't afford to leave it *too* long before you tell them,' Alex Meade said.

'I know I can't,' Mary replied. 'It's impossible to keep them imprisoned in this apartment for ever, and the moment they step out in the wider world, they're bound to hear it from someone else. And so, sometime soon – perhaps as soon as you leave – I *will* tell them.'

'I could do it,' Meade suggested, though it was clear from the expression on his face that it was not a job he would relish.

'You're a sweet boy, Alex . . .' Mary said.

'I meant it!' Meade protested.

'I know you did, but it really *is* my responsibility.' Mary took a deep breath, and then continued. 'But this is not what you're here to talk about. You came to ask me some questions, so please ask them.'

'Do you know anything about the case your husband was working on when he died?' Meade asked.

'*The* case?' Mary repeated. 'Patrick never worked on just *one* case in his entire career. He saw abuse and corruption everywhere, you see, and he wanted to end it all at once. He did the work of ten men, but, of course, however hard he tried, he could never really hold back the tide.'

Jenny returned, clutching the tea tray so tightly that her knuckles had turned quite white.

'Shall I . . . shall I pour it, ma'am?' she asked, laying the tray fearfully on the table, as if she thought that – even at this late stage in the process – something was about to go disastrously wrong.

'No, I'll serve, thank you,' Mary said.

But still Jenny lingered, almost – Blackstone thought – as if she was desperate to hear what they were talking about.

'Is there something else, Jenny?' Mary asked.

'I–I was wondering what the master would like for his supper, so I can begin . . .'

'The master will not be dining at home this evening,' Mary told her.

The news seemed to unnerve the girl. 'Then what shall I . . .? I mean, there's things . . .'

'One of the virtues that I've endeavoured to teach you is the ability to think for yourself,' Mary said, sounding much more like the mistress of the house now. 'And I thought I'd been fairly successful in that particular undertaking.'

'Oh, you have, ma'am.'

'Then I see no need to break off my conversation with these gentlemen in order to give you specific instructions. Look around the apartment, see what needs to done, and do it.'

'Yes, ma'am,' Jenny said, then she bobbed down into an awkward curtsy and fled.

'She's normally much better than this,' Mary said. 'In fact, of all the maids who've passed through this apartment, she's one of my biggest successes.'

'It's probably our unexpected visit which has unsettled her,' Blackstone suggested.

'It probably is,' Mary O'Brien agreed. She shook her head

sadly from side to side. 'She'll have to go, of course – the poor little thing. I simply can't afford to keep her on now that we won't be receiving Patrick's salary any more. I'm not even sure the *rest of us* will be able to go on living here.'

Meade coughed. 'I'd . . . I'd be more than prepared to loan you some money,' he said.

'I couldn't take it,' Mary said immediately.

'Why ever not?'

'Because I have no means of ever paying you back.'

'I wouldn't *want* you to pay me back.'

Mary O'Brien fixed Meade with a penetrating gaze. 'You offered to give Patrick that same kind of loan, didn't you, Alex?' she asked.

Meade squirmed like a bug under a microscope. 'I'm a rich man,' he said. 'And I so admired what your husband was doing that I wanted to free him from the daily concerns of having to—'

'But Patrick wouldn't accept that kind of loan from you, would he?' Mary said, in a voice which would not be denied an honest answer.

'No, he wouldn't,' Meade admitted, like a guilty schoolboy who has realized there is nowhere left to hide.

'If Patrick wouldn't accept it, then neither can I.' Mary lifted the teapot. 'I'd better pour the tea before it goes cold.'

'I know you said that your husband always worked on several cases at once,' Blackstone said, 'but I was wondering if there was one case that he was giving special attention to.'

'Patrick never talked about his work at home,' Mary said. 'I think he was trying to protect me from the seedier side of life.' She paused for a moment. 'Why is it, Mr Blackstone, that all men – even a thoughtful, understanding man like my Patrick – so underestimate the characters of their women that they are forever trying to shield them? Some women don't *want* to be shielded.'

'No,' Blackstone agreed, thinking of one of *his* women – Dr Ellie Carr – with whom he had once hoped to make a life. 'Some women don't.'

'I do know, if this is of any help to you, that Patrick has been spending a great deal of his time recently in the Lower East Side,' Mary O'Brien said. 'But the person who you should really be talking to about Patrick's investigations is his partner, Sergeant Saddler.'

There was another moment's awkward silence, then Alex Meade said, 'That's true. But the problem is, you see, no one at police headquarters seems to know where he is.'

'They wouldn't,' Mary O'Brien replied.

'What makes you say that?' Blackstone asked.

'When Sergeant Saddler heard the news about my husband's murder, he was naturally terrified that exactly the same fate was in store for him, and so he went into hiding.'

'How do you know that?' Meade asked.

'He rang me.'

'To tell you he'd gone into hiding?'

'To offer me his condolences. And to tell me that if I needed him, he would come to me – at whatever the risk to himself.'

'So you know where he is?' Blackstone asked.

'No, he thought it would be putting me in too much danger to know that. But he did give me a telephone number at which he could be reached.'

'And may we have that number?' Meade asked.

'Of course,' Mary O'Brien said.

NINE

I n his soldiering days, Blackstone had never thought of the platform on an Indian railway station as merely a place to wait for the arrival of a train. Instead, he had seen it as a vast stage, on which the drama of Indian life – with all its colour, diversity and sheer bloody confusion – had been enacted on a daily basis.

The cast – and the action – was almost invariably the same, wherever the stage happened to be located. Hours before the train was due to arrive, the platform would begin to fill up with its actors, and by the time the locomotive actually chugged slowly into the station, there would not be even a square inch of space free. Peasants, with sacks over their shoulders, would jostle for position. Low-level clerks, in sweat-sodden wing collars, would scowl their disapproval of such disorderly

manoeuvres, while indulging in those same manoeuvres themselves. Fathers carried small children above their heads to
avoid them being crushed, wives held on to their husbands to
stop being swept away in a sea of souls. And even before the
train had fully come to a halt, the scramble for a seat on it –
or simply a place to stand – had begun.

The station platform of the Third Avenue 'El' at Chatham
Square reminded him of those times. It was true there were
no brown faces on this platform, that the men were wearing
overalls rather than loose white jackets, and that instead of
being poked in the eye with the edge of a bag of rice, he ran
the risk of being barked on the shin by a bag of workman's
tools. But for all that, the crush was the same, the jockeying
for position was the same, and the smell of sweat – while not
exactly the same – was equally unpleasant.

'We could have taken a cab, but it would probably have
been slower,' Meade said. 'Anyway, I thought travelling on
the "El" was something you should experience at least once.'

'It was very thoughtful of you to give me the opportunity,'
Blackstone said, as a shift of bodies behind him almost pushed
him on to the track.

'Chicago's "El" is a very different world,' Meade said. 'The
trains are pleasanter, and they've electrified the track there,
but the people like J.P. Morgan – who own the New York "El"
– don't see the point in making any improvements while it's
still a moneymaking machine just as it is.'

The train appeared, its engine belching out smoke and cinders,
and the moment the doors had opened, the people on the platform surged forward, pushing those passengers who had intended
to disembark at this station further back into the carriages.

After an almost indecently short wait, the train set off again.
Its journey took it within a few feet of second- and third-floor
apartments, and as it passed them, the windows shook and
rattled. Through those windows, Blackstone saw the people
inside the apartments – men in shirtsleeves, women sewing,
a child playing with wooden horses on wheels.

'Guess why there's no "El" running up Fifth Avenue,' Meade
said, shouting to be heard over the noise of the rattling train.

'Because that's where the rich live,' Blackstone shouted back.

'Because that's where the rich live,' Meade agreed.

They reached 59th Street, and through a combination of

luck and elbowing managed to reach the platform before the train pulled out again.

On foot, they cut across town to Central Park, where they had arranged to meet Inspector O'Brien's partner, Sergeant Saddler.

'Why was he so insistent on meeting in the park?' Blackstone asked, as they walked.

'Because he knows he's safe from the Lower East Side gangs there,' Meade told him.

Blackstone nodded. 'Makes sense,' he said. 'Even a hot-headed kid sent out to prove himself isn't going to attempt to kill Saddler with so many potential witnesses around.'

'It's nothing to do with potential witnesses,' Meade told him. 'Saddler will be safe from the gangs in Central Park because he knows that no gang members will *be* in Central Park.'

'He *knows* that, does he?' Blackstone asked sceptically.

'Yes.'

'For a fact?'

'Certainly.'

'How can he be so sure?'

'He can be sure,' Mead said, 'because Central Park is *not* in the Lower East Side.'

'So what's to stop one of these gang members taking the "El", just like we did?' Blackstone asked.

'In theory, there's nothing at all to stop it,' Meade replied. 'But it just doesn't happen.'

'Why not?'

'Because they never even see it as an option. Their world is bounded by a few city blocks. It's all they know about, and all they care about. They're born there, live there, and die there – and they'd never dream of leaving it, even for a day. Their existence down on the Lower East Side is a violent one, right enough, but they're not afraid of violence and they're not afraid of an early death – it's the unknown which scares the shit out of them.'

They entered the park on the south-eastern side, and stood with their backs to the Pond.

'The first superintendent of this park was a man called Olmsted,' Meade said. 'He was high-minded, upright and honest. He refused to be bribed or to give bribes, but even a good man like him couldn't stop Tammany Hall using the park's construction to its own advantage.'

'Is that right?' asked Blackstone, who was getting used to playing the role of hayseed stooge to Meade's smart city boy – and was even starting to enjoy it. 'And just how did Tammany Hall manage that?'

'It was easy,' Meade said. 'Tammany provided the labour for the works, so just by the act of giving men jobs which hadn't existed before, it was already buying their votes. But that wasn't enough for Boss Tweed, who was running the machine at the time. He came up with the brilliant idea of having not just one gang of labourers working on the job, but *two*.'

'Why did he need two gangs?' Blackstone asked, as he knew he was supposed to.

'Because one gang planted the trees in the daytime, and the other dug them up at night,' Meade said. 'Then the next day, the first crew would plant them again, and the next night, the second crew would dig them up again. So instead of giving a hundred men ten days' work, Tweed was giving two hundred men work for as long as he wanted to. And, of course, that raised the cost of the project – which meant there was more money for Boss Tweed to skim off.'

A large man in a tired blue suit appeared at the entrance to the park. He seemed edgy, and even from a distance Blackstone could tell that he was sweating heavily.

'Is that him?' Blackstone asked.

'Yes, that's Sergeant Saddler,' Meade agreed, and immediately turned around to face the water.

Meade was in charge, and Blackstone was more than prepared to follow his lead, but as he turned himself, he said, 'Why are we giving the sergeant the cold shoulder, Alex?'

'We're not. He knows we're here, and when he's made sure we're not being watched, he'll come over and talk to us.'

'I thought you told me the Lower East Side gangs wouldn't operate in Central Park,' Blackstone said.

'The gangs aren't the only killers in New York,' Meade replied.

They stood staring into the water for perhaps three minutes before Saddler decided it was safe to sidle up to them, and even then he said, 'Don't look at me. Look at the Pond.'

'Is there somebody here?' Meade asked.

'I don't think so,' Saddler replied, in a voice which seemed half-strangled. 'But when you're in my situation – when your boss has just been murdered – you don't want to take any chances.'

'Before we start talking about Patrick, why don't you tell Mr Blackstone about the extent of police corruption in New York City?' Meade suggested.

'Can't you tell him yourself?' Saddler asked.

'I *have* told him myself,' Meade replied. 'But I don't think he quite believes it's as bad as I say it is. And I can understand that, because if I came here from the outside, I don't think *I'd* quite believe it was that bad, either.'

From out of the corner of his eye, Blackstone saw Sergeant Saddler give a slight shrug.

'The whole thing stinks,' the sergeant said. 'Saloons are supposed to close at one o'clock in the morning. and stay shut all day Sunday, but that's bad for business, so instead they pay their local precinct twenty dollars a month and stay open. Then there are the brothels. They pay fifty dollars a month for protection. But that ain't the end of it – not by a long way. Sometimes the whores steal from their clients, and *sometimes* the clients complain about it to the police. It don't get them nowhere. The police never arrest the whores.'

'Why not?' Blackstone asked.

'Because the patrolmen get their cut of what's been stolen,' Saddler said. 'Then there's the supply racket.'

'What supply racket?'

'Brothels need all kinds of stuff to keep running. Booze, cigarettes, food, medicine, linen. But since the brothels are illegal, the precinct captains don't allow any of the legitimate businesses to sell them anything.'

'So where do they get what they need?'

Saddler laughed, though there was not much evidence of humour in it. 'They get their supplies from the *police*. The captains buy the stuff from the legitimate supplier and sell it on to the brothels for a profit.'

'Jesus!' Blackstone said.

'Then there are the opium dens – there are ten thousand of them in New York, and they all have to pay a bribe. Pushcart pedlars give patrolmen three dollars a week to stay in business. The sail makers on South Street pay just to hang out the canvas banners advertising their wares. The inspectors and captains take the biggest cut of the money, but everybody gets their share.'

'Is that why you joined the Detective Bureau?' Blackstone asked. 'To get away from all that?'

Saddler laughed again. 'Hell, no, Mr Blackstone! The reason that I joined the Detective Bureau was because there was *even more* money to be made there than there was in uniform.'

'How?'

'By working the rich areas, rather than the poor. See, Inspector Byrnes, who was the first Chief of Detectives—'

'Mr Blackstone knows who he was,' Meade interrupted.

'Inspector Byrnes figured out that the people who really needed protection – by which he meant the people who could really *afford* protection – were the bankers and stock-brokers in the Wall Street area. So one of the first things he did after he was appointed was to ask the brokers if they'd give him an office right there in the Stock Exchange – and seeing how that could work to their advantage, they agreed immediately. The next thing the inspector did was draw an invisible line around the area and send the word out on to the streets that no criminals would be allowed to operate inside it.'

'Well, no *common* criminals, anyways,' Meade said.

'That's right,' Saddler agreed. 'The criminals in wing collars and top hats, who worked in banks and brokerage houses, could come and go as they damn well pleased.'

The sergeant suddenly stopped talking, and glanced nervously over his shoulder.

'Something wrong?' Meade asked.

'I just got the feeling, for a second there, that we were being watched,' Saddler said.

'And are we?'

'No, I don't think so. It must just be my nerves playing me up. But, hell, who *wouldn't* be nervous in my position?'

'Who indeed?' Blackstone asked. 'Do you think you can stay long enough to finish your story?'

'If it don't take *too* long,' Saddler said. He paused, then admitted, 'I've forgotten what I was saying.'

'Byrnes drew an invisible line around the Wall Street area,' Blackstone prompted.

'Oh, yeah. But there's no point in drawing that line if you ain't going to enforce it – especially in a place like Wall Street, where everybody knows there are such rich pickings – so enforce-ment was just what the Detective Bureau spent most of its time doing. Course, paying so much attention to the Wall Street area meant that we didn't solve much crime anywhere else – but why should we, when there was no profit in it?'

'Just how much profit was there in guarding Wall Street?' Blackstone wondered.

'Plenty, especially for Inspector Byrnes. See, the sergeants just got cash from the brokers for protecting them, but what the inspector got was tips about which stocks to buy – and since the system's crooked, that advice was *never* wrong and those stocks *always* went up.'

'How much money *did* he make?' Blackstone asked.

'Hard to say for sure, but the Lexow Committee found one bank account of his with three hundred and fifty thousand dollars in it. They asked him to explain how a man who earned less than three thousand dollars a year could end up with so much money, and he couldn't explain it at all. But even then, he wasn't arrested. Even then, he hung on for a couple more years before resigning from the force.'

'You're being very frank about what you and others have done,' Blackstone said.

'Yes, sir, I am,' Saddler agreed earnestly.

'Why?' Blackstone asked.

'Tell Mr Blackstone about what happened to you to make you a new man,' Meade suggested.

'I heard the Reverend Parkhurst preach,' Saddler said simply.

'Reverend Parkhurst?' Blackstone repeated.

'He was the pastor who stirred up all the fuss about corruption and led to the Lexow Committee being formed,' Meade explained.

'The reason I happened to hear the reverend speak was that I was on the tail of this judas goat . . .' Saddler continued.

'This what?' Blackstone asked.

'Judas goat. It was another one of Inspector Byrnes' ideas. See, we didn't always charge everybody we arrested – not even all the guilty ones. Sometimes, we'd let a suspect go, but we'd follow him, and see who he talked to. Then we'd rearrest him, and work him over until he gave us something on the people he'd been associating with.'

'Something real – or something he'd simply made up to avoid further beating?' Blackstone asked.

'Didn't really matter, as long as it gave us grounds to arrest *them*. Then we'd let the judas goat go again, as long as he promised to give evidence against his friends. You see how it works?'

'Yes,' Blackstone said. 'By using the judas goat, you make several arrests instead of just the one.'

'And that looks good on paper,' Saddler said. 'And not just *on* paper, but in the *newspapers*. Most of the citizens of New York thought Inspector Byrnes was their saviour. And only the Detective Bureau – and the poor devils we'd arrested – knew the real truth.'

'You were telling us about hearing the Reverend Parkhurst preach,' Meade reminded him.

'Oh, yeah. The goat realized I was on his tail, so he dived into the Madison Square Presbyterian Church. And I followed him, and sat down beside him. And do you know what I said to him – right there in the *House of God*?'

'No.'

'I said to him, God forgive me, "When this service is over, you'd better tell me something I can use – or I'm gonna break both your arms." Then Reverend Parkhurst stepped into the pulpit, and even before he started to speak, it was like a bright shining light had entered my world. And as he spoke – about how there was all this vice in this modern Gomorrah, and about how the police were feathering their own nests instead of stamping it out – that light grew brighter and brighter. And when the service was over, I looked afresh at the poor wretch next to me, who'd been driven by poverty to become what he was, and who I'd been determined to abuse. And I wept. I left that church a new man, Mr Blackstone, and, though I may be guilty of the sin of pride in even saying this, a better man.'

'Is that when you met Inspector O'Brien?' Blackstone asked.

'It's when I *sought out* Inspector O'Brien,' Saddler replied. 'I was now a true believer, floating in the midst of a sea of heathens. I'd already given all the money I'd made through graft and corruption to the Reverend Parkhurst's church, but I knew that, without support, I would slip back into that trough of depravity from which the Reverend Parkhurst's words had raised me. And I also knew that only one man could give me that support – Inspector O'Brien.'

'And so, a legendary team was born,' Meade said.

Saddler laughed again, bitterly this time.

'Legendary?' he repeated. 'I don't think so. Alexander the

Great, who conquered most of the known world, was a legend. George Washington, who brought America its freedom, was a legend. And what have we done? Built up cases – against a handful of patrolmen – which were *so* strong that even a Tammany-appointed judge couldn't ignore the evidence. Sent one sergeant to jail, and forced one captain into retirement. That's no more than skimming the frothy top off the scum. But what drove us on was the hope that one day – *one day* – we would land that really big case which would truly shake this city to its rotten core.'

'What were you working on just before the inspector was killed?' Meade asked.

'We had several investigations running.'

'Like what?'

'There was a fantail gambling ring in Chinatown that a couple of patrolmen were taking a percentage from. There was a sergeant who was selling off the bicycles belonging to the Police Bicycle Squad—'

'But nothing earth-shattering?' Meade interrupted. 'Nothing that would *truly* shake this city to its core?'

'No,' Saddler replied hesitantly.

'You don't seem entirely sure of that,' Meade pressed.

'I think Inspector O'Brien might have been working on something he hadn't told me about,' Saddler admitted.

'Hadn't *told* you about?' Meade repeated, incredulously. 'But you were his partner. And I know, from the things that he said to me about you, that he would have trusted you with his life.'

'And I like to think that I'd earned that trust. But Inspector O'Brien simply wasn't himself for the last few days of his life.'

'How had he changed?' Blackstone asked.

'He was on edge. Not exactly irritable with me – Mr O'Brien was too much of a gentleman for that – but like he was so stressed that he *wanted* to be angry. Then there were moments when he was hopeful, too – like you sometimes are when everything looks black, but you think there might just be a ray of sunshine on the horizon.'

'*He seemed excited. Or perhaps nervous. I do not know which one it was,*' Schultz, the fat German in Bayern Biergarten, had said.

'If he *was* working on something big, why *didn't* he tell you about it?' Meade asked.

'Maybe because he thought it would be dangerous for me to know too much. Maybe he was keeping me in the dark to protect me. Inspector O'Brien was that kind of guy.'

'So there's *nothing* you can tell us?' Meade asked disappointedly.

'No.'

'Think about it!'

'Like I told you—'

'This whole case might hang on one small scrap of information that only *you* can give us. Without that information, the killer may go free. So please, think about it,' Meade implored.

For perhaps two minutes Saddler was silent. Then he said, 'There maybe is one thing.'

'Yes?'

'This happened three or four days ago. I was leaving headquarters and heading for home, when I realized I'd left my door key on my desk. When I got back to the office, the inspector was on the phone. He didn't see me, and just carried on talking. I didn't mean to listen to what he was saying, but it was kind of hard to avoid it.'

'What *did* you hear him say?' Meade asked.

'He said, "Let's cut to the chase. We both know you're up your elbows in slime, and that one day you're going to go to jail for it. But if you'll help me out with this one thing, I might be able to make the situation a little easier for you when your fall eventually comes." The man on the other end of the line said something, and the inspector said, "Yes, I thought you'd see it that way, Senator Plunkitt." Then he noticed me standing there, and he hung up without another word.'

'And you're sure that's what he said? "I thought you'd see it that way, *Senator Plunkitt*"?' Meade asked excitedly.

'I'm sure,' Saddler confirmed.

For a few moments Meade was silent, then he said, 'What are your plans for the future, Sergeant Saddler?'

'Simple – to get the hell out of this city before whoever killed the inspector tracks me down.'

'And where will you go?'

'I got a sister who married and moved out of state. She'll look after me for a while.'

'Where exactly is she living?' Meade asked.

Saddler shook his head. 'I won't tell you.'

'But if I need to contact you . . .'

'It's for your own protection, because Inspector O'Brien was right – the less you know, the less you're in danger. If you do need me to come back to the city to help make your case, get in touch with Mrs O'Brien.'

'Because she'll know where you are?'

'Yeah. She'll *always* know where I am. Her husband gave me back my self-respect, and, if necessary, I'll lay down my life for her.'

Meade reached into his pocket, and extracted a buff-coloured envelope.

'Take this,' he said, slipping it surreptitiously to Saddler.

'What is it?' the other man asked.

'Money. It's not a fortune, by any means, but it will keep you going for a while.'

'You're a good man, Sergeant Meade,' Saddler said, putting the envelope in his pocket.

'No,' Meade countered, 'if there's one good man here, it's *you*, Sergeant Saddler.'

TEN

Alex Meade was unnaturally silent as he and Blackstone left the park, and his silence continued as they walked along 59th Street.

Blackstone decided to say nothing himself. He knew that there are times when a man needs to be left alone to think, and he was perfectly content to wait until the sergeant's brain had sorted through all the information that Sergeant Saddler had given them.

Finally, as they approached the Third Avenue 'El', Meade came to a sudden, decisive halt.

'Senator Plunkitt!' he exclaimed, as if he was revealing a great universal truth which, until that moment, had been deeply hidden.

'What about him?' Blackstone asked.

'Who would ever have thought that we could possibly have gotten *so* lucky *so* soon in the investigation, Sam?'

'Have we been lucky?' Blackstone asked. 'I didn't know that.' He smiled. 'But maybe if you told me who Senator Plunkitt *is*, I'd have more of an idea what you were talking about.'

'Senator Plunkitt is a political fixer without an equal in the whole of New York City,' Meade replied. 'He's the man that all the other politicians – all the other *election stealers* – watch carefully, in order to learn how it should really be done. He's an Irishman . . .'

'Now why doesn't that surprise me?' Blackstone asked drily.

'The man wasn't even *born* in this country, and yet, by the time he was twenty-eight years old was already a state assembly man, a New York City alderman, a police magistrate and a county supervisor.'

'It is quite impressive to have been all those things by such a young age,' Blackstone admitted.

'You're not listening to me, Sam,' Meade told him. 'He hadn't *been* all those things at such a young age.'

'I thought you just said . . .'

'He *was* all those things. At one and the same time! And he was drawing salaries from all of those positions. And how was that possible?'

'*You* tell *me*.'

'It was possible because he could fix elections like nobody else could, and so he had the full backing of Boss Tweed's Tammany Hall for whatever he wanted to do. And this, Sam, is the very man who Inspector O'Brien wanted to see just a few days before he was gunned down.'

'From what Sergeant Saddler overheard O'Brien say to Plunkitt on the phone, it doesn't sound as the inspector was after Senator Plunkitt himself,' Blackstone cautioned.

'No, it doesn't,' Meade agreed. 'But it *does* sound as if Patrick thought that Plunkitt had certain information which would be useful to his investigation, don't you think?'

'Possibly.'

'And why *wouldn't* Plunkitt have that information? He's been in city politics for nearly forty years now. If anyone in New York knows where all the bodies are buried, it's him.'

'That does seem likely.'

'Which means that we need to have a talk to him ourselves, every bit as much as Patrick did.'

'That's possibly true,' Blackstone agreed. 'But why should *he* want to talk to *us*?'

'For the exact same reason that he agreed to talk to Patrick O'Brien,' Meade said, as if it was obvious to him, and he was surprised it wasn't equally obvious to his companion.

'Maybe it would be better if you spelled it out a little more simply for me,' Blackstone suggested.

'Plunkitt knows that he's bound to fall one day – even the mighty Boss Tweed himself was eventually arrested and died in jail. And when Plunkitt does fall, he's going to need the support of people who, if they're not exactly on his side, are at least willing to give him the odd break. Besides, we've got *even more* leverage than Patrick had.'

'Have we?'

'Of course we have. Patrick went to see the senator, and now Patrick's dead.' Meade's eyes narrowed. 'That's a pretty suspicious sequence of events, don't you think?'

'It's not a sequence at all – it's just two events,' Blackstone pointed out. 'Besides, I'm sure there are a lot of people who've been to see Plunkitt in the last few days who *didn't* end up dead.'

'Yes, there are bound to be,' Meade agreed, brushing the argument aside with a wave of his hand, as if it were of no consequence at all. 'But how many of those people who've been to see him were New York police inspectors who had based their entire careers on investigating municipal corruption?'

'At a rough guess, I'd say only one.'

'*Of course* it's only one. Don't get me wrong, I'm not suggesting that Plunkitt had anything to do with Patrick's death himself, but Plunkitt *is* bound to worry that *we'll* try to link him to it, isn't he? And that alone should be enough to make him want to cooperate with us, at least to the extent that he'll tell us what it was that he told Patrick.'

There were times when Alex Meade could sound wise beyond his years, Blackstone thought. But there were also times – and this was one of them – when quite the reverse was true; when – like a small child – he seemed to believe that he could achieve anything he wanted to, simply *because* he wanted to.

And it was precisely because he was in the second kind of mood at that moment that Meade was able to paint such a rosy picture of a future meeting with Senator Plunkitt.

Certainly, Plunkitt had agreed to see O'Brien, but O'Brien had been an inspector who already had a formidable reputation, rather than an inexperienced young sergeant with an English detective, (who was still learning the rules of the game), in tow.

And even if the meeting *did* take place, Blackstone was far from convinced that Meade could use O'Brien's death to put pressure on the Irish-born senator – because any man who had played Tammany's game so successfully, for nearly forty years, was highly unlikely to be *that* easily intimidated.

'So what should we do now?' Meade asked, his enthusiasm still bubbling over. 'I suggest we go straight down to the Lower East Side, and trace the route Inspector O'Brien took last night.'

'Trace the route?' repeated Blackstone, who was suddenly feeling incredibly weary.

'That's right.'

'And how, exactly, do you *propose* to trace it?'

'We'll go around all the saloons and brothels, and ask the people there if they saw Inspector O'Brien last night. Then, by putting all the sightings together, we should be able to plot out . . .'

'How many saloons and brothels are there on the Lower East Side?' Blackstone asked.

Meade shrugged. 'I've never actually thought about it before, but I suppose there must be thousands of them.'

'And if we really put our backs into it, how many of them do you think we should be able to get round tonight?'

'Two or three dozen,' Meade said, starting to sound a little less sure of himself.

'And do you think that most of the *people* we talk to in those two or three dozen places are going to be forthcoming?'

'I beg your pardon?'

'If they *did* see Inspector O'Brien last night, are they likely to *admit* that they did?'

'They might admit it,' Meade said, though he was not even convincing himself.

'Or are they more likely to lie, in order to avoid being dragged into the middle of a police murder investigation?' Blackstone asked.

'They're more likely to lie,' Meade admitted. 'At least, they'll lie at first. But the more we question them, the more they'll begin to realize that it would be better for them if they started telling the truth.'

'And how long do you think it would *take* us to question one of these people?'

'Two or three hours.'

'So what you're talking about is questioning three or four people, from each of two or three dozen saloons and brothels, for up to two or three hours per person,' Blackstone said. 'Have I got that right, Alex?'

Alex Meade grinned self-consciously. 'It's not really one night's work, is it, Sam?'

'No,' Blackstone agreed. 'It isn't. The more you learn about police work, Sergeant Meade, the more you'll discover that most of it is no more than a long drawn-out grind.'

'You're quite right, of course,' Meade said, humbly. 'And anyway, I shouldn't be telling you what *I* think we should do, I should be asking what *you* think we should do. Because I do want to learn from you, Sam – I *know* I can learn from you. So what *do* you think . . .?'

'I think you should take me to my lodgings, while I've still got the strength to stand up,' Blackstone said.

The hotel was on Canal Street. It was called, as the desk sergeant had promised, the Mayfair Hotel, but with its cracked paint and peeling wallpaper, it was as different to any building in *London's* Mayfair as it could be.

Alex Meade was mortified by the state of the place.

'I knew that no hotel on Canal Street was ever going to be as swish as the hotels you find on Fifth Avenue,' he said. 'But even so, Sam . . .'

'The department probably booked me in here because it was no more than a short walk to the Mulberry Street police station,' Blackstone said. 'And as far as the place itself goes, it's perfectly fine.'

Better, in fact, than his lodgings in London, he thought, because while no Scotland Yard inspector ever lived in a grand style, most of them managed to live better than a man who donated half his salary to Dr Barnardo's Orphanage.

'This has nothing to do with being close to Mulberry Street,' Meade protested. 'Some clerk in the office booked you in here because it was *cheap*. And that's just typical of the stuffed shirts and pen-pushers who make this kind of decision. They simply don't have anything like enough respect for *real* policemen, but *I* do – so why don't you let me see if I can find you a room somewhere a little classier?'

'And who'll pay for this classier room?' Blackstone wondered. 'Will it be the police department? Or will it be you?'

Meade bit his lower lip. 'Why does no one ever seem to want to take my money?' he asked plaintively.

'Maybe because, since you're offering it so willingly, they think there has to be a catch,' Blackstone suggested.

'And do *you* think there's a catch, Sam?'

'No, I don't. But I don't want you running around, trying to find me a classier room, either. Not when you've got better things to do with your time.'

'Like what?' Meade asked.

Blackstone suppressed a sigh. 'Like trying to find out exactly where Inspector O'Brien went last night.'

'But that can't be done in one evening,' Meade countered. 'You said yourself that it was a long, drawn-out grind.'

'I said it *could be* a long, drawn-out grind,' Blackstone replied. 'But who knows, you could get lucky.'

Meade's eyes lit up with newly rekindled enthusiasm. 'Do you really think I might get somewhere?'

Not a chance! Blackstone thought.

'It's a possibility,' he said aloud.

Meade hesitated for a second, torn between his desire to see Blackstone treated properly and his urge to throw himself back into the investigation.

'Well, if you're sure you're happy with the accommodation that has been provided . . .' he said finally.

'I am.'

'Then I'll see you first thing in the morning?'

Meade's last words were meant to sound like a statement, but they came out as a question. As if he couldn't quite *believe* that Blackstone would still be there in the morning. As if he feared that the magical policeman from London – from whom he hoped to learn so much – would simply melt away in the night.

'I'll be here,' Blackstone promised.

'Until tomorrow, then,' Meade replied, sounding a little relieved.

Blackstone nodded. 'Good hunting,' he said.

* * *

The Third Street 'El' ran right past Blackstone's hotel bedroom window, so that now, instead of being one of the travelling watchers – as he'd been earlier in the day – he had become one of the stationary watched. For several minutes, he sat looking at the faces rushing by in the elevated trains. Occasionally, he waved – though no one ever waved back.

He did not mind the noise that the 'El' itself produced or the rattling of window-frames it left in its wake. He was a Londoner, brought up on noise, and – in a way – he embraced it as a comforting familiarity in a land where everything else seemed strange.

He had told Meade that he was exhausted, and he had not been lying. But now he found that sleep – perversely – would not come to him, and he continued to sit on his bed, smoking and listening to the cockroaches scuttling along the floor.

And, as he sat there, his mind travelled back over the some-times-hazardous journey which had been his life.

He had given serious consideration to coming to America when he had left the orphanage. But instead, he had joined the army and fought in a bloody war in Afghanistan – a war in which many of his comrades had died, and he had almost been killed himself.

He had had a second chance to cross the Atlantic when he left the army, but once again he had chosen a different course, and become a Metropolitan policeman – had deliberately plunged himself into a world of depravity and cruelty, where he had seen many things he would now rather forget, and had once, incidentally, saved the life of a queen.

He wondered what would have happened if he *had* decided, on either of those two occasions, to come to America.

Would he still have been the same man he was now – a man battered by life, but still able to face himself in the shaving mirror? Or would the country have changed him – for better or worse – as it seemed to have changed so many other men?

When sleep finally came, he fell almost immediately into a dream about a woman.

He *often* dreamt about the women he'd loved:

Hannah – who had loved him in return, but had betrayed him to the assassins anyway, and who had died herself in the process.

Agnes – who had betrayed him to her Russian paymaster,

and who he had last seen on a lonely railway station in the
middle of Central Russia.

And Dr Ellie Carr – who had not betrayed him to any *man*,
but to her love of her *work*.

Sometimes only one of his women would appear in his
dreams. On other occasions, though, they would *all* be there,
merging into one another and then drifting apart – so he was
no longer sure which of them he had truly loved, or whether
he would have continued to love *any* of them, if fate had
allowed him to.

But that night he did not dream of Hannah, Agnes *or* Ellie.
That night – for reasons he was quite unable to explain to
himself when he woke up – he dreamed of Jenny, the O'Briens'
timid parlourmaid.

ELEVEN

The shoeshine stand was on 13th Street, half a block
from where Meade and Blackstone were standing, and
the shoeshine boy was kneeling down, buffing the shoes
of a large man in a frock coat and silk top hat.

'That's him,' Alex Meade said. 'That's George Plunkitt.'

'Did you have any trouble in getting him to agree to meet
us?' Blackstone asked.

'None at all,' Meade replied airily. 'Like I told you yesterday,
after Inspector O'Brien's death he must be a worried man –
though not half as worried as he'll be after *we've* been talking
to him for a while.'

But he didn't look worried – at least, from a distance.

'Do you know what was one of the first – and of the most
important – things that I learned in the army?' Blackstone
asked. 'It was to avoid the temptation to start shooting at the
enemy the moment you catch sight of him.'

'Is that right, Sam?' Alex Meade said, though his thoughts
were clearly focused much more on Senator Plunkitt than they
were on Blackstone's military experiences.

'And believe me, it's not an easy temptation to resist,'
Blackstone continued, speaking as if he had gained Meade's

full and enthusiastic attention. 'You see the man charging towards you, and you know his greatest wish in life is to get close enough to you to kill you. Your own blood is racing and you desperately want to pull the trigger. But there are two very good reasons why you shouldn't do it.'

It seemed to have finally occurred to Meade that this was more than merely idle chatter.

'You're making a point here, aren't you, Sam?' he asked.

'I'm trying to,' Blackstone admitted.

Meade sighed. 'All right, what are the two reasons you shouldn't pull the trigger?'

'The first is that the closer he gets to you, the more you can see of him, and the bigger a target he becomes.'

'Sure. Makes sense.'

'But the second one is even more important. You see, he *knows* you're pointing your rifle at him. He *expects* you to fire it. And because of that, he knows he has no choice but to keep on running. And maybe that will work out for him. Maybe he'll be able to dodge the bullet and be on top of you before you have time to fire again.'

'Well, I guess that's war for you,' said Meade, who had never had any military training.

'But if you *don't* fire, it unnerves him even more than a bullet flying past his ear would,' Blackstone continued. 'Because he's not sure what the rules *are* any more. And that will affect the way he acts. Sometimes the uncertainty will slow him down. Sometimes it will make him start to waver from side to side. But whatever he decides to do, he'll start making mistakes – because you've robbed him of his clear sense of purpose.'

Meade grinned. 'I get it,' he said.

'You do?'

'Sure! You're saying I shouldn't go into this meeting with Plunkitt with all guns blazing.'

'That's exactly what I'm saying,' Blackstone confirmed.

'Relax, Sam,' Meade said. 'I'll run rings around the man.'

I very much doubt that, Blackstone thought.

George Plunkitt had a barrel chest and legs as thick as small tree trunks. His broad face was dominated by a large nose and a thick black moustache which looked as if it could have served as a heavy-duty scrubbing brush.

But, as they drew closer to the man, it was his eyes that fascinated Blackstone the most. They had the sharpness of a fox's, and the cunning of a peasant's – but what they totally lacked was any sign of the worry that Meade expected them to be showing. If they revealed anything at all, Blackstone decided, it was a sort of amusement which, while it was not exactly contemptuous, was certainly a long way from respectful.

Meade reached into his pocket for his shield.

'Senator Plunkitt?' he asked crisply. 'I'm Detective—'

'You're little Alex Meade,' Plunkitt interrupted. 'Well, well, well. Seems a long time since I last dandled you on my knee at a Tammany Hall picnic, don't it? So how's your daddy gettin' on, Alex?'

Meade swallowed, as if not sure what to say next. But a question had been asked of him, and – almost against his will – he found his good breeding forcing out an answer.

'My father's doing fine, Senator,' he said.

'Well, I'm pleased to hear that,' Plunkitt said. 'Be sure to give him my best wishes the next time you see him.'

'I will,' Meade said awkwardly. He paused for a second, to regroup his forces, then continued. 'Considering the nature of this meeting, Senator, you might prefer to hold it in your office.'

'Now, I'm just a simple man from the peat bogs, but I always thought that an office was the place where you did your business,' Plunkitt said. 'Did I get that wrong, Alex?'

'No, you didn't get it wrong, Senator,' Meade said, miserably.

'Well, then, we're in the right place, ain't we?' Plunkitt said, waving his hand expansively up and down the street. '*This* is my office, boy,' he said. 'Always was, an' always will be.' He looked down at the shoeshine boy. 'Ain't that the plain simple truth, Antonio?'

'It is, Senator,' the boy agreed, as he continued to polish.

'A fine young man, and the best shoeshine in New York City,' Plunkitt told Blackstone and Meade. 'Why, I'd walk miles out of my way just to have this lad shine my shoes.'

The boy gazed at Plunkitt with a look which came close to adoration on his face, but the Senator's attention had already been transferred to a Jewish tailor who was walking past with a bolt of cloth under his arm.

'See you at the bar mitzvah, Jake,' Plunkitt called out.

'It'll be an honour to have you there, Senator,' the other man called back.

Plunkitt turned back to Meade. 'So, you're the one who asked for this meeting, let's hear what you got to say.'

'Inspector O'Brien, the policeman who's just been killed, was conducting an important investigation just before he died,' Meade began.

'I would hope *all* our city officials are *always* engaged in important work, 'cos we sure as hell wouldn't want to pay them their fine salaries for doin' *unimportant* work,' Plunkitt replied.

'And we know he came to see you, which would suggest that he considered you to be connected – if only in a minor way – with that investigation,' Meade pressed on.

'I was sorry to hear of the inspector's death,' Plunkitt said. 'I sent the widow some flowers and a note which said if there was anything I could do for her in her time of woe, she only needed to ask.'

'You haven't answered my question, sir,' Meade said.

'I wasn't aware you'd asked one,' Plunkitt countered.

'Did Inspector O'Brien think you might be connected with the investigation he was conducting?'

'To tell you the truth, I don't rightly know,' Plunkitt replied. 'When I spoke to him on the telephone, I certainly thought that might be the case. But then I spent half an hour with the man, and if he had a point he wanted to make – or a question he wanted to ask – he never got around to it.'

'So what did the two of you talk about?' Meade asked sceptically. 'The weather?'

'As a matter of fact, we did,' Plunkitt said. 'Inspector O'Brien was of the opinion that it was even hotter this summer than it was last. We also talked about whether this American League they're thinkin' of founding will ever turn baseball into a national sport.' He paused for a second. 'An' the Oklahoma Territory,' he added. 'We discussed that, too. He thought it was about ready for statehood, and I didn't.' Plunkitt smiled. 'So you see, while it was an amiable conversation on the whole, we did have our disagreements.'

'And he gave no indication that he suspected you might be involved in anything illegal?' Meade persisted.

'No indication at all. But if you were to ask me what I thought he *believed*, deep down inside himself, I'd guess he

believed what men like him *always* believe when they see
men like me, with our big houses an' our yachts.'

'And what's that?'

'That I was probably one of the rottenest apples in the barrel.'

'And *are you* one of the rottenest apples in the barrel?'
Blackstone asked.

Plunkitt looked at him, with an amused smile playing on
his lips.

'Who's your friend, Alex?' he asked.

'Inspector Sam Blackstone,' Meade said.

'I didn't know we'd got any Inspector Blackstone workin''
for the New York Police Department.'

'He's not a New York policeman – he's from Scotland Yard.'

'Now ain't that interestin'?' Plunkitt said. 'Why are you
here, Inspector? Are there so few Irishmen left for you to
persecute in the Old Country that you have to come over here
in search of new ones?'

A working man, carrying a bag of tools in his hand, had
arrived on the scene, and was now waiting patiently to be
noticed.

'Are you here about your boy, Walter?' Plunkitt asked.

'Yes, Senator.'

'I talked to the precinct captain this mornin'. The charges
have been dropped, an' he'll be home in time for supper.'

'Thank you, Senator,' the workman said. 'I don't know how
I'll ever repay you.'

'Don't want no repayment,' Plunkitt said. 'Just want you
to remember to put your tick in the right box come next election day.'

'I will, Senator,' the workman promised. 'You have my
word on that.'

'An' your word's as good an assurance as any man should
need, Walter,' Plunkitt said.

The workman walked away, and when he was just out of
earshot, Plunkitt said, 'We were talkin' about rotten apples,
weren't we, Mr Blackstone?'

'We were,' Blackstone agreed.

'Then listen to what I have to say about how things work
here in New York City, an' you might just possibly end up a
wiser man.' He turned to Meade. 'Cards on the table, Alex?'

'Cards on the table,' Meade agreed.

'You hear that your Inspector O'Brien has been to see me, which must mean he's investigatin' me . . .'

'I never suggested . . .' Meade began.

'Hear me out,' Plunkitt said imperiously. 'He must be investigatin' me, which, in turn, has to mean I must be runnin' scared. An' it ain't a big step from that to thinkin' I paid somebody to put a bullet in the inspector. Ain't that right?'

'I never thought that,' Meade protested.

Plunkitt smiled. 'Maybe you did, an' maybe you didn't. But now I've gone an' planted the thought right there in your head, you got to admit it's a possibility, don't you?'

'Yes, I suppose it *is* a possibility,' Meade admitted, reluctantly.

'No, it ain't.' Plunkitt said. 'Because Inspector O'Brien didn't scare me one little bit. I honestly don't think he was even *there* to scare me, though I still ain't got no idea what he *did* want. But say that *had been* what he wanted – say he'd intended to frighten the livin' bejesus out of me, it still wouldn't have worked.'

'No?' Blackstone asked sceptically.

'No,' Plunkitt replied. 'You see, the problem with people like him – with all them do-good reformers – is that they don't draw the distinction between honest graft an' dishonest graft.'

'*Is* there a difference?' Blackstone asked.

'A world of difference,' Plunkitt said. 'Dishonest graft is when you set about blackmailin' gamblers, saloon keepers, disorderly people, etc. I've never gone in for that, and neither have any of the other men I know who have made big fortunes in politics.'

'So what's *honest* graft?' Blackstone asked.

'I've got some time on my hands, so I'll give you a couple of examples,' Plunkitt said graciously. 'My party's in power in this city, so when they're goin' to make public improvements, I'm one of the first to hear about it. So supposin' they're goin' to build a bridge. I get tipped off, and I buy as much property as I can where the approaches to the bridge are goin' to be. Then, when the city needs the land – 'cos the bridge ain't no good if there's no way to reach it – I sell my land for a good price. And ain't it perfectly honest to make a profit on my investment and foresight? Of course it is. Well, that's honest graft.'

'If you say so,' Blackstone said in a flat voice.

'Then take another case,' Plunkitt continued. 'The city was goin' to fix up a big park. I heard about it, and went looking for land in the neighbourhood. There wasn't any land goin' at a price I was prepared to pay, 'cept for a big piece of swamp. Well, I took that swamp fast enough, and held on to it. Things turned out just like I thought they would. They couldn't make the park complete without Plunkitt's swamp, and they had to pay a real good price for it. You find anything dishonest in that, Mr Inspector?'

'I don't know the law in America,' Blackstone said.

'You surely don't,' Plunkitt agreed.

A thin woman in a faded dress had arrived, and was standing where the workman had stood earlier.

'I've paid your rent for this week, Eliza, but I ain't goin' to do it again, so you better tell your Lew to get off that fat ass of his an' go out an' earn some money,' Plunkitt said.

The woman smiled weakly. 'Thank you, Senator,' she said.

'My pleasure,' Plunkitt told her. 'An' it ain't just in land that money's to be made,' he said to Blackstone and Meade. 'For instance, when the city's repavin' a street and has several hundred thousand old granite blocks to sell, I'm on hand to buy them. An', believe me, I know just what they're worth. How do I know? Never mind that. Anyways, I had a sort of monopoly on this business for a while, but then one of the newspapers, which are always stirrin' up things that are none of their concern, tried to spike it for me. How? It persuaded some outside men to come over from Brooklyn and New Jersey and bid against me. Well, there we all are in the auction room, me, an' the outside men, an' the newspaper reporters, who are just waitin' to see me get my butt kicked. So what did I do?'

The story was interrupted by the arrival of yet another suppli-cant, a young man in a shabby suit.

'The booze has been delivered for the wake, Senator,' he said.

'Glad to hear it,' Plunkitt told him. 'Now that's top-dollar Irish whiskey I sent over. Treat it with the respect it deserves.'

'We will, Senator.'

'Which is just another way of sayin' that if everybody ain't rollin' drunk by the time I arrive, I may start thinkin' that I've wasted my money.'

The man in the shabby suit grinned. 'No worries on that score, Senator. We'll be drunk, right enough.'

'So, where was I, Alex?' Plunkitt asked.

'Granite blocks,' Meade reminded him.

'That's right. So what did I do? I went to each of the men the newspaper had persuaded to bid against me, an' I said, "How many of these 250,000 stones do you want?" Well, one said 20,000, another wanted 15,000 and some of the others wanted 10,000 each. So I said, "All right, let me bid for the lot, and I'll *give* each one of you all you want for nothin.".. They agreed, of course. So the auctioneer says, "How much am I bid for these 250,000 fine pavin' stones?" And I says, "$2.50." "$2.50!" he screams. "That's a joke! Give me a real bid." But he soon found out the bid was real enough. My rivals kept as silent as the stone I was biddin' for. I got the lot for the price I bid, an' gave them their share, An' that's how the attempt to do Plunkitt down ended – an' that's how *all* such attempts end.'

This wasn't just the *New* World, Blackstone thought, it was a very *different* world.

'Now when these reform administrations come into office, like they do once in a while, the first thing they do is spend money like water, tryin' to find out about the public robberies they talked about during their campaigns,' Plunkitt continued. 'And guess what? They don't find nothin'. The books are always all right. The money in the city treasury is all right. Everything is all right. All they can show is that Tammany heads of departments looked after their friends, *within the law*, and gave them what opportunities they could to make honest graft. Now, let me tell you, that's never goin' to hurt Tammany with the people. Every good man looks after his friends, and any man who doesn't isn't likely to be popular. If I have a good thing to hand out in private life, I give it to a friend of mine. So why shouldn't Alderman X do exactly the same in public life?'

'So Inspector O'Brien's corruption investigation didn't bother you?' Blackstone said.

'That's what I'm sayin'. I knew he was never goin' to uncover what I done wrong, because I never done nothin' wrong.' Plunkitt smiled. 'Which brings us right back to where we started, which is that I had no reason on God's green earth to have the man hit. Any more questions you'd care to ask, Alex?'

'No,' Meade said weakly. 'Thank you for your time, Senator.'

'My pleasure,' Plunkitt told him. He turned to Blackstone again, and fixed him with his piercing eyes. 'Say, for the sake of argument, that my worst enemy was given the job of writin' my epitaph when I'm gone. An' say, for argument's sake again, that he tried to work out the worst possible thing he could write about me. You followin' me so far?'

'I'm following you so far,' Blackstone agreed.

'An' say he wasn't allowed to lie. Say he could write anythin' about me as long as it was the truth. Do you know what the worst thing he could come up with would be?'

'No,' Blackstone said. 'What would it be?'

A fresh smile spread across the senator's broad face. '"George W. Plunkitt",' he said. '"He seen His Opportunities and He Took 'Em."'

TWELVE

I t wasn't Blackstone's normal practice to start drinking that early in the morning, but when he saw the look of mute appeal in Meade's eyes as they passed the saloon on 12th Street, he quickly decided that even if *he* didn't need the boost that a shot of alcohol would give him, the sergeant certainly did.

He sat Meade down at a table, went over to the bar, and ordered a draft beer for himself and a whiskey for the sergeant. When he returned to the table, Meade was gazing down speculatively at his hands, as if wondering if they were up to the job of strangling him.

'Cheer up,' Blackstone said.

'Cheer up?' Meade repeated bleakly, grabbing the shot glass as a drowning man might clutch at a straw, and knocking the whiskey back in a single gulp. 'Cheer up! Plunkitt ran rings round me. You warned me he might, but I was such an arrogant little prig that I wouldn't listen to you.'

'He's been in the game a long time,' Blackstone said consolingly. 'He was at it before you were even born.' He hesitated for a second, before asking, 'Did Plunkitt really dandle you on his knee at one of the Tammany Hall picnics – or was that just a tactic to knock you off balance?'

'I don't know,' Meade admitted. 'He may have dandled me on his knee! He may even have ruffled my goddam hair and told me I was a sweet kid. I don't remember.'

'But you did *attend* Tammany picnics?'

'We attended a few of them,' Meade said, with the shame evident in his voice. 'My father despises the whole Tammany crowd – but if you want to do business as a lawyer in New York City, you sometimes have to force yourself to be pleasant to them.'

'You do what you have to do,' Blackstone said. 'I sometimes have to force myself to be pleasant to my assistant commissioner – and that man is the scum of the earth.'

'Really?' Meade asked gratefully.

'Really,' Blackstone confirmed.

But he was thinking, even so, I'd rather cut my own arm off than go on a *picnic* with Todd.

'Why am I so stupid?' Meade wailed. 'Why did it have to turn out that Plunkitt was the organ grinder and I was no more than the monkey? And what would Clarissa have thought of me if she'd been there? Would she *ever* have considered marrying me after that?'

'Clarissa *wasn't* there,' Blackstone said firmly. 'And the way things turned out wasn't your fault. You can only do serious damage to the enemy if you have the right ammunition – and we didn't.'

'Do you think he was telling the truth?' Meade asked. 'Do you think the only graft he's involved in *is* what he calls "honest graft"?'

'I don't know,' Blackstone admitted. 'But even if it is true – even if every cent he's ever made has been, strictly speaking, legal – that still doesn't make him exactly a choirboy, does it?'

Meade forced a smile on to his face. 'No,' he agreed. 'Not even a defrocked one.'

'Because he'd never have had the opportunity for this "honest graft" of his if he hadn't been an important politician,' Blackstone continued. 'And he'd never have become an important politician in this city if he hadn't used all possible means – legal *and* illegal – to fix elections.'

Meade's smile had been growing in strength as Blackstone spoke, and now he looked positively amused.

'Have I said something funny?' Blackstone asked.

'Not exactly,' Meade replied. 'Or rather, it's not what you said that was funny, so much as it's the fact that it was *you* who said it.'

'You've lost me,' Blackstone admitted.

'You remember me meeting you down at the docks, don't you?' Meade asked.

'Of course I do.'

'And you remember me saying that there were no real detectives in New York City?' Meade paused, and suddenly looked a little troubled. 'I was maybe being a little disloyal to Inspector O'Brien when I said that,' he continued, 'but I've always thought of him as a moral crusader rather than a true detective.' He paused again. 'Anyway, you remember me saying that about the Detective Bureau?'

'Yes, I do.'

'And you didn't believe me, did you?'

'Well, I . . .' Blackstone began, uncomfortably.

'Now imagine that instead of talking about the Detective Bureau, I'd talked about Senator Plunkitt. Imagine if I'd delivered *then* that little speech on Plunkitt that you delivered just *now*. You'd have thought I was a prime candidate for the funny farm, wouldn't you?'

Good God, Meade was right, Blackstone told himself. He *would have* thought the sergeant was a candidate for the funny farm. But now his whole view of the city – his whole way of *thinking about it* – had altered.

And how long had that *taken*?

Amazingly – incredibly – it had taken less than a day and a half!

Yet, in some ways, he was starting to feel as if he'd never existed anywhere else – as if New York City had been his entire universe for as long as he could remember.

So maybe the city *did* actually have the power to change people, without them even really noticing it happen.

And maybe that power was both its greatest strength and its greatest weakness.

'What's on your mind, Sam?' he heard Meade say.

Blackstone grinned self-consciously. 'I was worried about becoming a new man without ever having got the old one quite right.'

'I'm sorry?'

'Doesn't matter,' Blackstone said. 'Shall we get back to the matter of Senator George Plunkitt?'

'Sure.'

'The one thing I'm absolutely sure of is that when he said he had no real idea why Inspector O'Brien visited him, he wasn't lying.'

'But he *had* to know,' Meade protested. 'Otherwise, none of it makes any sense.'

'None of *what* makes any sense?'

'I knew Patrick O'Brien well. Very well indeed. Given the opportunity to speak to Plunkitt, he wouldn't have wasted that time by talking about the weather, or baseball, or if Oklahoma should be a state.'

'But that's just what Plunkitt says he *did* talk about,' Blackstone said. 'And I believe him.'

'Well, I don't,' Meade said stubbornly. 'Patrick was one of the most direct men I've ever met.'

'Perhaps, but . . .'

'No,' Meade corrected himself, 'he was *the* most direct man. If he had accusations to make, he'd make them, without even stopping to think about the consequences that might have on his own career. And if he wanted help or information, he'd come right out and ask for it, even if he knew there was a good chance of his request being turned down.'

'But there might be circumstances when . . .'

'His opinion of himself wasn't based on what others thought of him, or what they were prepared to do for him. He was his own man, you see. He was *always* his own man.'

'Maybe not *always*,' Blackstone cautioned. 'Sergeant Saddler did say he'd been acting strangely for the last few days of his life.'

'But *why* wouldn't he tell Senator Plunkitt what it was he wanted?' Meade asked, still fretting over the point like a wild dog worrying a dead sheep, and *almost* conceding that George Plunkitt had been speaking the truth. 'And what *was it* that he wanted?'

'I don't know,' Blackstone said crisply, 'but we're not going to find out by sitting here, are we?'

'So what's your plan?' Meade asked.

Yes, what *was* his plan? Blackstone wondered. Where *did*

they go after they'd come up against the brick wall which was
Senator Plunkitt?

'*My* plan is to follow your *plan*,' he said. '*My* plan is go
back to the Lower East Side, and see if we can pick up
O'Brien's trail.'

'So you think it's a good plan, do you?' Meade asked, with
suspicious innocence.

No, not really, Blackstone thought. In fact, not at all. But
it's the *only* plan we've got.

'It could work,' he said aloud. 'Longer shots than that have
been known to come off.'

'The reason I'm asking, Sam, is that when you told me to
go down to the Lower East Side last night, I got the distinct
impression it wasn't because you thought it was *good* plan –
it was because you were looking for an excuse to get me out
of your hair for a while.'

'That's what you thought, was it?' Blackstone asked, non-
committally.

'Yes, that's what I thought. And after I'd left you at the
luxurious Hotel Rat-trap on Canal Street, and I was walking
through the Lower East Side, I began to see the hopelessness
of the plan – as it stood – for myself.'

'As it stood?' Blackstone repeated.

'That's right,' Meade agreed. 'And I started to realize that
we desperately needed to come up with something that
would give us an extra edge. And that's when I had my
idea.'

He was deliberately teasing, Blackstone thought. But after
the morning the boy had had, what was wrong with letting
him have his bit of fun?

'What idea?' he asked.

'This,' Meade said, reaching into his pocket, taking out a
small poster, and laying it flat on the table between them.

The banner along the top of the poster screamed:

Have you seen this man?

And beneath it was a photograph of the man it referred to.

It came as a shock to Blackstone to realize that though he'd
been investigating O'Brien's death for a day and half – and
had built up an image of him through what others had told

him – he had not, until that moment, had any real idea of what the man himself looked like.

Now he studied the picture carefully, and was forced to concede that Meade's description had been perfectly accurate, for while O'Brien had not been particularly good-looking, he had a presence about him which shone through even in a grainy photograph.

There was more text underneath:

Inspector Patrick O'Brien was murdered on the evening of Tuesday, 26th of July. The New York Police Department are anxious to speak to anyone who saw him on the afternoon or evening of that day.

Please contact Sergeant Meade at the Mulberry Street police headquarters.

Big Reward for Information Leading to an Arrest.

'I thought of putting "substantial reward",' Meade said, 'but they're very suspicious of long words on the Lower East Side. And anyway, "big" should certainly get their attention.'

'And how big *is* "big"?' Blackstone wondered.

Meade shrugged. 'Depends who earns the reward. If the information comes from a Bowery wino, I can pay him out of the change in my pocket. If it comes from a prosperous East Side merchant, I'd probably have to empty my bank account in order to raise a large enough sum to make him talk.'

'So you're offering this reward yourself?'

'I am,' Meade agreed – almost defiantly, as if he expected Blackstone to tell him that he was acting like a complete fool.

But Blackstone didn't. Instead, he said, 'The idea only came to you last night, and you've already had the poster printed?'

'That's right.'

Blackstone whistled softly. 'Then it's been a very quick job,' he said. 'Even with the backing of Scotland Yard, I'd never have got it done anything like as quickly in London.'

'Maybe not,' Meade agreed. 'But this is a city in which money not only talks, but talks in a very loud voice indeed. You really should have learned that by now, Sam.'

'How many posters did you have printed?'

'A thousand.'

Blackstone whistled again. 'That's very good,' he said. 'But they're no use to us just sitting in a big stack. We need to get them distributed around the streets as soon as possible.'

'They've *already* been distributed,' Meade said. 'I hired a team of bill stickers at the same time as I went to the printers. They've been plastering the posters all over the Lower East Side since early this morning.'

Blackstone clapped him on the shoulder. 'Good work!' he said.

Meade positively beamed. 'Do you know,' he said, 'I'd almost given up hope of *ever* hearing you say that.'

THIRTEEN

I n Alex Meade's considered opinion, Inspector Michael Connolly had been a very poor street detective, and made an even worse head of the Detective Bureau, a position he had held ever since Thomas Byrnes had left the police department with his $350,000 bank account still intact.

The man himself was in his late forties, and was rapidly losing the battle with both his expanding waistline and his receding hairline. He was a traditionalist in many ways, preferring chewing tobacco to either cigars or the newfangled cigarettes, and still believing – like his predecessor – that the best psychological tool to employ in an interrogation was the old-fashioned billy-club.

And as he looked across his desk at the two men standing before him, he seemed to be very, very angry indeed.

'Who the hell is this guy, Sergeant Meade?' Connolly demanded, pointing at Blackstone.

'He's Inspector Samuel Blackstone of New Scotland Yard, London, England, sir.'

'Inspector Samuel Blackstone!' the chief of detectives repeated contemptuously. 'Just look at him! The man dresses like a bum. And not even an *American* bum.'

That was a bit rich, coming from a fat, balding man with chewing-tobacco stains all down the front of his shirt, Blackstone thought.

But he wisely kept his peace.

'So what's this *English* bum doing here?' the chief asked.

'Availing me of his experience in my inquiries, sir,' Meade said. 'As you may already know, Commissioner Comstock asked me to investigate Inspector O'Brien's murder—'

'Oh, I *do* know,' Connolly interrupted him. 'I know because he told me so himself. Not *asked* me if it would be all right, you understand. *Told me!* He thinks that because he's a goddamn commissioner, he can ride roughshod over the chain of command in this department. Well, maybe he can – for a while. But as soon as I've had the chance to talk to the *other* three commissioners – the ones who know how things *should* be done – it'll suddenly be a completely different story. You'll be *off* the investigation and a new team of more senior – more *experienced* – detectives will be *on* it.'

'But I'm not off it yet?' Meade asked.

'So this Limey's av . . . av . . . What the hell was it you said that he was doin'?' Connolly asked, ignoring the question.

'Availing me of his experience in my inquires.'

'Availing you of his experience! And that's what Commissioner High-and-Mighty Comstock wants him to do? Avail you?'

'Yes, sir.'

'Jesus Christ, you'd have thought the War of Independence had never happened,' the chief of detectives said in disgust. 'You'd have thought that George Washington had never kicked the Brits' butts right back in the Atlantic Ocean.' He paused for a second to chew on his tobacco. 'But we ain't here to talk about your Limey friend.'

'No, sir?'

'No, sir!' the chief echoed him. He reached into his drawer, took out one of the O'Brien posters – much the worse for wear after having been torn off a wall – and slammed it down on his desk. 'Did you authorize this?'

'Yes, sir, I did.'

'Sure you did,' Connolly agreed. 'This is just the kind of cockamamie idea you *would* come up with!'

'Has anyone responded to it, sir?' Meade asked.

'*Responded* to it!' Connolly repeated. 'What's that supposed to mean? Why don't you *ever* speak plain straightforward American, for God's sake?'

'Has anyone come here with information?' Meade clarified.

'No.'

'No?'

'But there's a whole crowd o' bums in the holding cells who *say* they've got information.'

'You've locked them up?' Meade asked, alarmed.

'No, I ain't locked them up. The cell doors are open, an' they can walk outta here any time they want to. Only they ain't gonna walk out, are they? 'Cos they want this *big reward* you promised them.'

'Yes,' Meade said. 'I expect they do.'

'But there ain't gonna *be* no big reward. Any why? Because you're personally gonna throw all these bums out on to the street again. And when you've done that, you're gonna get your ass down to the Lower East Side an' tear down all these fly-posters.'

'If you say so, sir.'

'I *do* say so.'

'And when would you like me to tell Senator Plunkitt that those were your orders, sir?' Meade asked. '*Before* I throw the bums out and tear down the posters, or *after* I've done it?'

'And what – in the name of all that's holy – has Senator Plunkitt got to do with it?' Connolly asked.

'It was all his idea,' Meade explained. 'He's the one who's posting the reward.'

Connolly looked suddenly troubled. 'Why didn't you tell me this before, Sergeant Meade?'

'You never gave me the chance to, sir.'

Connolly screwed up his face, as if searching for some way to get out of the hole that he'd so readily dug himself into.

'I still think the whole idea's crazy,' he said finally, 'but Senator Plunkitt has served this city faithfully for nearly forty years, and his opinion is certainly always worth listenin' to. So if he thinks there's even the slightest chance you might turn up something with these posters of yours, well, I'm more than willin' to bow to his experience.'

'Thank you, sir,' Meade said. 'Where would you like me to conduct the interviews?'

'Where will you talk to the stinking bums, you mean? Inspector O'Brien's office is in the basement – you can use that.'

'Do you think that's such a good idea, sir?'

Connolly sighed in exasperation. 'Yeah, I think it's a good idea. Why *wouldn't* it be a good idea?'

'Because the office is probably still full of confidential files from Inspector O'Brien's investigations,' Meade said, with the same disarming innocence as Blackstone had seen him employ so effectively before.

Connolly blinked. He only did it once – but once was more than enough.

'Inspector O'Brien's confidential files probably *are* still there in the office,' he agreed. 'But we all know what a careful man the inspector was, and I'm sure all those files of his are safely under lock an' key.'

'No doubt you're right, sir,' Meade agreed.

'Did you see the look on Connolly's face when I mentioned Patrick's confidential files?' Meade asked Blackstone, once they were standing in the corridor outside the chief of the Detective Bureau's office.

'Yes, I did see it,' Blackstone replied. 'It would have been rather hard to miss it.'

'Either Connolly's had the files removed himself, or he knows who *did* have them removed,' Meade said.

'True,' Blackstone agreed, 'but it doesn't do us any good to know that, because in either case, they're probably lost and gone for ever.'

'You may be right,' Meade replied. 'Not that it matters anyway – because we don't really need them any more.'

'Don't we?'

'No, we don't! We'll get all the information we need from the people who are waiting to talk to us in the basement.'

Meade's spring of optimism was a perpetual source of wonder, Blackstone thought. Cover it with a large rock – the missing files, for example, or the dead end that their talk with Plunkitt had led them to – and for a while it was silent. But that did not mean that the spring had been truly dampened down. Rather that it was simply building up enough pressure to throw the rock high into the air, and so free itself again.

'Weren't you taking a big chance by telling Connolly that Senator Plunkitt was the one behind the reward?' Blackstone asked.

'Taking a chance? Not a bit of it!' Meade said airily. 'If the chief of detectives rings Plunkitt up – and I don't think he will – the senator will confirm everything that I've said.'

'Why?'

'Because, by that time, my father will already have rung Plunkitt up himself, and told the senator what to say.'

'And that's all it will take?' Blackstone asked, amazed.

'That's all it will take,' Meade confirmed. 'You see, guys like Plunkitt treat favours owed to them in the same way misers treat gold coins. Their greatest pleasure in life is to build up a big old chest full of them.'

'So Plunkitt will do it because your father asks him to, and then your father will owe Plunkitt?'

'Sure.'

'And doesn't putting him in debt to the senator bother you at all?'

'Hell, no!' Meade said. 'It's highly unlikely that Plunkitt will ever call the favour in.'

'You think so?'

'I do. See, the miser doesn't want to *spend* his gold – he just wants to *have* it. And sometimes, late at night, he'll open the chest and let all his gold coins trickle through his fingers. I think Plunkitt's like that, too – he likes to let all the favours that he's owed trickle through his fingers, then he just sits back and thinks about how rich he is.'

'You're forgetting one thing,' Blackstone said.

'And what's that?'

'It's still just possible he was involved in whatever O'Brien was investigating. And if he *was* involved in it, then the last thing he'll want to do is anything that may help us catch the inspector's killer.'

'Men like him are so arrogant they don't think anything can touch them, even if they're as guilty as sin,' Meade said. 'And after I allowed him to run rings round me this morning . . .'

'What?'

Meade grinned sheepishly. 'OK, after he ran rings round me, whether I wanted him to or not, he's got us marked down as two guys who couldn't find their own assholes – even if he gave them a detailed map. But we're gonna prove him wrong on that, ain't we?'

'I certainly hope so,' Blackstone said.

'So shall we go downstairs and see what our bait's hauled in for us?' Meade suggested.

'Why not?' Blackstone agreed.

*   *   *

The people whom Meade hoped would make Inspector O'Brien's files unnecessary had been herded into the three cells closest to the door.

They were a mixed bunch, Blackstone noted – men and women, young and old. Some of them were dressed more or less respectably, though a fair number wore clothes which would have been pushed to pass themselves off as rags. But there was one thing that united them all – the look of expectant greed which shone in their eyes when they saw Meade arrive.

A young patrolman stood guard over this motley crew.

'Exactly how many of these people are there, Officer Turcotte?' Alex Meade asked.

The patrolman shrugged. 'Don't know for sure,' he admitted. 'I kept countin' till I reached thirty, then I kinda lost interest.'

Blackstone did his own headcount, and estimated there were around fifty of the 'informers'.

And how many of these informers would be a complete waste of time? he asked himself.

Around *fifty* would be as good a guess as any, he decided.

'I'll be interviewing them in Inspector O'Brien's office,' Meade told the patrolman. 'I want to see them one at a time, and I'll leave it up to you to choose what order I see them in. Is that all right with you?'

'Sure,' Turcotte agreed.

But it was clearly *not* all right with some of the current residents of the cells, who had overheard the conversation.

'Why should *he* choose?' demanded an old woman who was wearing a thick shawl, despite the heat.

'Yeah, it should be first come, first served,' said a younger woman in a floral hat. 'An' *I* was here first.'

'The hell you were,' called out a voice from behind her. '*I* was here first. Ask the cop.'

'I got another important appointment to go to,' said a man who, from the downtrodden look of him, had never had an appointment – important or otherwise – in his entire life.

Meade waited until the noise had died down. 'Anyone who doesn't like the arrangement I've suggested is perfectly free to leave now,' he said, gesturing towards the stairs with his hand.

But none of the people in the cells took him up on the offer.

They all had the scent of money in their nostrils, and they were determined not to leave without at least getting a chance to take a bite at it.

'It feels strange,' Meade said uncomfortably.

'What does?'

'To be sitting here in Patrick O'Brien's office, behind Patrick O'Brien's desk.'

'*Somebody* always has to step into dead men's shoes eventually,' Blackstone pointed out.

'I know they do,' Meade agreed, still sounding ill at ease. 'But that person, whoever he is, should be worthy of filling those shoes – and I don't feel worthy of filling Patrick's.'

'You'll fill them well enough, given time,' Blackstone assured him. 'And even if you don't, it won't be through lack of trying.'

'Sometimes, you know, you're almost like a father to me, Sam,' Meade said emotionally.

'Then maybe I'll take you out on a Tammany Hall picnic,' Blackstone countered.

Meade grinned. 'Yeah, I was getting kinda maudlin just then, wasn't I?'

'Yeah, you kinda were,' Blackstone agreed, smiling as he imitated the young detective sergeant.

Meade squared his shoulders and turned his attention to the stack of plain white paper which was on the desk in front of him. He peeled off the top sheet and wrote '1' on it in pencil.

'Send in the first of the informants,' he called out to Officer Turcotte, who was waiting in the corridor.

Turcotte shepherded the potential informant into the room. It was a man somewhere in his late thirties. He was unshaven, had bad teeth, and emitted an essence of eau de vie de sewer, even from a distance.

'Name?' Meade said.

'Dickie Thomas.'

Meade wrote it down.

'Occupation?'

'Well . . . you know, Sergeant.'

'No, as a matter of fact, I don't,' Meade replied sharply.

'I do a bit o' this, an' I do a bit o' that.'

'Address?'

'I'm kinda *between* addresses at the moment.'

'No fixed abode,' Meade wrote down. 'So what have you got to tell me, Mr Thomas?'

'I seen him.'

'Inspector O'Brien?'

'That's right.'

'Where?'

'O'Malley's Saloon.'

'When?'

'Tuesday night.'

'Give me all the details.'

'O'Malley was standin' behind the counter, and this cop walks up to him, bold as brass, and asks for his bribe money. Well, O'Malley says business is bad, an' he can't afford to pay this week, and this inspector says in that case he'll be closing the place down.' Thomas paused for a second. 'I just had a thought,' he continued unconvincingly.

'Well, that must be a novelty,' Meade said.

'You what?'

'Tell me about this thought you've just had.'

'Ain't it obvious?'

'Not to me.'

'It was *O'Malley* what killed him.'

'And why should he have done that?'

'To stop him from closin' the place down, o' course.' Thomas held out a dirty hand, palm up. 'Can I have my money now?'

'I don't think the inspector was ever in O'Malley's Saloon,' Meade said. 'I think you made all that up.'

'I didn't,' Thomas told him. 'I swear I didn't.'

'And the *reason* I think you made it all up was because I know for a fact that, when Inspector O'Brien went out collecting bribes, he always wore his lucky green hat.'

'What?'

'He always wore his lucky green hat when he was collecting his bribes. And you never mentioned that.'

'Didn't I?' Thomas asked. 'I thought I did.'

'No.'

'Then I must just have forgotten to.'

'So he was wearing the hat?'

'Yes, he was. He definitely was.'

'With the pink feather in the hatband?'

'That's the one.'

'And with the small wooden duck, sewn on to the crown?'

'I . . . er . . . don't think I saw that,' Thomas said uncertainly. 'Maybe it had fallen off before he went into the saloon.'

Meade screwed up the sheet of paper, and threw it into the bin.

'Officer Turcotte, please show this man out, and then bring me the next one,' he said.

'O' course, the little wooden duck!' Thomas said wildly. 'Painted yellow, wasn't it? I didn't notice it at first, because the lightin' in O'Malley's Saloon is very poor . . .'

'No, it isn't.'

'An' besides, my eyesight ain't what it was.'

But despite his protest, Thomas knew as well as Meade did that the game was up, and when the officer grabbed hold of his arm and hauled him to his feet, he did not resist.

Meade did not seem in the least discouraged by the way that the interview had gone.

'When you're panning for gold, you have to sift a lot of silt before you get to the nugget,' he said.

'True,' Blackstone agreed.

But he was thinking that sometimes there wasn't even a nugget there for you *to* find.

FOURTEEN

Meade wrote '27' at the top of the clean white sheet of paper and then looked up at the girl.

She was perhaps nineteen or twenty, but she was wearing as much powder and rouge as a woman with sixty years of ravages to hide. Her dress was of good quality material, and had been cut not-so-much to show off her figure to its best advantage as to put her merchandise on display. She could, perhaps, have been called a lady, but only if the words 'of the night' were added as a qualification.

'Name?' Meade said.

'Trixie,' the girl supplied.

'*Full* name?'

'I'd rather not say.'

'Occupation?'

'Entertainer.'

'Address?'

The girl hesitated. 'I'll give my address, and I'll give you all the information you want, but you have to keep my name out of it, because if Mad . . . if my employer ever finds out I've been talking to you, I'll be out on the street before I've had time to turn round.'

'We'll keep your name out of it,' Meade promised.

The girl gave him the address.

'And that's a brothel, is it?' Meade asked.

'No, of course not!'

'Then what is it?'

'Well, I suppose you'd call it an exclusive club for discriminating gentlemen,' Trixie said primly.

'If you can't be honest with me, then I'm not interested in talking to you,' Meade said impatiently. 'Is it a brothel or isn't it?'

'It's *sort of* a brothel,' Trixie said reluctantly.

'So where exactly did you see Inspector O'Brien on Tuesday?' the sergeant asked.

'In the club,' Trixie said. Then, when Meade glared at her, she looked down at the floor and murmured, 'In the brothel.'

'When?'

'Around half past five on Tuesday afternoon.'

'Describe him to me,' Meade said.

Trixie shrugged. 'What can I say? He looked exactly like the man in the picture.'

Meade shook his head. 'That's not good enough. You have to convince me that you really saw him.'

'He was wearing a brown suit and a straw boater, but he took the boater off once he came through the door, which not every gentleman who visits us does.' Trixie giggled. 'Sometimes they even keep their hats on when they've taken *everything else* off.'

Meade laid down his pencil, and scrunched up the piece of paper he'd been writing on.

'Thank you for your time,' he said.

'Don't you want me to tell you what this inspector did?'

Meade shook his head again. 'There's no point in hearing

any more, unless you convince me that it really was Inspector O'Brien you saw. And I really don't think you can do that.'

'But I still get the reward, don't I?' Trixie said anxiously.

'I'm afraid not,' Meade said. 'Officer Turcotte will show you out.'

'Hold your horses,' Trixie told him, starting to sound desperate. She closed her eyes for a second, and when she opened them again, she said, 'I remember now – he was wearing a ring on his index finger.'

'How did you happen to notice that?'

'It was jewellery, wasn't it?'

'So?'

'So I always notice jewellery.'

'Describe the ring to me.'

'The band was gold . . .'

'Yes?'

'It had a red stone in it. I think that the stone might well have been a ruby.'

'Go on,' Meade said, both encouraged and encouraging.

'And it had something carved into it.'

'What kind of something?'

'Some kind of animal.'

'*What* kind of animal?' Meade asked sceptically. 'An elephant? An elk? A duck-billed platypus?'

Trixie giggled. 'I don't even know what a duck-billed thingy looks like,' she said. 'But it wasn't an elephant or an elk. It was some kind of big cat. I think it might have been a lion.'

Meade reached for a fresh sheet of paper, rapidly scribbled a few words on it, then slid it across to Blackstone.

Mary gave him that ring, Blackstone read. *She said he had the* heart *of a lion.*

Trixie had watched the whole thing, and now a smile came to her face. 'I got it right, didn't I?' she asked. 'It was him!'

'Yes, it was,' Meade agreed. 'I want you to tell me exactly what happened, Trixie. Start at the beginning, and don't leave anything out.'

'Well, half past five is a very quiet time at the club,' Trixie said. 'You see, we get the gentlemen who like to visit us during their lunch hour, and we get the gentlemen who always come in the evening – either before or after dinner – but at that time of the afternoon . . .'

'I get the point,' Meade said.

'So since there's not much business to be had, most of the girls are off-duty then. So there were only two of us there when Imre showed this particular gentleman into the parlour.'

'Who's Imre?' Blackstone asked.

'The doorman. Not that he'll ever admit that's what he is. He *says* that he's Madam's business manager, but you can take that with a pinch of salt, because he *also* says he's a Hungerarian count.'

'Do you mean Hungarian?' Blackstone asked.

'That's right,' Trixie agreed, as if, Hungarian or Hungerarian, it was all the same to her. 'Anyway, Imre led the gentleman into the parlour. And do you know what he says then?'

'No.'

'He says to the inspector, "I'm sorry there's not much choice, sir." What a pig! As if me and Lucy weren't enough choice for *anybody*!'

'What did Inspector O'Brien say?'

'He says that he's not there to . . . to . . .'

'To avail himself of the services that the house offered?'

'That's right, he's not there for that, he's just come to see Madam. Well, Imre tells him that Madam only ever sees very special clients who she's known for a long time.'

'What happened then?'

'O'Brien keeps on saying it's very important he sees her. And Imre keeps on saying he can't and that if he wants to take one of us upstairs, he's very welcome, but if he doesn't, he has to leave. And let me tell you, when Imre orders somebody to leave, that's just what they do, because he's six feet four and built like a brick shithouse.'

'So Inspector O'Brien left, did he?' Meade asked, his disappointment very obvious.

'No, he didn't. That's when he reaches into his pocket and pulls out his detective shield. I don't think he *wanted* to show it at all, you know – I think he'd just decided that if he didn't, Imre would give him the five-second bounce and he'd end up lying in the street.'

'What did Imre say when he saw the shield?'

'He shrugs his shoulders, to show it doesn't impress him. Well, he is a *count*, after all – though I can think of another

word which sounds rather like "count" but would describe him
much better, if you know what I mean.'

'I know what you mean,' Meade said.

And Blackstone was amused to note that the young sergeant
had reddened slightly.

'Anyway, Imre says it makes no difference whether O'Brien
is a cop or not, because we pay our protection money directly
to the local precinct captain. And that's when this inspector
suddenly loses his temper – but not for the reasons you might
think.'

'No?'

'No. He isn't exactly angry. He's – what's the word? –
he's outraged. He says it's a disgrace that *any* policeman
should take bribes from a whorehouse. But I don't see
what's wrong with it myself. It's the way it's always been
done.'

'You see what a state we're in?' Meade asked Blackstone
in a low whisper. 'We've reached such a level of corruption
that it doesn't even *seem* like corruption any more.'

'What was that?' Trixie asked.

'Nothing. Carry on with your story.'

'Well, Imre starts to look worried, and he takes a step or two
backwards, because *now*, if it comes to a fight, the inspector's
so full of rage that you can see Imre thinks he might just win.'

'*Did* it come to a fight?'

'No, the inspector forces himself to calm down – you could
see him do it – and when he is calm, he becomes all crisp
and official. He says there are two choices. Either Imre takes
him to see Madam or else he'll be arrested on the spot for
keeping a disorderly house.'

'And what did Imre do?'

'What would *you* have done? He asks the inspector to wait
there while he goes and sees if Madam is available. And the
three of us – me, Lucy and the cop – are left alone in the
parlour.' The girl giggled again. 'It was too funny for words.'

'Funny? How?'

'Well, you could tell that he wasn't a regular at that kind
of establishment, and he seems very uncomfortable being there
at all. So me and Lucy try to make him feel more at home.'

'How did you do that?'

'I pat my hand on the chaise lounge and ask him if he'd

like to sit between us. He says, "No, thank you." He's very
polite about it, but very firm. And then he just stands there,
in the centre of room, fiddling with the rim of his hat and
gazing up at the ceiling. Then he sees what's *painted* on the
ceiling, and he quickly looks down at the floor.' Trixie chuckled
throatily. 'It's a good job that Madam didn't get any of them
erotic carpets she was thinking of buying, ain't it?'

'Did Madam invite him into her apartment?' asked Meade,
who was growing redder by the minute.

Trixie shook her head. 'Oh, no. Like I said, she's very
particular about who goes in there.'

'So she came into the parlour instead?'

'That's right.'

'And what did she say?'

'She asks him what he wants, and when he tells her he just
wants a private word, she leads him across to the far end of
the room, where the escritoire is.' Trixie paused. 'That's French
for "writing desk".'

'I know,' Meade said.

'Anyway, they talk for about five minutes – only, it's in a
whisper, so we can't hear. Then Madam opens the drawer of
the escritoire, and takes out a sheet of paper. She writes something on it and hands it to the cop.'

'And did that seem to satisfy him?'

Trixie frowned, as if there was only one activity that she
was used to hearing the word 'satisfy' applied to.

'How do you mean?' she asked.

'Did he seem pleased?'

'Yes, he did.'

'And what did he do with the piece of paper?'

'Folded it up and put it in his pocket.'

'And then?'

'And then he left – in a great hurry.'

'Was that because he wanted to get away from the brothel
as quickly as he could?'

Trixie frowned again. 'I don't think so. It was more of a
case of him wanting to get to somewhere *else* quickly.'

'What did Madam say to you when he'd gone?'

'She smiled at us, in a funny sort of way . . .'

'What do you mean by "in a funny sort of way"?'

'I don't know,' Trixie said perplexedly. 'Like she'd found

something funny, I suppose. And then she says, 'It's always nice to be of service to the police force, isn't it, girls?'

'And what do you think she meant?'

'I've no idea.' Trixie paused for the briefest of instants. 'Do I get the money now?'

Meade laid a ten-dollar bill on the table. 'Regard that as a down payment,' he said.

'A what?'

'A down payment. An advance. If your information checks out, there'll be more.'

'Funny way to do business,' Trixie complained. 'In my game, you make sure you have all the money in your hand before you so much as open your . . .' She paused again. 'How much more *will* there be?

'A hundred dollars,' Meade promised.

Trixie beamed with pleasure.

'Now that's a better way to make a living than lying on your back with your eyes closed, pretending you're reading *Harper's Bazaar*.'

By the end of a long afternoon, Meade had screwed up 68 pieces of paper, and had only one – Number 27 – still in front of him.

'So what do you think, Sam?' he asked Blackstone.

'I think that even though Plunkitt thought that he and O'Brien talked about nothing of any consequence, your inspector managed to squeeze an important piece of information out of the senator without Plunkitt even knowing he'd done it,' Blackstone replied.

'You see!' Meade said triumphantly. 'I told you Patrick wouldn't have wasted his opportunity, didn't I? I told you he wasn't just talking about the weather and the state of baseball.'

'You also told me that he was the most direct man you'd ever met,' Blackstone pointed out. 'And he doesn't seem to have been very direct in the way he handled Plunkitt.'

Meade looked a little crestfallen. 'Yes, well, I did say he was direct, but maybe, on just this *one* occasion, he realized that being direct wouldn't work.'

Or maybe you didn't know him as well as you believe you did, Blackstone thought. Maybe he was much *less* of a saint –

and much *more* of a clever, practical policeman – than you ever imagined.'

'I wonder just what it was that Plunkitt let slip without knowing he'd even done it,' Meade said.

'We've no way of knowing,' Blackstone replied. 'And now that Inspector O'Brien's dead, we may *never* know. But it doesn't really matter, anyway.'

'Doesn't it?'

'No. Because while each link in the chain, like the meeting with Senator Plunkitt, may be of some interest in itself, what's really important – what we're actually looking for – is what lies at the end of it. And we find *that* by following the chain link by link.'

'And the next link is the brothel where Trixie works?' Meade asked.

'Exactly.'

'Being the man that he was, Patrick must have hated ever crossing the threshold of that brothel,' Meade said. 'But he forced himself to go there anyway – because his sense of duty told him that he had no choice.'

'And once he *was* there, he picked up *another* piece of information – which led him to the next link in the chain.'

'But this time he felt he could be more direct in his approach – more like his true self. He asked the madam for exactly what he wanted, and – according to Trixie – the madam wasn't the least bit worried about giving it to him. She even seemed to be amused by the whole process.'

'She may not have realized how important that piece of information actually was,' Blackstone said. 'In fact, it may *not* have been of the slightest importance at all to *her*.'

'But from the way he acted when he'd got it, it seems to have been very important to Patrick's investigation.'

'And perhaps important enough to someone else, for that person to decide that O'Brien had to die.'

'We need to find out what it was that the madam wrote on that piece of paper,' Meade said.

'We certainly do,' Blackstone agreed.

FIFTEEN

The street they were walking up was only a short distance from Madison Square. Trees had been planted – a few yards apart – along its entire length, and the sidewalk appeared to be recently repaved. And as they passed by the brownstone houses, Blackstone noted that while they were similar to the ones on the street where Inspector O'Brien had lived, *these* had only a single bell-pull by their front doors.

'Nice area,' he said to Meade.

'Yes, it's a thoroughly respectable neighbourhood populated by moderately prosperous families,' Meade replied. 'And that, of course, is why it was such a smart move for the madam to open her brothel here.'

They were back to playing the I-know-this-city-and-you-don't game again, Blackstone thought with a smile.

'Why was it a smart move?' he asked.

'For two reasons.' Meade paused. 'You'd say that Trixie is a *fairly* high-class whore, wouldn't you?'

'I can't speak for New York, but she would certainly be fairly high-class if she worked in London.'

'Which would suggest, wouldn't it, that the place where she works is a *fairly* high-class brothel?'

'I would assume so.'

'And when you're running that kind of business, you want it to be in an area where your potential clients will feel safe – an area much like this one.'

That made sense, Blackstone agreed. A gentleman's pleasure between the legs of a willing whore could be quite spoiled by the thought that, once he stepped outside, he was likely to be robbed at knifepoint.

'You told me there were two reasons,' he said to Meade. 'What's the second one?'

'I pointed out to you the people who live on this street are all moderately prosperous. But moderately prosperous is not the same as being rich. And in New York City, if you're not rich, you're not *powerful*.'

'So while the residents might not much like the idea having a brothel virtually on their own doorsteps, there's not a great deal that they can do about it,' Blackstone said.

'Exactly,' Meade confirmed. 'As long as the police bribes are paid in full, and on time, the brothel's here to stay, however they might feel. But if it was located a few blocks west of here, close to Fifth Avenue, then people like the Vanderbilts and the Astors would see to it that, however big a bribe the madam was prepared to pay, it wouldn't stay open for even a day.'

They had reached the brothel. The front door was open, and standing in the doorway was a tall man in a frock coat and top hat.

That would be Imre, Blackstone thought.

Trixie had said the doorman was built like a brick shithouse, and he couldn't have come up with a better description himself. And yet, even allowing for the man's size and obvious strength, Inspector O'Brien's righteous anger had been enough to have him worried.

There were four steps leading up to the front door, and the moment Meade mounted the first one, the doorman took a step forward himself.

'I am afraid that we are not open, gentlemen,' Imre said in heavily accented English.

Meade looked up at the house. Lights were blazing at most of the windows, and the sound of a tinkling piano was drifting down the hallway.

'Looks open enough to me,' the sergeant said.

'It is a private party,' the doorman told him firmly.

Blackstone, still standing on the sidewalk in partial shadow, was beginning to think there was something familiar about Imre. In fact, he was *certain* there was something familiar about him. But, for the moment at least, he couldn't quite put his finger on it.

Meade reached into his pocket and produced his detective's shield.

'I don't really give a damn if it's the Republican Party Convention that's going on in there,' he said. 'I'm Detective Sergeant Meade of the Detective Bureau, and I'm investigating the death of Inspector Patrick O'Brien.'

'So what?'

'So, in pursuance of that investigation, I'd like to come inside and speak to the owner of this establishment.'

Imre took a quick step back, so that he was now clearly *inside* the house again.

'Do you have a warrant?' he asked.

'No, as a matter of fact, I don't,' Alex Meade admitted. 'But I can easily get one, if I have to.'

Imre smirked. 'I don't think you will find it easy at all,' he said. 'And without a warrant, you may not come into the establishment nor may you talk to anybody at all.'

There was a filing cabinet which occupied a good part of Blackstone's policeman's brain, and now one of the drawers suddenly flew open – and a single file fell out.

'Hello, Freddie,' he said. ''Ow's tricks, me ole mate?'

'Freddie?' Imre repeated. 'I do not know of whom you speak.'

'Have you heard from either of the Wilkins brothers recently?' Blackstone asked.

Imre peered into the gloom at the foot of the steps.

'Is that you, Mr Blackstone?' he asked, with a slight wobble entering his voice.

Blackstone stepped out into the light.

'None other,' he said grandly. 'Let me introduce you to French Freddie,' he continued, turning to Meade. 'Not that he's *always* been French Freddie. For a while, he was Eric the Dutchman, and before that Sven the Swede. And before even *that*, when he was a kid growing up in the East End of London, he was plain Horace Grubb.' He returned his attention to the doorman. 'As far as I can recall, you've never been a Hungarian before, Freddie, but then, I suppose, you must be running out of nationalities to impersonate.'

'Listen, Mr Blackstone . . .' the doorman began.

'With Freddie's build, he made an ideal collector for the Wilkins brothers, who ran a particularly nasty little gang down in Whitechapel,' Blackstone said, ignoring the doorman and talking to Meade again. 'Then, one day, when he'd been out on his collecting round, he completely disappeared. And so, as it happened, did the bag stuffed full of money.'

'That was really quite a coincidence,' Alex Meade said, playing along with him.

'Wasn't it, though?' Blackstone agreed. 'A few weeks later,

a body was fished out of the Thames, and it had Freddie's wallet in its pocket.'

'And you thought he was dead?' Meade asked.

'Not for a split second,' Blackstone replied. 'And, as a matter of fact, neither did either of the Wilkins brothers.' He fixed the doorman with his gaze again. 'Did you really think, even in your wildest dreams, that you could fool a couple of sharp villains like them, Freddie?'

'I . . . I . . .' Freddie-Imre gasped.

'They put a price on your head, Freddie. Would you like to guess how much they were offering for information on your whereabouts?'

'No, I . . .'

'A thousand pounds! Just think of that. *One thousand pounds*. It's a fortune, isn't it?'

The doorman nodded numbly.

'And, of course, it's much more than the amount of cash that you actually did a runner with,' Blackstone continued. 'But as far as the brothers are concerned, you see, what you really stole from them wasn't their money at all – it was their *reputation*. And they knew that the only way to get that reputation back was by subjecting you to a particularly slow and painful death – preferably in front of witnesses.'

'Listen, Mr Blackstone, there's no need to—'

'But they couldn't kill you, could they?' Blackstone ploughed on. 'And why couldn't they? For the very simple reason that they had absolutely no idea where you were. But they *will* know, as soon as I send them a telegram.'

'Yer . . . yer wouldn't do that to me, Mr Blackstone,' the doorman gasped. 'Yer *couldn't* do that to me. Yer a copper, sworn to up'old the law.'

'But I wouldn't have to *be* a copper if I had a thousand pounds in my pocket, now would I?' Blackstone asked. 'With a thousand pounds I could buy myself a nice little farm somewhere in the countryside and sit back while other people did all the work for me.'

'Please, Mr Blackstone . . .' the doorman said.

'It does seem very hard on poor Freddie to condemn him to death after he's built up a new life for himself in America,' Meade said solicitously. 'Isn't there any alternative, Sam?'

'Well, I suppose we *could* reach some kind of deal instead,' Blackstone mused.

'What kind of deal?' the doorman asked miserably.

'You do something that I want you to do, and in return I *won't* do something you *don't* want me to do.'

'How d'yer mean?'

'We'd very much like to enter this house, but without a warrant we can't come in unless we're invited in. So why don't you do that, Freddie? Why don't *you* invite us in?'

'The boss will have my guts for garters if I do anyfink like that,' the doorman protested.

'No, she won't,' Blackstone said dismissively. 'But the Wilkins brothers would. They'd have your guts flying from a flagpole – and if they did it just right, you'd still be alive to see it.'

The doorman bowed his head in defeat.

'Please come inside, gentlemen,' he said, *almost* back to being Imre the Hungarian count again.

The door to the main salon led off the hallway. It was slightly ajar and Blackstone caught the briefest glimpse of three naked girls – who were entertaining their invisible audience by playing leapfrog – before Imre ushered them onwards.

The hallway itself was decorated with thick crimson wallpaper, its plushness relieved, every yard or so, by a piece of French Second Empire furniture or a gilded mirror.

'Now this is what I *call* a brothel,' Meade said, perhaps in an attempt to compensate for his earlier blushes.

Imre led them into a small parlour which was slightly less flamboyant than anything else they'd seen so far.

'If you wouldn't mind waiting here, gentlemen, I'll see if Madam is available to grant you an audience,' the doorman said, stepping back into the hallway and closing the door behind him.

Meade looked at Blackstone quizzically. 'Did these Wilkins brothers of yours really put a price on his head?' he asked.

Blackstone shrugged. 'Not as far as I know. I actually believed someone else had drowned Freddie and stolen the money. And so, I assume, did the brothers. And even if they had put up the money, they're in no position to pay it now – as Freddie would know if he read the English papers.'

'They're in prison?'

'They *were* in prison, after I arrested them towards the end of last year,' Blackstone said. 'But it was a very short stay indeed – it usually is when you're hanged.'

The door opened again, and a woman, who could only have been the madam, entered the room.

She was in her mid-to-late forties, Blackstone guessed. She had a huge bosom, which must have been a great asset to her while she was working her way up the ranks, but now merely provided a steady income for someone employed in the corsetry industry.

The woman smiled warmly at them. 'I am Mrs de Courcey,' she said. 'And you are . . .?'

'Detective Sergeant Meade, and my colleague from England, Inspector Blackstone.'

'An Englishman!' Mrs de Courcey exclaimed. 'How utterly charming. Do take a seat, gentlemen.'

They sat.

'I'd like to ask you—' Meade began.

'Before you ask me anything, I would like to apologize for the behaviour of my doorman,' Mrs de Courcey interrupted. 'Despite his size, he is a very gentle soul, and though he may have appeared rude to you, I'm sure that was not his intention. He sometimes forgets that he is no longer a Hungarian count,' she continued in a lower voice, as if imparting a great secret, 'and that he has now risen to an even higher station in life – that of a free American citizen.'

The pretty little speech had been aimed solely at impressing Meade, Blackstone thought. And it had worked, because the sergeant looked as if he were now struggling against the impulse to jump to his feet, stand to attention, and salute an invisible flag.

It was interesting, too – though hardly surprising – to note that Freddie had not revealed to his employer that his fake identity had been tumbled by the copper from London.

'What Imre *should* have said to you is that members of New York Police Department – and their guests – are welcome in this house at any time of day,' the madam said earnestly, but then, with just a hint of lasciviousness entering her voice, she added, '*or night.*'

Despite his best intentions, Meade's face had coloured slightly – and the madam had intended that, too.

'We need to know what was on that piece of paper you gave to Inspector O'Brien,' Meade said in a rush.

Mrs de Courcey arched an eyebrow. 'To whom?'

'To Inspector O'Brien,' Meade repeated. 'He was the policeman who visited you on Tuesday.'

The eyebrow remained arched. 'May I ask what it is that leads you to believe that?'

'We have information.'

'And who informed you?'

'I'm afraid I can't say.'

Mrs de Courcey sighed. 'One of the many drawbacks to being a successful business woman in this city is that one does tend to acquire enemies,' she said regretfully. 'There are even some people, you know, who are so jealous of my good fortune that they will do anything – including telling outrageous lies – in an effort to bring me down.'

'We don't think it is a lie,' Meade said.

'And I am telling you, with my hand on my heart –' Mrs de Courcey paused to slowly rub her ample bosom – 'that the gentleman in question was never here.'

Meade was even less in command here than he'd been when he was dealing with Senator Plunkitt, Blackstone thought. The woman had stirred up his patriotism, then embarrassed him with sexual innuendo, and the result was that now he was being *far* too soft on her.

'You need to get one thing straight,' the Englishman said harshly. 'We're here looking for Inspector O'Brien's killer. That's *all* we're concerned with, so we have no interest at all in nailing a woman who, however elegantly she speaks, is no more than the madam of a whorehouse.'

Mrs de Courcey looked outraged. 'I . . . I've never . . .' she began.

'Shut up and listen,' Blackstone ordered her. 'You have two choices. The first is to tell us what you told Inspector O'Brien, and we'll leave it at that. The second is to refuse to tell us, but that would be a mistake, because when we find out what it was ourselves – and we *will* find out – we'll be coming after you.'

By a truly valiant effort, Mrs de Courcey had recovered most of her composure and now she turned to Meade, smiled, and said, 'We Americans pride ourselves on being direct, and we tend to see the English as reserved. Yet so often, it's quite the reverse, don't you think?'

But the spell she had cast over Meade had been broken.

'Doesn't matter how he *chose* to say it,' the sergeant told the madam. 'What's important is that *what* he said was quite true. You do only have two choices.'

'No, I don't,' said Mrs de Courcey, who had not *quite* given up the battle for Meade's soul. 'Although,' she added softly, 'you're quite right that those would be my choices if things had happened as you say they did. But, you see, they simply did not. This Inspector O'Reilly of yours—'

'It's *O'Brien*, as you know very well,' Blackstone snapped.

'This Inspector *O'Brien* of yours never came here, so I could not possibly have given him an addr—'

Then Mrs de Courcey fell silent.

'An address?' Blackstone asked, pouncing on the word. 'Who said anything about it being an *address* you'd given him?'

The woman still said nothing.

'You'd like to take back the words if you could, wouldn't you?' Blackstone taunted. 'But it's too late now.'

'What else *could it* have been that I was supposed to have written?' Mrs de Courcey demanded, and her voice was suddenly coarser. 'A love poem from the whore to the cop? Instructions on how to cure the clap? It has to be an address – only I didn't write nothin'!'

'We could arrest you, you know?' Meade said.

'Grow up, sonny!' Mrs de Courcey said contemptuously. 'But do it somewhere else – 'cos I want you *out* of my knocking shop right now!'

'I'll pull that bitch in for questioning if it's the last thing I do,' Meade said angrily, as they walked away from the brothel.

He was whistling in the dark, Blackstone thought.

'You'll never get a judge to sign the warrant,' he said aloud.

'I will if I pick the right judge – and offer to pay him the right bribe.'

'I'm not sure there *is* such a thing as the *right* judge,' Blackstone said, hating the thought of putting the rock back on top of Meade's spring of optimism, but knowing that it had to be done.

'You don't know this city like I do,' Meade said stubbornly. 'As I've told you often enough before, money talks.'

'Of course it does,' Blackstone agreed. 'But we both know that all men aren't *really* equal, and neither is all money. There's *some* money which has greater powers of persuasion than the rest.'

'What the hell are you talking about?' Meade demanded.

'What's the first question that the judge you try to bribe is going to ask his clerk?'

Meade thought about it. And as he did, his expression grew gloomier and gloomier.

'He's going to ask whether or not Mrs de Courcey pays her bribes on time,' he said finally.

'Exactly. And if she does – and I'm *sure* she does – what's his next move going to be?'

'He'll turn down the bribe. It'll really cut him up to do it, but he'll do it anyway.'

'Why?'

'Because the web of corruption works on a perverted kind of trust, and if Mrs de Courcey's bribes didn't get her the protection she expected, the other madams would start asking themselves whether it was worth them paying their bribes.'

'And if that happened, the whole system would collapse,' Blackstone said. 'And nobody involved in it wants that.'

'You're right, of course,' Meade said. 'You're *always* so damned right.' He took a deep breath. 'I'm going to go down to the Lower East Side. Do you want to join me?'

'All right,' Blackstone said. 'But why, in particular, do you want to go there now?'

'Because it's a festering boil on the ass of New York City – and that makes it the perfect location for getting disgustingly drunk in.'

SIXTEEN

He was lying flat out, on a cast-iron bed with a rather lumpy mattress – that much he had already established – but other than that, Sam Blackstone had no real idea of where he was.

Slowly it started to come back to him. He was in New York City. He was in a hotel – the Mayfair Hotel on Canal Street.

Locating himself should have made him happier, but it didn't. He was feeling rougher than he could remember feeling for a long, long time. A smithy seemed to have been established inside his head while he'd been sleeping, and the blacksmith was already hard at work, hammering out innumerable horseshoes and using his brain as the anvil. Even worse than that, a tannery had been set up inside his mouth, so that now he seemed to be in imminent danger of being poisoned by his own breath.

His back ached. His legs ached. Whenever he looked towards the light streaming in from the window, he noted that his vision was blurred – but he didn't do much of that, because the light made his pupils burn.

He lay on the bed, trying to retake control of his body, and thinking about the previous night.

He and Meade had probably visited at least ten or twelve saloons on the Lower East Side, and had a minimum of two drinks in each one. In Kleindeutschland, they had supped foaming steins of beer. In one of the less salubrious saloons on 5th Street they had drunk a whiskey which would have made embalming fluid taste good. They had been accosted by scores of prostitutes of all colours. They had been invited into several opium dens. That he had ever found his way back to his hotel when this excess was over had been little short of a miracle.

And why had they done it? he asked himself, as the blacksmith in his head eased off for a second.

They had done it because – though neither of them was prepared to openly admit it – they both knew that their investigation was dead, and they were attending its wake.

The trail that the investigation had been following had ended – decisively – with Mrs de Courcey, and they would never be able to pick it up again. The killer – or killers – had got away with murdering an outstanding police officer. And Mrs O'Brien, struggling to bring up three children alone, would be left with the bitter knowledge that she would never find justice for her husband.

The smithy in his head appeared to have closed for the day, and even the tannery was not quite as active as it had formerly been. Blackstone slowly swung his legs off the bed, and placed his feet gingerly on the floor. When nothing disastrous happened, he stood up, and was pleased to find that he did not immediately fall over again.

He would live, he told himself – though he was still not entirely sure whether that was good or bad.

'Detective Sergeant Meade hasn't reported for duty yet,' said the desk sergeant at Mulberry Street, in an uncharacteristically cheery voice which made Blackstone really hate him. 'It seems that he's come down with a case of food poisoning.'

Blackstone nodded – carefully. 'Thank you,' he said.

'If it *is* food poisoning that he's suffering from, then he probably caught it from the same bottle that you did,' the sergeant said, after looking at Blackstone more closely.

And then he chuckled.

'What a wonderful sense of humour you Americans do seem to have,' Blackstone said sourly.

The sergeant didn't seem to notice the barb. 'Would you like to see the girl now?' he asked. 'Or don't you feel up to it yet?'

'What girl?'

'The one who came in over an hour ago, and said that she wanted to speak to you.'

'To speak to *me*? Or to speak to *Sergeant Meade*?'

'She said she wanted to see the Limey.'

Who could she be? Blackstone wondered.

Jenny the little housemaid?

There was no logical reason he could think why it *should* be her. But then there was no logical reason why she should have made an appearance in his dream, either!

'Did she look like a domestic servant?' he asked.

'No,' the desk sergeant replied. 'She looked like a whore.'

Not Jenny then, but Trixie, Blackstone thought, and was surprised to find that he felt strangely disappointed.

'Like I said, she's been waitin' for over an hour,' the desk sergeant told Blackstone. 'Do you want to see her? Or should I tell her to get her ass the hell out of here?'

'I'll see her,' Blackstone said. 'Where is she?'

'In the interview room, third door on the left,' the desk sergeant replied, jerking his thumb in roughly the right direction.

*   *   *

Trixie was wearing even more powder and rouge than she had been the day before, but Blackstone suspected there was good reason for that.

'I've come to return this,' she said, sliding the ten-dollar bill quickly across the table.

'Why?'

'Because . . . because I lied.'

'Lied about what?'

'I lied about that policeman coming into the club on Tuesday. He never did.'

'Then why did you *say* he did?'

'Because I wanted the reward.'

'And now you *don't* want it?' Blackstone asked.

Trixie shrugged. 'I still want it,' she admitted, 'but my conscience won't let me keep it.'

Or *somebody* wouldn't let her keep it, Blackstone thought.

'So Inspector O'Brien was never in the brothel?' he asked.

'That's what I said.'

'So how was it that you were able to describe the ring he was wearing so accurately?'

For a moment, Trixie was lost for an answer. Then she said, 'I didn't say I hadn't seen him – I only said I hadn't seen him in the club.'

'Then where *did* you see him?'

'Out on the street.'

'On the *street*?'

'That's right, I was out shopping, one day last week, when he stopped me and said he wanted to know about the club. It was when he was showing me his shield that I noticed the ring.'

It was more than obvious to Blackstone that the girl was lying.

Inspector O'Brien had stopped her in the street and asked her about the brothel!

O'Brien had shown no curiosity about the place at all until *after* he'd had his conversation with Senator Plunkitt. And even then, he'd known so little about the establishment – and this according to what Trixie herself had said the day before – that he hadn't been able to ask for the madam by name, and had felt distinctly uncomfortable even being there.

But though Blackstone knew that Trixie was lying – and though she knew that he knew she was lying – they both also knew that it would be almost impossible for him to ever prove it.

'Shall I tell you what *I* think happened?' Blackstone suggested.

Trixie shrugged again. 'Tell me if you want to. I don't mind – one way or the other.'

'I think that after we left last night, your madam started to ask herself where we could have got our information from. And being a smart woman, it didn't take her too long to work out that it could only have come from one of three people – you, Imre or the other girl.'

'Lucy.'

'Lucy. But she trusts Imre, so it had to be one of you two girls who'd been talking. Did Imre beat both of you up to get a confession or were you the only one who got the pounding?'

'Nobody got beaten up.'

'So if I was to scrape all that paint off your face, I wouldn't find any bruising?'

'You might find a couple of bruises,' Trixie admitted. 'But that's only because I walked into a door.'

'If you stick to your original story – the *true* one – we'll protect you,' Blackstone promised.

'Like you did last night?' Trixie asked bitterly.

She had a point, Blackstone thought.

'We made a mistake by showing your madam that we knew too much of what had gone on,' Blackstone said – although the mistake had been all Meade's, because he himself would have never have been anything like as explicit. 'I'm sorry for that, but it won't happen again. We'll put you in a hotel, somewhere they won't be able to get at you.'

But his heart was only half in it, because he knew even if she *did* stick to her original story, it would do very little to help the investigation now.

'And how would I earn a living if you were hiding me away?' Trixie asked.

'We'd give you some money.'

'But nothing like as much as I earn by doing what I do now,' Trixie pointed out.

'Probably not,' Blackstone agreed.

'Do you know why I asked to see you instead of the boy who gave me the money?'

'No, I don't.'

'It was because you were older – and maybe wiser – and I thought you'd understand the position I'm in.'

I do, Blackstone thought sadly. I understand it only too well.

But still, he heard himself say, 'The position you're in?'

'I don't exactly like being a whore,' Trixie said seriously, 'but it's the only job that's open to a girl like me where you can make a decent living. And I want to get on in the business. By the time I'm Madam's age, I want to own a place like hers. And I won't get that by taking money off the police – I'll get it because I'll be earning enough to *give* the police money.'

'Listen, Trixie, things will change – things will get better,' Blackstone said. 'The world won't always be as corrupt as it is now.'

But again, his heart was not in it, because he knew there had been corruption – and prostitution – for over five thousand years before he'd been born, and he was sure they'd still be around five thousand years after he died.

'Take the money back, Trixie,' he urged, sliding the ten-dollar bill back across the table.

'No,' the girl said firmly.

'Why not?'

'Because if they find out that I've still got it, they'll think I didn't do what they told me to.'

The door swung open, and the desk sergeant entered the room.

'Sergeant Meade's called again,' he said.

'Is he feeling any better?' Blackstone asked.

'Wouldn't know about that. He didn't say. But what he *did* say was that you should get yourself over to the New York Hospital, which is on 15th Street, as quick as you can.'

'As quick as I can?' Blackstone repeated.

'Yeah,' the desk sergeant agreed. 'He seems to think that somebody you want to talk to is dying.'

The building was five storeys high and had a sloping slate roof. There were small mock-turrets at each end of the roof and a larger one over the principal entrance. It could easily have been part of a prestigious university, or perhaps the home office of a successful insurance company. But it was neither of these things. It was, instead, the New York Hospital, and when Blackstone finally burst through the front door, he had been running so hard that it felt as if his lungs were on fire.

'Meade!' he gasped at the nurse behind the reception desk. 'Detective Sergeant Meade. He sent me a message to come here.'

The nurse – who had seen so many dramas from behind her desk that they now scarcely seemed like dramas at all – merely nodded.

'He's waiting for you on the third floor,' she said and pointed. 'Use those stairs.'

Who was it that was dying? Blackstone asked himself, as he took the stairs three at a time.

Not the sergeant himself, obviously.

But *whoever* it was, it had to be somehow connected to the investigation, or Meade would never have called him.

He passed the second floor, his heart beating out a furious tattoo, his head pounding.

Could it be Mrs de Courcey? he wondered.

Or Senator Plunkitt?

Was he about to hear a deathbed declaration from one of them which would crack the Inspector O'Brien murder case wide open?

He had reached the third floor and paused to catch his breath.

Ahead of him was a long corridor which smelled strongly of both carbolic soap and desperation.

And halfway along the corridor, shrouded in their own misery, sat a man and a woman.

As they saw him approaching them, Alex Meade and Mary O'Brien stood up.

'What happened?' Blackstone asked.

'It's Jenny!' Mary O'Brien moaned. 'Poor little Jenny. She's slashed her own wrists.'

Blackstone felt his stomach knot.

'But she's not dead, is she?' he asked.

And even as he was speaking the words, he was thinking to himself, of course she's not dead, you bloody fool! If she was *dead*, there'd be no reason for us to be here.

'No, she's not dead – but she *is* in a pretty bad way,' Alex Meade said grimly.

'How did it happen?' Blackstone demanded.

'I–I took the children out to Central Park this morning,' Mary O'Brien sobbed. 'I thought it might cheer them up a little. I thought that the fresh air would be good for them. I asked Jenny if she wanted to come, too, but she said that she didn't.'

'You mustn't blame yourself, Mary,' Meade said soothingly.

'I should have *made* her come with us, shouldn't I?' Mary said, ignoring him. 'I'm the mistress of the house and she's the servant. I should have insisted that she came.'

'You weren't to know what would happen,' Meade told her.

'Wasn't I?' Mary asked fiercely.

'No, you've—'

'When I told her that because of Patrick's death I was going to have to let her go, I saw how *depressed* she was. So I should have known then. I should have damn-well *known*!'

'Who found her?' asked Blackstone, as the policeman who never entirely left him took control of his head again.

'Mrs . . . Mrs Kenton. She's the part-time cleaner who helps Jenny with the heavy work. She . . . she wasn't due to arrive until eleven o'clock, but for some reason she got there at about half-past ten.' Mary shuddered. 'The doctor said that if she'd arrived even a few minutes later than that, poor little Jenny would already have been dead.'

She bowed her head and seemed unable to go on.

'As I understand it, this Mrs Kenton behaved truly admirably,' Meade said, trying his best to sound cool and efficient. 'The first thing she did was to apply tourniquets to the girl's arms to stop the bleeding, then she bandaged her wrists. And having taken things as far she could herself, she stuck her head out of the window and shouted to a passer-by that he should summon an ambulance.'

There was one question that almost seemed too crass to ask, but Blackstone knew that he had to ask it anyway. He gestured to Meade that they should move a little distance away from Mrs O'Brien.

'It's a terrible thing to have happened,' he said, as the knot in his stomach continued to tighten up. 'A truly ghastly thing. But what I don't really see is why *we're* here.'

'We're here because Jenny wants to see us,' Meade said. 'Or, to be accurate, she wants to see *you*.'

'What?'

'She keeps losing consciousness, but every time she comes round, the first thing she wants to know is why you're not here.'

She was the second girl in an hour who'd asked to see him, Blackstone thought, as he felt the heavy weight of responsibility pressing firmly down on his shoulders.

He already knew why Trixie had asked for him. She'd
thought he'd have a better – and more sympathetic – understanding of her situation than Alex Meade would have done.

But what possible reason could the servant girl – who had
only met him once – have for being so desperate to talk to him?

The girl was unconscious, and was dressed in a white surgical
shift which was only slightly paler than her own complexion.

The bed she had been laid on was no more than the standard
size, yet it seemed far too big for her. She looked lost in it,
Blackstone thought. She looked as if she was *drowning* in it.

'What are her chances?' he asked the doctor, a youngish
man who looked as if he had not slept for days.

'Not good at all,' the doctor replied. 'She doesn't appear
to have had a particularly robust constitution to begin with,
and she's lost a great deal of blood. We've no idea what state
her vital organs are in – they could be failing even now, for
all we know – but she's so weak that we daren't risk trying
any explorations.'

'Tell me something – anything – that I can pin a little hope
to,' Blackstone demanded.

The doctor thought about it. 'If she manages to live through
the day, I might start being a little more optimistic of a
recovery,' he said finally.

'Well, *that's* something, isn't it?' Blackstone asked.

'But if she died without ever recovering consciousness again,'
the doctor continued, 'I wouldn't be in the least surprised.'

Blackstone thought back to the dream he had had, only two
nights earlier. Not a dream of Hannah or of Agnes, or even
of Ellie Carr, but of Jenny. It had puzzled him at the time that
she should have a key to his sleeping world, and it puzzled
him even more now.

The girl groaned.

'She seems to be coming round,' the doctor whispered. 'Go
and stand by the bed, where she can see you.'

Blackstone did as he'd been instructed, and arrived there
just as Jenny opened her eyes.

She smiled weakly at him. 'Hello,' she said.

'Hello, Jenny,' Blackstone replied.

'I'm an orphan,' the girl told him.

'I know.'

'I don't ever remember having a papa of my very own, but I saw this picture of a gentleman in a magazine once, and he looked so nice and kind that I cut it out and kept it.'

'Did you?' Blackstone asked, feeling as if his heart would break.

'I've still got it. I used to look at it sometimes and pretend that *he* was my papa. Isn't that silly?'

'No, it's not silly at all,' Blackstone said, as a wave of helplessness and inadequacy swamped him. 'It's sweet.'

'And when you came to the apartment that time, with your friend, you reminded me of my magazine papa.'

So *that* was what this was all about, Blackstone thought.

'I wish I *had* been your papa,' he said. 'I would have been *proud* to be your papa.'

'Would you . . . would you hold my hand?' Jenny asked timidly.

Blackstone looked to the doctor for guidance, and the doctor mouthed back that it would be all right, as long as he was very, very gentle.

Blackstone took Jenny's hand, and the girl gripped his with what little strength she had left in her.

'You slit your own wrists, didn't you, Jenny?' he asked softly. 'Nobody helped you. Nobody else was involved.'

'Nobody,' Jenny confirmed, almost dreamily. 'I did it all by myself.'

'Tell me how you did it.'

'I waited until the mistress had taken the children off to Central Park, and then I went into the kitchen and took a sharp knife out of the drawer. I . . . I . . .'

'Gently, Jenny,' Blackstone cooed. 'Take it gently.'

'I took the knife back to my bedroom. I wanted to get it all over and done with straight away, but somehow I–I just couldn't. I must have sat staring at that knife for hours before I got up the courage to use it.'

Not hours, though it may have felt like it, Blackstone thought. But *an* hour at least.

He could almost see her, sitting there on her bed, looking at the sharp knife she was holding in her trembling hands, and willing herself to find the strength to end it all.

'If I'd done it just a few minutes sooner, I'd have been dead by the time Mrs Kenton arrived,' Jenny said plaintively. 'When you see her, tell her I'm sorry for upsetting her, will you?'

'There'll be no need for that,' Blackstone said, with feigned heartiness. 'You'll be able to tell her yourself in a day or two.'

'No, I won't,' Jenny said, with a certainty that was quite chilling. 'You *know* I won't.'

'*Why* did you do it, Jenny?' Blackstone asked, still softly. 'Whatever possessed you to want to end your life?'

'I did it because I'm no good,' Jenny told him. 'I did it because I'm a very wicked person.'

'No, you're not,' Blackstone said soothingly.

'You don't know,' Jenny said, with as much passion as her weak state would allow. 'You've no idea.'

Up until perhaps a minute earlier, he'd firmly believed that the reason she'd asked to see him was because he'd become her new father figure – a living breathing replacement for the picture she'd cut out of the magazine.

And that was probably just what *she* believed, too.

But there was so much more to it than that, Blackstone was now starting to realize.

Jenny knew she was going to die, and something deep within her – perhaps the soul she was probably only vaguely aware she even possessed – was driving her to unburden herself before death took her.

And *that* was why he was there.

Not as a replacement for the man whose picture she cut from the magazine at all, but as a father figure in a much more traditional sense – as a priest, who was supposed to hear her confession and grant her absolution.

'I'm sure you could never have done anything that other people would consider even remotely wicked,' he said.

'Wicked,' Jenny mumbled, almost deliriously. 'Wicked.'

'But if you want to tell me about these *so-called* terrible things that you think you've done, I'll be happy to listen,' Blackstone assured her.

'I betrayed the master,' Jenny said. 'He was never anything but kind to me, and I betrayed him.'

The knot in Blackstone's stomach was now so tight that he was finding it difficult to breathe.

'How did you betray him?' he asked.

But from the strange look which had come into Jenny's eyes, he doubted she could even hear him any more.

'He's dead because of me,' Jenny whimpered. 'He's dead because I betrayed him.'

'Jenny, listen to me!' Blackstone said desperately. 'Try to hear what I'm going to say to you.'

But it was hopeless – she was too far gone now.

'It wasn't a bullet that killed the master,' Jenny whispered, her voice so faint that he had to lower his head closer to her mouth to even hear what she was saying. 'It was me!'

Her grip on his hand had been growing weaker and weaker as she spoke these last few poignant words, and now there was no grip left at all.

The doctor, who had been watching the whole scene from a distance, now stepped forward and placed a finger on Jenny's neck.

He shook his head sadly. 'She's gone, I'm afraid.'

Blackstone just stood there, looking down at the dead girl.

'You can let go of her hand, now,' the doctor said.

'What?'

'She can't feel you any longer, so there's no point in you continuing to hold her hand.'

No, there probably wasn't, Blackstone thought. And yet his own hand seemed reluctant to release its grip.

'There are things to do,' the doctor said, a hint of impatience entering his voice. 'We have to wash her and lay her out. We're going to need the bed.'

Blackstone forced his fingers to open and Jenny's arm flopped back on to the bed.

He turned and walked towards the door, and as he did so, he felt his eyes start to prickle. It was a long time since he could last remember crying – but he was crying now.

SEVENTEEN

There was only enough space for a single bed, a night-stand and a small wardrobe in Jenny's bedroom, but given her former life at the orphanage, thought Blackstone – who knew all about orphanages himself – it must have seemed unimaginably luxurious to the girl.

He looked down at the blankets and sheets which covered the narrow bed, and which were themselves covered with a dark brown stain.

How Jenny had bled!

How she must have lain there in quiet despair, watching her life slowly seep away!

'Where are Isobel, Emily and Benjamin?' he heard Meade ask from somewhere behind him.

'At the moment, they're with Mr and Mrs Barlow, our neighbours,' Mary O'Brien replied. 'But they can't stay there for much longer.'

'Why not?'

'It wouldn't be fair to the Barlows. They're very willing to help, but they're old people, and it must be a strain on them having even three *well-behaved* children around.'

'So if they can't stay with the neighbours, what *are* you going to do with them?'

'The children must come back to the apartment.'

'Is that wise – after what's just happened here?'

'This is their home,' Mary said firmly. 'And if it contains unhappy memories – as it unquestionably does – they must learn to come to terms with them. Because you can't live your life by running away from unpleasantness or pretending it never happened.'

'I still think you should consider . . .' Meade began.

But Mary had left his side and was already standing next to Blackstone and looking down at the bed.

'I'll have to clean this up before they get back,' she said. 'I can at least spare them that.'

'If there's anything we can do, you know that you only have to ask,' Meade said.

'I *do* know that, and I'm very grateful for it,' Mary told him. She began stripping the sheets and blankets off Jenny's bed. 'I'd like to throw these away, but I simply can't afford to. Still, the stains will hardly show if Jenny boils them really . . .' She faltered. 'Jenny *won't* be boiling them, will she?' she continued, with a choke in her voice. 'Jenny will never be boiling anything again.'

'Perhaps it might be a good idea if you sat down for a while,' Meade suggested.

'There's no time to sit down,' Mary said, collecting up the bedding in her arms. 'There's still far too much to do.' She

looked down at the mattress, and saw that the bloodstains had
left their mark there, too. 'The mattress is beyond saving,' she
decided. 'It will just have to be burned. Could you gentlemen
. . . could you take it down the basement for me, and ask the
janitor if he wouldn't mind putting it in the furnace?'

'Of course,' Meade said.

'Be glad to,' Blackstone told her.

When Blackstone and Meade returned from the basement, they
found Mary pacing back and forth across the living-room floor.

'There's a bottle of whiskey on the table,' she said. 'Will
you please pour us all a drink, Alex?'

'I'm not sure that's . . .' Meade began.

'We must drink to Jenny's memory,' Mary said firmly. 'We
at least owe her that.'

Meade poured the three drinks, and handed one to Mary.

'Patrick always said that it was an insult to good whiskey
to drink it standing up, so do please sit down,' Mary said.

But she did not sit down herself. With her own glass of whiskey
held tightly in her hand, she continued to pace the floor.

'There is so much to do,' she said, not for the first time,
and in a voice which kept oscillating between the despairing
and the frantic. 'So very, very much to do. The orphanage
where Jenny was brought up was run by Presbyterians, you
know, and once she came to live with us, we went to great
pains to see that she continued to follow her chosen religion.'

Or, at any rate, the religion that had been chosen *for* her,
Blackstone thought, because in that – as in so many other
aspects of her life – she had been able to make very few
choices of her own.

Do you think the fact that she killed herself means she can't
be buried in consecrated ground, Alex?' Mary asked.

'I don't know,' Meade replied.

'It shouldn't. It's not *fair* that it should. But perhaps, even
if it does, I can persuade her pastor – who is also the orphanage
pastor – that she never *intended* to kill herself.' She looked
at Blackstone, perhaps hoping for some sort of support, but
the inspector could think of nothing to say. 'Or perhaps I can
tell him that she was just punishing her body in the same way
as the flagellants punish theirs.'

'I don't think Presbyterians do that,' Blackstone told her.

'No, I don't suppose they do,' Mary said. 'Or that she *did* intend to kill herself, but changed her mind at the last moment.' she continued, as if searching for something – *anything* – that they could agree on.

'Perhaps that's just what she did do,' Blackstone said, feeling as if the words were being torn from him.

But he didn't believe it. Not for a second.

Jenny had known what she was doing. Weighed down with her guilt over O'Brien's death, she had sought the only escape she thought was open to her – and had taken her own life.

'But even if the church won't bury her with all the trappings of religious ritual, she still has to *be* buried,' Mary said. 'Can she still have a funeral service, even if the grave is not consecrated?'

'I don't know,' Meade said for the second time.

'I must find out,' Mary said. 'I must arrange for the burial. I must send out the notices.' She stopped pacing, as if a new, terrible thought had suddenly struck her. 'There is *no one* to send notices to,' she wailed. 'She was an orphan. She had no family of her own. She had no friends . . .'

'No friends at all?' Blackstone asked.

'There was one,' Mary remembered. 'A girl called Nancy – Nancy Greene – who she was in the orphanage with. This Nancy went into service at a big house on Fifth Avenue, and Jenny used to go and see her once a month.'

'Do you have an exact address for the girl?' Blackstone asked.

Meade shot him a questioning look, as if to say, why would you want the girl's address?

And Blackstone replied with a look of his own, which said, it's too complicated to explain now, but I'll tell you all about it later.

'Nancy's address?' Mary said. 'Yes, I must have it somewhere. We would never have allowed Jenny to leave the house without knowing exactly where she was going.'

'Well, if you give me the address, I'll go and see her myself, and break the sad news to her,' Blackstone promised. 'And while I'm there, I'll ask her to attend the funeral.'

'You're very kind,' Mary said. 'And you will come to the funeral yourself, won't you?' she added imploringly.

'Of course,' Blackstone agreed.

'I'll come too,' Meade said. 'And I'd be grateful if you'd allow me to pay for it.'

'Why?' Mary asked. 'You hardly knew the girl.'

Meade shrugged awkwardly, as he always did when he found himself in this sort of situation.

'It doesn't matter that I didn't really know her,' he said. 'I'd still like to pay for her funeral.'

'The reason you're making the offer is to save me bearing the expense myself, isn't it?' Mary asked.

'Partly,' Meade conceded.

Mary took a deep breath. 'I still have a little money left. Not much – but enough to see Jenny buried decently.'

'But you have all your other expenses to consider,' Meade protested. 'Your children . . .'

'Jenny lived in this house,' Mary said. 'It would be hypocritical of me to say I regarded her as fully a part of the family – but I was fond of her, and I want to do the right thing. Do you understand that? *I* want to do the right thing!'

'I understand,' Meade said.

'Did Jenny ever leave the house alone, apart from going to see Nancy?' Blackstone asked.

'No.'

'Didn't she go to church?'

'Of course she did. Patrick insisted on that. He wasn't one of those Catholics who believe that anyone outside the True Faith is damned. Rather, he believed that when Jenny prayed, she prayed to the same God as we do.'

'But, surely, if she went to a different church, that meant she went out alone every Sunday,' Blackstone said.

Meade was growing more and more perplexed and even Mary was looking a little puzzled.

'We always take . . . we always *took* . . . a cab to church,' Mary said. 'We'd drop Jenny off at her church on the way to ours, and pick her up on the return journey home.'

'Can I ask you something else?' Blackstone asked.

'Yes.'

'Did your husband ever bring any of the work connected with his investigations home with him?'

'What?' Mary said, as if she had absolutely no idea what he was talking about – as if this latest tragedy had blanked out all memory of anything that had gone before it.

'Did he bring home any files?' Blackstone persisted. 'Or
notebooks? Or anything else that might be tied in with the
cases he was working on?'

Again, Meade gave Blackstone a quizzical look, and again
Blackstone signalled that all would be explained later.

'Yes, he did sometimes bring files home,' Mary said. 'But
he always took them away again in the morning.'

'So they were here overnight.'

'Yes.'

'Where did he keep them?'

'He had an office. A room next to Jenny's bedroom. Hardly
a room at all in fact. More of a cupboard.'

'And did he keep it locked?'

Mary thought about it. 'The door *does* lock,' she said finally.
'But I don't think he ever locked it himself. Why should he
have? This was his home.' She frowned. 'Why are you asking
all these questions, Mr Blackstone?'

'Because—'

'Because, even though *I* seem to have forgotten it, *you* are
still investigating my husband's murder?' Mary interrupted.

'Yes,' Blackstone agreed.

'And I'm keeping you away from pursuing that investigation,' Mary said, sounding angry – though only with herself.
'I'm keeping you away from it because I'm a poor weak
woman who can't cope with even the smallest difficulty
without having a man to lean on.'

'You're not weak,' Blackstone told her. 'And this is no *small*
difficulty you have to deal with.'

'Patrick would be ashamed of me,' Mary said bitterly.

'I'm sure he would un—'

'And rightly so. I'll find Nancy's address for you,
Mr Blackstone, and then you must both return to your
investigation.'

'We can't just leave you alone like this,' Meade said.

'I won't *be* alone. I have very good neighbours who will
help me if I ask them to.'

'You said they were rather old and—' Meade began.

'But even if I hadn't,' Mary interrupted him, 'it is not your
job, Alex, to cosset me – it is *your* job to find my husband's
killer.'

*   *   *

The barman in Murphy's Saloon had suggested that they order shots of whiskey to accompany their beers, but they had already been forced to drink some whiskey at Mary O'Brien's house – and even without that, after their previous evening of excess, they had decided that their livers deserved a break.

As Blackstone sipped at his beer, he made a concerted effort to assess his own mental state.

He was sure that the defeatism of the previous evening – the defeatism he had woken up with that morning – had been quite vanquished.

But what had replaced it? What was it that was now driving him so hard that he felt he was once again charging on all cylinders?

It was anger, he decided – pure, unadulterated anger!

'Do you want to tell me *now* why you were asking Mary about the times when Jenny left the house?' Alex Meade asked, after they'd been sitting in silence for some time.

'All right,' Blackstone said.

'And while you're about it, would you mind explaining why you were so interested in whether or not Patrick took work connected with his investigations home with him?'

'The two things are closely connected,' Blackstone said. 'Some investigations run along dead straight lines, but this one is circular – and Jenny's a big part of one of the arcs.'

'Well, thank you for explaining that to me,' Meade said. 'Everything is *so much* clearer now.'

Blackstone dipped his finger in his beer, and drew two arcs on the table. 'These are two parts of the same circle,' he said.

'That's obvious enough,' Meade agreed.

'The one on the left is what O'Brien did on the last day of his life, and the one on the right is the reason that Jenny killed herself. Neither of them mean much on their own, but if we can find some way to join them up, they'll make a sense which is *so* obvious that we'll be surprised we didn't see it right away.'

'Tell me about Jenny's arc,' Meade said, starting to get interested.

'Certainly,' Blackstone agreed. 'The last thing she said to me before she died was that she had betrayed O'Brien and got him killed. But what she *didn't* say was *how* she'd betrayed him, or *who* she'd betrayed him to. And now I think I have the answers to both those questions.'

'Go on.'

'I wanted to know just how much freedom Jenny actually had. Now, we know she went to church on Sundays, but the O'Briens dropped her off at the door and picked her up at the door, so that's really no kind of freedom at all.'

'Agreed,' Meade said.

'But she was much freer when she saw this girl Nancy, so if she betrayed O'Brien to anyone, it had to be to her.'

'But Nancy, according to Mary O'Brien, is just an orphan girl – like Jenny herself.'

'What is it that makes all of us important, if only for the briefest of moments?' Blackstone asked.

'I don't know.'

'It's who we're *connected* to, and what we can extract from that connection. Caesar's wife had power *because* she was Caesar's wife. The attitude of the desk sergeant in Mulberry Street changed towards me when it began to occur to him that maybe I'd got Commissioner Comstock's ear.'

'But what's all that got to do with Jenny?' Meade wondered.

'Jenny wasn't *just* a maid, she was *the* maid of a crusading New York police inspector, and . . .'

'And Nancy, whatever her *official* position is in society, could also be connected to someone important,' Meade said excitedly.

'Exactly,' Blackstone agreed. 'Nancy may be working in the house of another policeman . . .'

'That's highly unlikely, Sam, given that the house in question is on Fifth Avenue.'

'Or the house of a politician. Or she may even have a lover with a criminal background.'

'And whoever this person is – let's call him Mr X – he wanted to know what Patrick O'Brien was getting up to?'

'Yes. But how would he find out about that? And, more importantly, how could *Jenny* help him?'

'Patrick brought files home and kept them in his unlocked office, next to Jenny's bedroom!'

'And Jenny either copied them, or memorized them, and passed the information on to her friend Nancy.'

'Who herself then quickly passed on that information on to Mr X,' Meade said.

'I imagine Jenny was doing it as a favour for a friend, or to earn a few dollars,' Blackstone said. 'She knew what she was doing was wrong, but she didn't think that it was *terribly* wrong. And why would she? Once she'd passed the information on, nothing world-shaking ever happened. Life went on much as before. And if Inspector O'Brien was ever puzzled over how the people he was investigating seem to know so much about that actual investigation, he never said anything about it to Jenny.'

'But then she passed on something which showed Mr X just how much danger Patrick's investigation was actually putting him in,' Meade said.

'In fact, he was in *so much* danger that he decided the only way out of the situation was to have O'Brien killed,' Blackstone added.

'And Jenny must have finally understood the chain of events – must have realized that it was the information that she'd passed on which had caused his death?'

'"He's dead because of me",' Blackstone said, bleakly quoting the dying girl's words. '"He's dead because I betrayed him. It wasn't a bullet that killed him. It was me".'

'Brilliant!' Meade said. '*Absolutely* brilliant! You must be pleased as punch with yourself, Sam.'

And under normal circumstances he would have been. But Blackstone knew these were *not* normal circumstances – and now there was no room in him for any emotion but anger.

He remembered leaving the orphanage himself, and how big, confusing – and frightening – the outside world had seemed to him. But then the army had taken him under its wing, and he had slowly learned how to handle freedom and accept responsibility.

Jenny had been taken under a wing as well – under the well-meaning wing of the O'Brien family. But it hadn't been anything like as big and all-encompassing as the army's wing, and others had been able to slip under it too. And once they had done that, they had exploited her.

Jenny was blameless, in both O'Brien's death and her own. It was the man who had used her who was responsible for both.

'Are you all right?' Meade said worriedly.

'I'm fine,' Blackstone replied, unconvincingly.

He looked down at the table. His two arcs had dried into sticky smudges, so he drew them afresh.

'To add to the left-hand arc – to be able to join it to the right one – we need to know the address that Mrs de Courcey gave to O'Brien,' he said.

'True, but the woman refuses to even admit that Patrick had been to the brothel,' Meade pointed out, 'and yesterday you said—'

'What I said yesterday is neither here nor there,' Blackstone told him. 'Yesterday I hadn't watched Jenny die, and I was too willing to give up easily. But I'm not willing any longer. The bitch will talk. I'll *make* her talk!'

'How?'

'You believe that everything that happens in New York City is lubricated by money, don't you?' Blackstone asked.

'Absolutely,' Meade agreed.

'So let's see how Mrs de Courcey feels when the money starts to dry up,' Blackstone suggested.

EIGHTEEN

Precinct Captain Michael O'Shaugnessy liked to think of himself as a plain straightforward man who would always rather use his fists than his brain, and, having clubbed his way up through the ranks, he had long ago lost count of the number of heads he had broken.

Now he was sitting pretty, with a country estate and an ever-expanding bank account, but he was not one of those men who repudiated the past which had made him the man he was, and whenever he heard one of the officers serving under him refer to him as 'Bull', he took it as a compliment.

In general terms, he could best be described as a man who travelled life's highway in a state of brutish happiness. But he was not feeling happy that morning. In fact, he found the two men sitting opposite him, on the other side of his desk, distinctly unsettling.

They unsettled him because he was not meeting them through any choice of his own, but because he had been *ordered* to meet them by that damned Commissioner Comstock. And since he hadn't been able to contact any of the other three commissioners – who worked maybe one day a week *between* them – he had felt compelled to obey the order.

They unsettled him because one of them was Detective Sergeant Alexander Meade, a far-too educated man whose father had very good political connections, and who was well known to regard straight-down-the-middle honesty as something of a virtue.

And they unsettled him because the other man – the Limey cop in the shabby suit – had a determination and intensity about him which would have unsettled *anybody*.

'I'm a busy man,' said O'Shaugnessy, who firmly believed that, when in doubt, you should always take the offensive. 'So say what you gotta say, an' then leave me to do my work.'

Meade nodded. 'Of course, sir,' he replied, deferentially. 'And may I just say that we really appreciate the fact, as busy as you are, you've still managed to find the time to—'

'You've already wasted thirty seconds,' O'Shaugnessy told him. 'Get to the goddam point!'

Meade swallowed. 'As you probably already know, sir, we – that is, Inspector Blackstone and I – have been asked by Commissioner Comstock to investigate Inspector O'Brien's murder and—'

'Listen, kid, I'm sorry O'Brien got killed,' O'Shaugnessy interrupted. 'An' I'm sorry for his wife and children, too. But any man who goes around disturbin' existing practices is just askin' for trouble.'

'And deserves what he gets?' the Limey asked, with a voice you could have cut diamonds with.

'Yeah, I suppose you could say that,' Captain O'Shaugnessy agreed, because he was sure as hell not going to be intimidated – or made to feel he'd been put in the wrong – by an *Englishman*.

'Did you know that a large part of the investigation that Inspector O'Brien was conducting just before he died was focused almost exclusively on you – and the bribery you're involved in, sir?' Meade asked.

So what? O'Shaugnessy asked himself.

Why should that bother him, when there wasn't a captain in the whole of New York City who made a secret of the fact that he accepted payments for the services he performed?

How *could it* be a secret, even if he wanted it to be, when there were so many people involved in the process – the saloon keepers and brothel owners who paid the bribes; the patrolmen who collected the bribes; the sergeants who peeled off their percentage before passing the bribes up to the captain; the inspectors, superintendents, judges and politicians at the end of the chain, all of whom, unlike hard-working precinct captains, did virtually nothing to earn their share . . .

The inspectors, superintendents, judges and politicians!

O'Shaugnessy felt his heart beating just a little faster, because it *could be* argued, if you were of a mind to, that some of their share – which they didn't earn, but certainly *expected* – had never actually reached them, and was now residing in the bank account with the name O'Shaugnessy on it.

If that snooping son of a bitch, Inspector Patrick O'Brien, had found out about that, and if the information ever did actually reach those people higher up the chain . . .

But then Captain O'Shaugnessy realized it was never going to happen, because after O'Brien's death, certain actions had been taken which made it *impossible* for it to happen.

And it was this realization which immediately turned what could have been a stressful meeting into an opportunity to have some good bullying fun at the expense of the hoity-toity sergeant and the skinny Limey.

'So you're sayin' Inspector O'Brien had some files on me, are you?' O'Shaugnessy asked.

'A great many files,' Meade said.

'In fact, there's a whole drawer-full of them,' the Limey added with conviction.

'An' have you got them now?' O'Shaugnessy asked.

'We have.'

O'Shaugnessy smiled. 'Do you know, boys, I simply don't believe you.'

Meade turned to Blackstone. 'Captain O'Shaugnessy must have heard the rumour that all the files which were in Inspector O'Brien's office have disappeared,' he said lightly.

'Perhaps he even went so far as to *help* them to disappear himself,' the Limey suggested.

O'Shaughnessy's grin widened. 'An' let's just say you're right in suspectin' that I had somethin' to do with their disappearance,' he told the Limey. 'Let's go even further, an' say I had a big fire in that stove over there in the corner – even though it *is* midsummer, an' almost hot enough to roast a pig on the sidewalk – how are you goin' to prove that what I burned was Inspector O'Brien's files?'

'The good captain thinks that he's completely in the clear,' the Limey said to Meade.

'But that's because he doesn't know about all the files that Inspector O'Brien kept in his office at home,' Meade said to the Limey.

O'Shaugnessy felt another twinge of misgiving.

'So just what was in these files of his?' he asked, praying that Sergeant Meade wouldn't suddenly start quoting certain bank account numbers or lists of property deeds.

And Meade didn't!

All he *did* say was, 'I'd prefer not to reveal that at the moment.'

Which, as far as Captain Michael O'Shaugnessy was concerned, was a mistake.

A big one!

'You ever play poker, Alex?' the captain asked.

'I have been known to.'

'An' I'll just bet that every time you do, you go home with a hole in your pocket. See, boy, the second you said you'd prefer not to reveal that, I knew you were bluffin' – I knew that though you were pretendin' you'd got a full house, you were holdin' no more than a pair of deuces. At best! An' you ain't gonna bring down Bull O'Shaugnessy with a pair of deuces.'

'Perhaps you're right,' Meade agreed quietly. 'Or perhaps I've got *such* a good hand that I don't want to lay it on the table yet.'

'And anyway, the poker analogy doesn't really hold up,' the Limey said calmly.

'The *what* don't hold up?' O'Shaugnessy asked.

'The poker analogy. If you're playing poker, then the hand you have is the hand you have. It's fixed – unless you're foolish enough to try and deal off the bottom of the deck – and there's nothing you can do about it. Bribery and corruption isn't like that at all. Firstly, there are many more cards in the deck, and secondly, you can draw them at any time.'

'Am I just being a dumb ole Irishman, or is this guy talking a load of horseshit?' O'Shaugnessy asked Meade.

The sergeant smiled sweetly. 'Oh, he's definitely not talking horseshit, sir, and if you didn't understand it that's probably because he didn't explain it clearly enough.' He turned to Blackstone. 'Try again, Sam,' he suggested.

'If we lay out all the mistakes you've made on the table for you to see,' the Limey said, 'you'll immediately start going round cleaning them up. And once you have cleaned them up, they won't *be* mistakes any more. Which is the last thing we want – because without your mistakes, you're no use to us.'

'Let me be quite clear on this,' O'Shaugnessy said. 'You're threatening me, ain't you?'

Meade turned to the Limey again. 'Told you he'd be bound to catch on eventually,' he said.

They seemed so sure of themselves – so much at ease – O'Shaugnessy thought. So maybe they really *did* have something on him. But, hell, he was a *precinct captain*, and he was damned if he was going to be threatened by a *detective sergeant* and a *Limey*.'

'I've had enough of listening to your crap!' he said. 'I want you out of my office. Now!'

Those few words – delivered harshly by a captain renowned for his violence – should have been enough to have the two men scurrying away like a pair of frightened rabbits.

Yet they weren't! Meade stayed perfectly still and the Limey actually crossed his legs as if he was settling in for a long session.

'Have I got to call in a few of my boys to *help* you out of the office?' O'Shaugnessy demanded.

'You *could* do that,' the Limey said.

But there was something in his voice which suggested that doing it would be a mistake, and almost against his own will, O'Shaugnessy heard himself saying, 'You've got five seconds to come up with a reason why I shouldn't.'

But it was at *least* ten seconds before Blackstone spoke again, and when he did, he said, 'A smart man would cover all his options. Are *you* a smart man, Captain O'Shaugnessy?'

'Smart enough,' O'Shaugnessy said. 'Smarter than any goddamn Limey, that's for sure.'

But he didn't *quite* believe it himself. And even if he *was* smarter than Blackstone, he still felt uncomfortable. There was a power about the Limey that went beyond mere brute force – a power which meant that even if you were beating the shit out of him, he would, somehow, still be in charge.

'A dumb man would argue that even if we have strong evidence against him – and you're right, we may *not* have strong evidence, it *could* all be a bluff – it still wouldn't matter,' Blackstone said. 'The dumb man would argue that given the level of corruption in this city, we'd only have a very slim chance of bringing him down even with *top-class* evidence.' He paused. 'How big a chance would you say we have, Alex? Twenty per cent?'

'More like twenty-five per cent,' Meade said.

'So the *dumb* man would throw us out of his office, just as you've been threatening to do,' Blackstone continued. 'The *smart* man, on the other hand, would say to himself, "Is it worth running the risk, even if that risk may only be twenty-five or thirty per cent, when, if I do these people a little *favour*, I can have a zero per cent risk?".'

O'Shaugnessy felt a sense of relief he hadn't even known he *needed* to feel. So all these guys wanted was a bribe. They were firmly back in his world – a world in which he was a captain, and they were nothing. And maybe he would pay them the bribe, not because he had to, but because it was reassuring to know that, deep down, everybody was the same.

'How much do you want?' he asked. 'And remember, boys, don't be too greedy.'

'You haven't been listening, Captain,' the Limey said coldly. 'We don't want money – we want a favour.'

'What kind of little favour?'

'Do you play chess, Captain?' the Limey asked.

What was it with this guy? O'Shaugnessy wondered. First it was analogies and now it was chess.

'I wouldn't be surprised if you *hadn't* played,' the Limey said. 'It *is* quite a stretching game.'

'I've played,' O'Shaugnessy said, because he'd be damned before he admit to this Limey bastard that there was *anything* he couldn't do.

'Then you'll know that on a chess board, you have sixteen pieces under your control, but that they're not all of the same value.'

'Sure,' O'Shaugnessy said, unconvincingly.

'The names we give to the major pieces are bishops, rooks and knights, but we might as well call them sergeants, politicians and judges – and their main job is to protect the king at all costs.'

'That would be you, Captain O'Shaugnessy,' Meade said.

'I knew that,' O'Shaugnessy growled.

'And as well as the major pieces, there are the minor ones,' the Limey continued. 'The pawns. The little people. There may be knights and bishops left on the board when the game ends, but the pawns have usually all gone, because that's their role in life – to be sacrificed when necessary.'

'What the hell *is* this Limey talkin' about?' O'Shaugnessy asked Meade.

'It will all be clear in a moment,' Meade promised.

'And in this case,' Blackstone continued, 'the pawn we want you to sacrifice goes by the name of Mrs de Courcey.'

'You want me to arrest her?' O'Shaugnessy asked.

'No, nothing like that. All we want you to do is to starve her out for a few days.'

'Starve her out? How?'

'Stop selling her booze, cigarettes and food, and make sure no one else does, either.'

'That all?'

'Not quite. We'd like you to post a couple of patrolmen outside the brothel, to prevent her clients from going in.'

'She pays me good money to look after her,' O'Shaugnessy said.

'She's a pawn,' Blackstone said dismissively. 'You're not there to serve her interests – she's there to serve yours.'

'An' what are all the other madams who pay me goin' to think, if I treat her like that?'

'They'll think that you've decided to make an example of her,' Blackstone said.

'What d'ya mean? Make an example of her?'

'When I was in the army, I used to have to watch men being flogged,' Blackstone said. He stood up, and raised his hands above his head. 'The soldier was tied up like this, and the shirt was ripped from his back.' He lowered his arms again. 'Then the flogging would begin.' He swung his right arm, as if slashing a whip through the air. 'The whip would bite into the flesh, and blood would begin to pour out of the gashes.'

O'Shaugnessy and Meade looked on, mesmerized. They could almost see it happening – could almost hear the whip as it whistled through the air, and the dull thud it made when it landed on the naked flesh.

'Sometimes the man being flogged would be guilty of a serious infraction of military discipline,' Blackstone continued. 'But sometimes the flogging was hardly merited at all – sometimes the man would have committed only the most trivial of offences.' He paused for a moment and lowered his whip hand to his side. 'Tell me, Alex, what do you imagine the men who were forced to watch this spectacle thought as they saw a man who'd done virtually nothing wrong being flogged to within an inch of his life?'

'That it wasn't fair?' Meade guessed.

Blackstone laughed. 'You poor simple child,' he said. 'I wouldn't have got that answer from you, would I, Captain?'

'No,' O'Shaugnessy agreed, 'you sure as hell wouldn't.'

'We were actually thinking two different things,' Blackstone said. 'The first was, "Thank God it's him who's getting the lash. and not me!" And the second was, "If he gets the skin ripped off his back for doing something like that, imagine what would happen to me if I *really* did something wrong!" Are you getting the point, Captain?'

Yeah,' O'Shaugnessy said pensively. 'I think I am.'

'It's called military discipline in the case of the floggings,' Blackstone continued. 'But it doesn't have to involve a whip, and it doesn't only apply to the army. Whores can be disciplined just as easily as soldiers can.'

'Go on,' O'Shaugnessy said.

'The other madams won't be *outraged* if you starve Mrs de Courcey – they'll be *scared*. They'll be falling over themselves not to offend you *in any way*, and the next time you decide to raise the amount of money that you expect from them, they'll pay up without a murmur.'

It was a smart idea, O'Shaugnessy decided – and wondered why he hadn't already thought of himself. But he certainly wasn't going to admit how smart it was to the Limey.

'So what's it to be?' Blackstone asked. 'Are you prepared to gamble that we *can't* bring you down, however hard we try – or are you willing to take out a little painless insurance?'

'I don't mind tellin' you, boys, that it will be very bad for business if I do what you ask,' O'Shaugnessy said. 'An' the thing is, I don't even know *why* you want me to do it.'

'It might help us to find whoever killed Inspector O'Brien,' Alex Meade told him.

'Well, like I told you earlier, the man should never have rocked the boat,' O'Shaugnessy said reflectively, 'but when all's said and done, he was a cop – an' an Irishman – an' if this will help your investigation, I suppose I could go along with it. How many days do you want this starvin' out to last?'

'Five days should be about enough,' Blackstone said, calculating that if it worked at all, it would work in three.

'I'll give you three days,' O'Shaugnessy said. ''cos even *three* days is gonna seriously hurt my business interests.'

'We appreciate the sacrifice that you're making,' Blackstone said. 'If there were more police officers like you around, Captain O'Shaugnessy, New York City would be a much better place.'

'Is this Limey son-of-a-bitch takin' the mickey outta me?' O'Shaugnessy asked Meade.

'Now why would he want to do that, sir, when you've been so helpful?' the sergeant replied, deadpan.

'We did it!' Meade said jubilantly. He raised his beer glass high into the air. 'Here's to us!'

'Here's to us,' Blackstone agreed, clinking his own glass against the sergeant's.

'But it was touch and go,' Meade said.

'It was,' Blackstone agreed. 'Do you have any idea at all what the captain thought might actually be in Inspector O'Brien's non-existent files?'

'No, I don't have a clue,' Meade admitted airily. 'It could have been anything – he could be getting a cut from a burglary ring, or he might have a nice little embezzlement scheme running. But I was always sure it had to be *something*, because, however much money they're making, men like O'Shaugnessy just can't resist squeezing that extra drop of juice out of the system.'

'Ain't that the truth,' Blackstone agreed.

'That flogging stunt you pulled was a master stroke,' Meade said. He grinned. 'No pun intended.'

'It's kind of you to say so,' Blackstone told him. 'But with such an obvious thug as the captain, it wasn't too hard to guess that that kind of thing would appeal to him.'

'And will it work out as you promised him it would?' Meade asked. 'Will it bring the madams into line?'

'This is your city, as you're constantly reminding me,' Blackstone replied. 'What do you think?

'I think it would work if he only tried it once,' Meade said. 'But he won't stick to once, will he?'

'No, he won't,' Blackstone agreed. 'He'll decide that he's on to a good thing, and he'll push it to the limits.'

'Until the madams decide they can't take the strain any longer, and they club together and buy themselves a politician. And then Captain O'Shaugnessy can kiss his career goodbye. So we've not only got what we went in there to get, we've started a process which will eventually bring O'Shaugnessy down. Now that's what I call a *good* day's work.'

It *was* a good day's work, Blackstone agreed. They had worked very well together as a team and had got the result they wanted, and now they were entitled to a few moments of euphoria.

But as he drained his beer, so the feeling of well-being drained away, too, and by the time the glass was empty, his anger over Jenny's death had taken control of him again.

'So what do we do now?' Meade asked.

'We split up,' Blackstone said. 'I don't trust O'Shaugnessy as far as I could throw him . . .'

'Now there's a surprise.'

'So I want you outside Mrs de Courcey's brothel, round the clock, just to make sure he's sticking to his side of the bargain.'

Meade grinned again. 'How come I always manage to land the good jobs?'

'I suppose you're just lucky,' Blackstone replied.

'And while I'm involved in the very complicated task of standing there and doing absolutely nothing, what will *you* be doing, Sam?'

Blackstone reached into his jacket pocket, took out the piece of paper that Mary O'Brien had given him earlier, and read the address that she'd written down on it.

'What will I be doing?' he said grimly. 'I'll be paying a visit on the girl who's at least *partly* responsible for poor Jenny's death.'

NINETEEN

The van Horne family residence was on Fifth Avenue, not far from St Patrick's Cathedral. It had been closely modelled on the style of chateaux which could be found in the Loire Valley, but the architect – perhaps in an attempt to make it look more authentically French – had added so many Gallic refinements that it had become a parody which a real French aristocrat would have found truly laughable.

And the English aristocracy would have looked down *their* noses at it, too, Blackstone thought as he examined the building from across the street – but then the English aristocracy look down their noses at almost *anything*.

He crossed the road, and was faced with the choice of going up the steps to the front door, or down the steps to the servants' entrance. In England, he had long ago decided it was easier to use the servants' entrance, since that kept the inbreeds who lived upstairs happy, while bothering him not at all. But this was America, he thought whimsically, the land of the free, and – not wishing to insult anyone's democratic sensibilities – he chose the front door without a second's hesitation.

His ring was answered by the butler, a tall man with sandy hair and deep green eyes, and the look on his face was a clear message – as Blackstone had always suspected it would be – that democracy was all very well in its place, but could only be stretched so far.

'Yes?' the butler said quizzically.

'I'm Inspector Blackstone of New Scotland Yard,' Blackstone said, in his most official voice.

'Are you indeed?' the butler replied, in *his* most official voice. 'And I am Boone, though you may call me *Mr* Boone.'

So it was like that, was it? Blackstone thought.

'I have been seconded to the New York Police Department,' he said, 'and I wish to question the servants in this house in connection with a case I'm currently investigating.'

The butler's eyes flashed with what could possibly be amusement. 'Is that right?' he asked.

'Do you have the authority to admit me or will you need the permission of the master of the house?' Blackstone asked.

'Oh, I have the authority all right,' Boone said. 'But even so, it might be more proper if you were to speak with the mistress first.' A thin smile flickered across his lips so swiftly that Blackstone was not entirely sure it had even been there. 'It also might be more entertaining,' the butler added.

When Boone announced Blackstone's arrival in the upstairs salon, the mistress of the house, Mrs van Horne, was already waiting to receive him. She was a large woman, a fact which even her expensive and skilfully cut tea-gown could not disguise, and her attempt to sweep gracefully across the thickly carpeted floor put the inspector in mind of an elephant in a tutu. Not that she continued to sweep for long – as her eyes fell on his second-hand suit, she stopped in her tracks and quickly turned away, in search of something more salubrious to look at.

Blackstone waited patiently for the lady to muster the strength to face his repulsive self again, and finally she did.

'When my butler informed me that an English inspector of police wished to speak to me, I was most certainly not expecting that someone dressed in the manner in which you are dressed would be appearing before me,' said Mrs van Horne, her voice sounding slightly choked.

She speaks almost as elegantly as she moves, Blackstone thought. And this happens to be my *best* suit, lady. You should just see my other one!

'You're quite sure you *are* an inspector of police, are you?' Mrs van Horne asked sceptically.

'Ah, it's the clothes that have got you confused!' Blackstone said, as if enlightenment had just dawned on him.

'Confused?' Mrs van Horne repeated, confusedly.

'I should perhaps have mentioned earlier that I'm in disguise,' Blackstone explained.

'Disguise?' the lady echoed. 'And what, pray, are you supposed to be disguised *as*?'

'As one of the common people,' Blackstone said. And then, on the principle of in-for-a-penny-in-for-a-pound, he added, 'You see, it would never do to move among the criminal classes dressed in my ermine, would it?'

'Your ermine?'

'My robes of state,' Blackstone amplified. 'Didn't I mention that I was *Lord* Blackstone of Chucklebuttie?'

'No, you didn't. So you are a lord?'

'We prefer the term "peer of the realm",' Blackstone said, sounding slightly disappointed that the woman had not known that.

'Yet you still find the need to *work* for a living?'

'So it would seem, or I wouldn't be here.'

'Are you *poor*?' Mrs van Horne asked, putting the same emphasis on the last word as she might have put on *leper*.

Blackstone laughed. 'Of course I'm not *poor*. I follow the profession of police officer out of a strong sense of duty. It's what we *peers of the realm* call noblesse oblige.'

'What an extraordinary breed of people you English seem to be,' the lady said.

But the look of disdain had quite vanished from her face, and now she seemed to be regarding him almost as an equal.

'I assume that your butler told you of the reason for my visit, Mrs van Horne,' Blackstone said.

'Indeed. You wish to question one of my servants – a Norma Something-or-other.'

'Nancy,' Blackstone corrected her. 'Nancy Greene.'

'Just so. But I'm afraid that will not be possible, as Boone has just informed me that the girl is no longer in my employ.'

'Why did she leave? Was she dismissed?'

Mrs van Horne wafted her hand through the air in a way which suggested that it was an extraordinary question for him to have asked.

'I have absolutely no idea, though given the lack of respect that the working class are allowed to display towards their betters these days, it would not surprise me if she had been ungrateful enough to have simply removed herself from my service without so much as a by-your-leave.'

Blackstone was finally catching on. 'You have no idea who she is, have you?'

'Indeed I do not,' the lady said haughtily. 'I have *so many* servants in my household, you see, that I could not possibly keep track of them all, even if I were inclined to.'

Blackstone was growing bored with the game – and even more bored with the woman's pompous vulgarity.

'Could I speak to the servants now?' he asked.

Mrs van Horne nodded graciously. 'I must admit that my first thought, as you entered the room, was to refuse you permission to see them, since you did not seem *at all* like the *right* kind of policeman.' She paused. 'All four of the police commissioners for New York City have dined at this house, you know. And on more than one occasion!'

Then it must have been the food that brought them back for second helpings, Blackstone – because it certainly couldn't have been the company.

'But you changed your mind,' he said aloud.

'I beg your pardon?'

'Your first thought was to deny me permission.'

'Ah, yes, but having spoken to you more fully, I have decided it would be wrong to go by initial appearances.'

Mrs van Horne tugged gently on the silk bell pull, and the butler appeared instantly in the doorway.

'Lord Blackstone would like to interview the servants, Boone,' Mrs van Horne said. 'See to it.'

'Certainly, madam,' the butler said. He turned, and bowed slightly in Blackstone's general direction. 'If you would like to follow me, my lord, I will see to it that all you require is effected.'

Then he raised his head again, looked Blackstone squarely in the eye – and gave him a broad wink.

They were sitting at the breakfast table in the butler's parlour. They had taken off their jackets and were both savouring the taste of the vintage port which Boone had had sent up from the wine cellar.

'What happened upstairs was better than I'd ever hoped it would be,' the butler said. 'I was nearly in hysterics when you said you were a peer of the realm, and that fat sow actually believed you.'

'So you were listening at the door,' Blackstone said.

'Naturally I was listening at the door. We all have to take our amusement where we can find it.' Boone took a sip of his port. 'Of course, you wouldn't fool anyone with real class for a minute,' he continued, matter-of-factly. 'Even with a coronet on your head, a page boy walking behind you holding your train, and a company of heralds trumpeting your arrival, the

Quality would have had you marked down as a fake the moment they saw you.'

'I fooled your mistress,' Blackstone said.

'That just proves my point,' Boone replied. 'You have to be *born* into class. However much you might want to, you can't buy it and you can't acquire it through marriage. Which is why the master would still be a gentleman even if he lost everything and ended up living on the street. And why the mistress will never be anything but a tea merchant's daughter if she lives to be a hundred.'

'You're a snob,' Blackstone said.

'Damned right I am,' Boone agreed.

Blackstone took another sip of the ruby port. It really *was* an excellent vintage.

'Tell me about Nancy Greene,' he said.

Boone hesitated before speaking. 'If I'm going to do that, I'd first like to know *why* you're interested in her.'

For a moment Blackstone considered telling the butler a convenient lie, then he looked into Boone's sharp eyes and quickly realized that lying would never work with this man.

'I believe she has some information about the murder of Inspector Patrick O'Brien,' he said.

'You're not suggesting she was involved in it?'

'Not directly, no.'

'So she's *indirectly* involved?'

'We think so.'

'And if you find her, will she be punished for that indirect involvement?' Boone asked, and though he tried to give the impression it didn't matter to him one way or the other, he failed badly.

'No, I don't think she will be punished,' Blackstone said.

And he meant it, for while she was certainly guiltier than Jenny had been, her guilt weighed less than a feather when compared to that of the man who had murdered O'Brien, and the man who had *ordered* his murder.

Boone nodded, apparently satisfied by the answer. 'There are *positions* in this household that some people would almost kill for,' the butler said. 'Footmen, coachmen, valet, lady's maid and the like. But there are also *jobs*, and some of them are so vile that even a starving immigrant, straight off the boat, would think twice about taking them. That's why we sometimes fill some of those jobs with young girls from the orphanage.'

'Because they have no choice?' Blackstone asked.

'Because they have no choice,' Boone confirmed.

'And Nancy Greene had one of those jobs?'

'Yes, she did. She was a scullery maid, which is just about the lowest of the low. The scullery maid is the first one up in the morning, lighting the kitchen boilers, and she's the last one to bed, after she's finished cleaning up after everybody. She doesn't eat with the rest of the servants. What *she* gets given is the rest of the staff's leftovers. Now you might say that isn't fair – and I'd agree with you – but that's the way things have always been run, and it will take a better man than me to change them.'

'She must have hated it,' Blackstone said.

'She probably did,' Boone agreed. 'But *if* she did, she was too smart to show it.'

'Smart?'

'Resentful scullery maids remain scullery maids for ever. But the ones who cheerfully tackle whatever task they're given are the ones who get chosen for promotion – and Nancy had understood that within a couple of days of arriving here. She was ambitious, you see, and I did all I could to fuel that ambition.'

'How?'

'In all kinds of little ways. I'd compliment her on any work she'd done particularly well. I'd slip her the odd fifty cents once in a while. But most importantly, I made quite sure that when she was *entitled* to see her friend Jenny, she *did* see her friend Jenny.'

'I'm not sure I follow you,' Blackstone admitted.

'All servants are allowed half a day off once a week, but only if they can be spared without it affecting the smooth running of the household. And because Nancy was such a good little worker, Cook was always finding reasons she *couldn't* be spared, so that in the end, I had to put my foot down.'

'And you did that so she could see Jenny?'

'Yes.'

'Why?'

'Because Jenny had landed herself a cushy little job. It wasn't in a grand house like this is, but she was comfortable enough. And I wanted her to be an example for Nancy – a reminder of what she could become if she stuck at it.'

Blackstone laughed. 'So much for the stern and unyielding butler,' he said. 'You're nothing but a pussycat in disguise.'

'Oh, I can be stern and unyielding when I need to be,' Boone said seriously. 'If you don't believe me, just ask the staff. But when you see a kid like Nancy, you just want to help her.'

'So what went wrong?' Blackstone asked.

Boone sighed. 'I went down to the kitchen one morning about three weeks ago, and she'd simply disappeared.'

'And why do you think that was?'

'I don't know,' Boone admitted. 'But if I had to guess, I'd say that one day, when she was out walking with Jenny, she met a man – and that eventually this man persuaded her to run away with him. It happens from time to time – and it nearly always ends badly.'

'Do you think it's possible that any of the servants know more than you do?' Blackstone asked.

'It's possible,' Boone said. 'Though if they *do* know, they won't tell *me*.' He took another sip of his port. 'But I suppose there's a chance they might open up to you, an outsider, as long as I promise them that whatever they tell you will never get back to me.'

'And would you do that?' Blackstone asked.

'Why not?' Boone replied. '*I* can't get Nancy out of whatever trouble she's landed herself in, but you might just be able to. And from the impression I've formed of you, I think that if it's humanly *possible* for you to help her, you will. Am I wrong about that?'

'No,' Blackstone said. 'You're not wrong.'

TWENTY

The girl's name was Florence. She had a sallow complexion, thin, pinched features, and narrow, distrustful eyes. She was a scullery maid, as Nancy had been. But it did not take Blackstone long, as he sat across the

table from her, to work out that she was the *other* kind of
scullery maid that Boone had talked about – the sort who
would never get on.

'Cook told me that you were a friend of Nancy Greene's,
Florence,' Blackstone said. 'Is that right?'

The girl sniffed. 'I suppose I was. She used to help me with
my work, when I was fallin' behind.'

Blackstone smiled at her, though he didn't find it easy. 'And
I suppose that you helped her with *her* work, when *she* was
falling behind?' he asked.

'Nancy never fell behind,' Florence said resentfully. 'Nancy
always managed to finish her work in *plenty* of time.'

'And while you were working side-by-side, did you talk to
each other?' Blackstone asked.

Florence sniffed again. 'Not allowed to talk when we're
working. It's one of the rules.'

'But I'll wager the pair of you broke that rule now and
again, didn't you?' Blackstone cajoled.

'Maybe.'

'And when that happened, did Nancy tell you things?'

'Tell me things? Like what?'

'Like, for example, what she did when she went out for a
walk with her friend, Jenny, who she'd known at the orphanage?'

Florence's eyes narrowed even further, as if she was
expecting some kind of trap.

'They didn't do nothin',' she said. 'They walked. What else
can you do, when you ain't got no money?'

'You did hear Mr Boone say that whatever you told me
wouldn't get back to him, didn't you?' Blackstone asked.

'Yes.'

'So you can speak freely. You can tell me anything that
Nancy told you. I promise that it won't hurt her. It may even
be to her advantage. Do you understand that?'

Florence looked down at the table. 'Yes.'

'So let me ask you again. What did Nancy do when she
was out walking? Did she meet anybody?'

'Might have done.'

'Don't you *want* to help her?' Blackstone asked, exasperated.

Florence looked up.

'No,' she said, with a sudden fierceness entering her voice.
'Why *should* I want to help her? She's abandoned me, ain't

she? She's out there livin' high on the hog, an' I'm still stuck here. An' it's even worse for me now than it used to be, because she ain't here to give me a hand.'

'So you don't want to help her,' Blackstone said resignedly. 'But maybe you'd like to help yourself.'

'How do you mean?'

Blackstone took two dollar bills and one $5 dollar bill – Meade's money – out of his pocket, and laid them flat on the table. Florence gazed down at them, almost mesmerized, and licked her lips.

'*Did* Nancy meet someone when she was out walking with Jenny?' Blackstone asked.

Florence nodded. 'Yeah, a guy called Eddie.'

'Eddie what?'

'Don't know,' Florence said, as her hand began to creep slowly across the table towards the dollar bills.

Blackstone slammed his right hand down hard, over the money.

'Eddie what?' he repeated.

'Eddie Toscanini,' Florence said sulkily.

Blackstone lifted his right hand slightly, extracted one of the dollar bills with his left, and passed it across the table to Florence.

'And she saw him more than once, didn't she?' he asked.

'After the first time they met, it was every time that her and her friend went out.'

'And when she eventually ran away, it was this Eddie Toscanini she ran away with, was it?'

'Yes.'

Blackstone took out the second dollar, and dangled it in the air.

'Where did they run away *to*?'

'She told me that he lives on Little Water Street. I think that's near the Bowery.'

Blackstone released his hold on the second dollar bill, and the girl caught it in mid-air.

'And what does he do, this Eddie Toscanini?' Blackstone asked.

'What do you mean?'

'What's his job?'

'No idea,' Florence said. 'Listen, mister, I've told you all I know. Can I have the rest of the money?'

'No, you can't – because you're still holding something back,' Blackstone said sternly.

'I ain't. I promise I ain't.'

'You said that Nancy was living high on the hog, didn't you?'

'That's was just a manner of speakin'. I don't *know* anyfink. Anyway, whatever life she's havin', it must be better than bein' here.'

'You said she was living high on the hog,' Blackstone repeated. 'Which must mean that Eddie's got money, which in turn must mean that he's got some kind of good job.'

'Don't have to mean that at all,' Florence said stubbornly.

'All right, have it your own way,' Blackstone said, picking up the $5 bill and making as if to return it to his pocket.

'Wait a minute!' Florence said frantically. 'I *do* know what Eddie does, but I didn't want to say in case I got into trouble.'

'In trouble?' Blackstone repeated. 'With Mr Boone?'

'With Eddie,' Florence said.

'I promise you that whatever you tell me, I won't say it came from you,' Blackstone said, dangling the $5 bill in the air, just as he had dangled the single one.

'How do I know I can trust you?' Florence whined.

'You don't,' Blackstone told her. 'But if you do decide not to trust me, then you'll never get this money.'

'Eddie works as a runner for the Five Points Gang,' Florence said, the words spilling out of her mouth as she reached forward and snatched the $5 bill from Blackstone's hand.

If there were a prize for being the one place on earth that God had truly forgotten, Five Points would not have been a racing certainty to win, Blackstone thought – but it would certainly have been in with a chance.

The area owed its name to the fact that five streets – Anthony, Orange, Mulberry, Cross and Little Water – all met there, and it was at least as depressing as anything he had ever come across in London.

The houses were historical only in the sense that they were old. They were mostly three and four storey dwellings, which – like drunken men – lurched heavily against each other for support. The roofs had gaps in them, many of the windows were no more than holes in the walls to which ragged blankets had been nailed, and the doors hung crookedly on their hinges.

The streets which ran in front of these houses were no better than the houses themselves. They had been hurriedly constructed of cheap concrete slabs, many of which were broken or missing. In some of the alleys there was no paving at all, but only a compacted dirt floor that would become a river of mud in heavy rains. And everywhere there was garbage – a detritus that even the poverty-ravaged inhabitants no longer had any use for.

Blackstone stood and watched two uniformed policemen who – no doubt for a substantial fee – were escorting a group of middle-class people around the area.

How those respectable people gawped and pointed – as if they were viewing a freak show!

But at least freaks were *paid* for being stared at, Blackstone told himself. At least they got *something* out of their humiliation.

Not so the actual residents of Five Points. All *they* got from their well-dressed visitors was a reminder that somewhere beyond this decay there was a better life to be had – but that it was a life which was not for them.

Blackstone shifted his attention from the visitors to the inhabitants – and especially those who were boys, and aged around fourteen or fifteen. Some of these boys were prowling pointlessly up and down the streets, like bears confined in a cage that was far too small for them. Others loitered on street corners, looking out disinterestedly at a disinterested world.

There were dozens of such boys.

Perhaps even scores of them.

Any one of them could be a member of the six-hundred-strong Five Points Gang – any one of them could be the boy who Herr Schiller had seen gun down Inspector Patrick O'Brien.

And *this* was the place that Nancy had fled to from the van Horne mansion of Fifth Avenue. *This* – according to Florence, the envious scullery maid – was where she was now living high on the hog.

But if she *did* live there, he had certainly not been able to find her during the course of that early evening.

'Never heard of no Eddie Toscanini,' lied a youngish man, whose breath reeked equally of whiskey and tooth decay.

'There ain't no girl called Nancy livin' round here,' an old woman – who was so bent with age and poverty that she was almost doubled-over – mumbled unconvincingly before hobbling off.

But the youngish man and the old woman had at least *spoken* to him, Blackstone thought. They hadn't just lowered their heads and hurried on without saying a word, as most of the others who he had approached had done.

He did not blame any of the people for their reluctance to talk to him. In fact, he could quite understand why they acted as they had. Because even a man in a shabby suit had untold wealth in the eyes of the residents of Five Points – and that meant that he was not to be trusted.

The sun was starting to set. Soon it would be dark, and in Five Points it would darker than in most of the city, because street lighting seemed to be one more thing that the area was not deemed worthy of.

The darker it got, the more dangerous this place would become, he told himself – and while he was not afraid of danger, he had never been a man to recklessly court it.

He would return to Five Points the following day, after he had attended Inspector Patrick O'Brien's funeral, he decided.

But the next time he came here, he would not be alone. Next time he would bring with him someone who just might be able to turn his fruitless search into a successful one.

TWENTY-ONE

I t was a little after nine o'clock in the morning, and though the early mist blown up from the river had finally dispersed, a distinct chill still lingered in the air.

In the Calvary Cemetery, Queens, the funeral cortège was making its way slowly towards the chapel. It was led by the hearse, a truly splendid vehicle which was panelled in delicately lacquered wood and pulled by four jet-black horses. The hearse was followed by three private carriages. And behind the carriages were the rest of the mourners, who were making this solemn journey on foot.

Blackstone was at the very back of the cortège – *so* far back, in fact, that he might have been said not to have been part of it all. There were reasons for this. Religion – *any* religion – made him distinctly uncomfortable. Besides, he felt something of a fake even *being* at the funeral of a man he had not even known existed until he was already dead.

He wished that Alex Meade were there instead of him, while he himself manned the observation post outside Mrs de Courcey's brothel. But when he had suggested that, the sergeant would have none of it.

'I'm a New York City police officer, and you're not,' Meade had said. 'I'm the one with the shield.'

'But this isn't a police operation,' Blackstone had countered. 'Not an official one. I don't need a shield to make sure that O'Shaugnessy's keeping to his side of the deal.'

'Anyway, I know what to look out for, and you don't,' Meade had said, almost frantically. 'There are hundreds of ways to smuggle supplies into the brothel. Ways which I'd spot, and you'd miss entirely.'

It was all nonsense, Blackstone had thought.

But he hadn't argued the point further, because they both knew the *real* reason that Meade didn't want to go to the cemetery.

Blackstone looked beyond the cortège, to the chapel which lay ahead. It was an impressive and ornate structure, with a cupola at its centre, and a pair of elaborate towers, one each side of the arched doorway. It looked like no Christian building he had ever seen before. Rather, it reminded him of the mosques he had known during his soldiering days in India.

The cortège drew up in front of the chapel. Mary O'Brien and her family emerged from the first carriage, Commissioner Comstock and the Chief of the Detective Bureau from the second.

The third carriage had been carrying the six police officers in full dress uniform who were to act as pall bearers. They heaved Patrick O'Brien's coffin on to their shoulders and carried it into the chapel. The rest of the mourners soon followed them.

Now there were only two of them left out in the chill air – the driver of the hearse, and the policeman who was far away from home.

It was a strange funeral in some ways, Blackstone thought. The hearse and the carriages were lavish – almost in the extreme. Yet most of the mourners were, judging by their dress, from a humbler background.

He found himself wondering how someone in Mary O'Brien's financial position could have *afforded* such an expensive send-off.

And then he realized that, of course, she wouldn't have *needed* to.

Because Patrick O'Brien had been a serving officer, killed in the line of duty, and it would be the New York Police Department, not Mary herself, that would be footing the bill.

But that, apparently, was all the support that the department was prepared to give, for though there was a fair turnout of other mourners, there was a notable absence of policemen.

Blackstone recalled the funerals of brother officers that he had attended back in England. There had been rank upon rank of blue-uniformed men around the graveside, standing stiffly to attention and paying their last heartfelt respects to their fallen comrade. The sense of loss which filled the air had been enough to make a grown man cry – and many of the grown men there had, indeed, succumbed to it. And later, when they had finished politely sipping their glasses of port with the widow, they had taken over a whole pub and got blind drunk.

No one in the New York Police Force, it would appear, had liked the honest, upright policeman. No one would later drink to his memory. speaking of the dead man in terms which shifted from admiring to the maudlin and then going back to the admiring again.

No, it was even worse than that, Blackstone admitted to himself. Most of the officers, involved in illegal activities as they were, would be *glad* that he was dead – and it was looking more than possible that one of those officers had actually *ordered* his death.

'You look like a man deep in thoughts about mortality, which is about right for a funeral,' said a voice just to his side.

Blackstone turned to look at the speaker. He was a man who appeared to be only in his mid-thirties, though his complexion was already mottled with broken red veins.

'Are you a friend of Patrick O'Brien's?' Blackstone asked.

'A relative,' the other man replied. 'His cousin.'

Blackstone held out his hand. 'I'm Sam Blackstone.'

'And I'm the black *sheep* of the O'Brien family,' the other man said. 'The name's Dermot.'

'What makes you the black sheep?' Blackstone asked.

'Now isn't that just obvious?' Dermot replied. 'It's the drink that brought about my current status, sir!'

But he said it so lightly that Blackstone couldn't help smiling.

'Yes,' Dermot mused, 'in many Irish families there's serious competition for the title of chief drunk, but the O'Briens are a relatively sober lot, and I achieved my eminence without really trying.'

'Shouldn't you be in the chapel?' Blackstone asked.

'Wouldn't be welcome,' Dermot said. 'Oh, Patrick wouldn't have minded – he was always one to tolerate weakness in others – but his parents would. They're almost as ashamed of me as they are proud of their son.'

'And they *were* proud of him, were they?'

'Bursting with pride! And I'm proud of *them* for being proud of *him*.'

'Why's that?'

'Patrick's father is a cobbler, and his mother is a cleaner,' Dermot said. 'They're not as poor as they might have been if they'd stayed in the old country, but America's been no picnic for them, either.'

'Yes?' Blackstone said, still not quite getting the point.

'Patrick was a bright feller, and everybody knew it from the start. If he'd put his mind to it, he could have been a successful Wall Street lawyer by now, and his aged ma and pa could have been living in the lap of luxury. But he didn't *want* to be a lawyer. He wanted to be a policeman, and – by God – an *honest* policeman. And did his parents stand in his way? Did they try to persuade him to chase the big bucks? No, sir, they did not! They gave him all the support and encouragement that any son could wish for.'

'How do they get on with his wife?' Blackstone asked, curious.

'With Mary? They get on famously with her – and who wouldn't? And they adore them three grandchildren of theirs.'

The chapel doors opened and the pall bearers emerged, carrying the coffin on their shoulders.

'I'd better be going,' Dermot O'Brien said.

'Come to the graveside with me,' Blackstone urged him. 'The family won't mind.'

'Ah, there speaks a man who doesn't *know* the family,' Dermot said, without rancour. He looked briefly at the coffin and then at Blackstone again. 'Most Irishmen go to the wake and show their respect for the dead by getting roaring drunk,' he continued. 'Did you know that?'

'Yes, I did,' Blackstone said.

'But me, I'm a contrary sort of feller,' Dermot told him. 'For one day – and one day only – I'll be showing my respect for Patrick by staying sober.'

Then he turned, and walked quickly towards the cemetery gates.

Blackstone stood some distance from the open grave, watching as the priest closed his prayer book at the end of his final act in what – as with all funerals – was a series of final acts.

The priest stepped back, and Mary O'Brien – black veiled – took his place at the edge of the grave. Once there she stood perfectly still for a few seconds, gazing into the distance – as if already contemplating life without her husband – then she bent down, took up a handful of soil, and threw it on the coffin.

Her children followed her example. Isobel, the eldest daughter, seemed unable to even look into the grave, and when she released her soil, some of it missed completely, and landed instead on the edge of the hole. Emily, the younger daughter, *did* look into the grave, but with an expression on her face which said she had no idea what was going on, or why she was even there. Benjamin – who was both the baby of the family *and* the man of the family – behaved with a dignity which went well beyond his years, looking down at coffin with an intense sadness, but – though biting his lip – refusing to cry.

An old couple – almost certainly Patrick O'Brien's parents – stepped forward. Their obvious suffering was matched by their obvious pride – or so it seemed to Blackstone – and the moment they had retreated from the grave they gathered up their grandchildren and put their arms around them.

Other relatives and friends came next – enacting the same ritual, adding their own handfuls of soil to the grave in which the remains of Patrick O'Brien would soon be allowed to rest in peace.

And then it was all over. The mourners began to move away from the grave, and Blackstone himself was about to turn and take his leave when he saw Mary O'Brien make a discreet – but urgent – gesture which indicated that she wanted him to stay.

It was another five minutes before the handshakes and condolences were finally dispensed with and Mary was free to join him.

'Sergeant Meade sends his apologies,' Blackstone said. 'He wanted to be here himself, but he couldn't make it.'

He had left it vague, hoping that the widow would, too.

But that kind of evasion seemed not to be a part of Mary O'Brien's nature, and instead of simply nodding, she said, 'What

I think you mean, Inspector Blackstone, is that Alex is following up a lead in the investigation into my husband's murder.'

'Yes, that is what I mean,' Blackstone admitted.

'I'm glad he couldn't come,' Mary O'Brien said. 'He's worshipped my husband, you know, ever since Patrick addressed his Harvard debating society. He would have found the funeral *very hard* to take.'

She'd hit the nail on the head, Blackstone thought admiringly. Meade's staying away had had nothing to do with his being the best man to watch the brothel. He hadn't come to O'Brien's funeral because it would have been too *painful* for him to come.

'But it was very good of you to act as his representative,' Mary O'Brien said. 'I want you to know that it's very much appreciated.'

'It was the least that I could do out of respect for a fellow officer,' Blackstone replied.

And the moment the words were out of his mouth, he knew he'd made a mistake – knew that he'd inadvertently reminded Mary of something she'd probably been trying very hard to forget.

'It is a pity that most of his brother officers in the New York Police Department did not feel under the same obligation as you do,' Mary said, confirming his worst fears. Then she paused for a second, before continuing. 'Do you think I sound bitter?'

'Perhaps,' Blackstone said carefully. 'And if you are, then I think you have every right to be.'

'I'm not bitter at all,' Mary said, with what seemed to a fierce conviction. 'And shall I tell you why?'

'If that's what you want to do.'

'I have always believed that we must do the *right* thing, however much inconvenience – however much pain and suffering – that might cause us,' Mary told him. 'And Patrick – though he was sometimes weak, as we are *all* sometimes weak – did just that. So you see, Mr Blackstone, the fact that there are so few policemen here is not to be taken as an insult to his memory – it is a rather to be regarded as a tribute to the way in which he did the right thing, whatever the cost to himself.'

'I'm sure that's true,' Blackstone said.

But he was thinking, it still hurts you, though, doesn't it, Mary? You'd still have liked to see those ranks of blue standing by the grave.

'And now that I have buried my husband, I must bury poor

Jenny,' Mary O'Brien said. 'And I would like to do that as
soon as possible. I have a new life ahead of me – a hard one,
it is true, but one which must be lived, nevertheless – and I
can't begin that journey until Jenny is laid to rest.'

'I can understand that,' Blackstone said.

'I knew you would. You are a kind man. A sensitive man.
In that way, you share many of my husband's qualities.' Mary
paused for a second. 'Do you know *when* they will release
Jenny's body to me, Mr Blackstone?'

'No, I'm afraid not,' Blackstone admitted.

'But, surely, since you're a policeman yourself . . .'

'I've really no idea how they do things over here. But if
you asked me to guess, I would say they'll probably release
the body as soon as the post-mortem has been completed.'

Even viewing her through her veil, Blackstone thought that
Mary O'Brien looked shocked.

'The post-mortem?' she repeated.

'In England, it's customary, in a case like this. In America,
for all I know, it may even be a legal requirement.'

'Isn't the point of a post-mortem to find out how someone
died?' Mary O'Brien asked.

'Yes, it is.'

'But everyone *knows* how she died!' Mary protested.
'There's no doubt about it in *your* mind, is there?'

'None at all,' Blackstone answered. 'She slit her own wrists.
She even told me so herself.'

'Then why can't they spare the poor child that last indig-
nity? Why do they have to cut her open?'

'As I said, it's probably the law.'

'The law!' Mary replied scornfully. 'And when is the law
ever enforced in New York City? Only when it's convenient!
Do you think the Carnegie family or the Morgan family would
have to wait for a post-mortem before they were allowed to
bury their dead? Of course they wouldn't! Because they have
power! Because they have influence! But because I'm a poor
widow, I must wait – I must put off the moment when I can
leave the past behind me and begin the struggle that will be
the rest of my life. It's hard, Mr Blackstone. It's *very* hard.'

'I know,' Blackstone said, sympathetically.

'Make them give me Jenny's body soon,' Mary begged, and
she was crying now. '*Please* make them give me the body.'

'If I thought it would do any good, I'd certainly try,' Blackstone told her. 'But I'm only a visitor, and I have no influence here.'

'What about Alex Meade?' Mary asked. 'Do you think that *he* has any influence?'

'I would imagine he has some, even if it's only through his father,' Blackstone said. 'Though whether it's enough to get you what you want . . .'

'Then speak to him,' Mary pleaded. 'Ask him to do what he can – however little that might be.'

'I will,' Blackstone promised.

'And find my husband's killer, Mr Blackstone,' Mary said, with a certain firmness in her voice. 'Help me to close that door behind me, too.'

TWENTY-TWO

Small, scrawny children were playing lethargically in the dirt. Bent old women were hobbling painfully – and fearfully – away from the saloons, clutching bottles of the cheapest booze available in their gnarled and withered hands. Gangs of boys were gathered at street corners. Small groups of men gambled away money which could have been used to feed their families. Five Points looked much as it had done the day before, Blackstone thought – and as it would probably *always* look, until some more honest, more caring city council pulled the whole area down and replaced it with something fit for human beings to live in.

'I don't want to be here,' Florence, the peevish scullery maid, whined. 'I don't like it.'

'Stop complaining,' Blackstone said curtly. 'It's better than having to work in the kitchen, isn't it?'

'Why don't you take me somewhere fancy?' Florence suggested in a sickly sweet voice, as she ran her index finger up and down the lapel of his jacket. 'If you was nice to me, I could be *very* nice to you.'

Blackstone angrily brushed the girl's hand away.

She would end up as a whore, he thought. She would be driven to it by her own laziness.

But she would not be the kind of whore that Trixie

was – working in a fancy midtown brothel, servicing customers who had specially asked for her, and saving for the day when she could open an establishment of her own. No, Florence's future was altogether bleaker. She would become one of those women who lurked in the shadows on street corners, and whose only appeal was that she carried something between her legs which offered the men who used her some fleeting satisfaction at rock-bottom prices.

'Did you hear me? I said, why don't you take me somewhere fancy?' Florence repeated.

'Have you already forgotten why we're here?' Blackstone asked, his words edged with contempt.

'Course I ain't forgot,' Florence replied. 'I ain't *stupid*, am I? Yer want me to finger Nancy for you.'

'Exactly,' Blackstone agreed. 'And she won't *be* anywhere fancy, will she? Because, according to you, *this* is where she lives.'

Florence laughed unpleasantly. 'What a dump,' she said. 'I'll bet Nancy wishes that she was back in the big house. But she can't *go* back, can she? She's burnt her bridges, an' now she's stuck with it.'

'And you're very pleased about that, aren't you?'

'Why wouldn't I be pleased? She thought she could lord it over me, didn't she? Well, now she knows she can't.'

'Did she ever actually *say* anything to show that she wanted to lord it over you?' Blackstone asked.

'Well, no, she didn't *say* anything, not in so many words,' Florence admitted. 'But Mr Boone thought the sun shone out of her backside.'

'And why do you think that was?'

'Don't know.'

'Could it have been because she worked harder, and more cheerfully, than you did?' Blackstone suggested.

Florence shrugged. She was already bored with the subject and, besides, a new thought had already entered her mind.

'How much will I get paid for this?' she asked.

'Nothing,' Blackstone told her.

'Nothin'! I'm not doin' it for *nothin'*. If yer don't pay me, you'll never find Nancy. 'Cos I'll say I haven't seen her – even if I have.'

'You *have to* find Nancy,' Blackstone told her coldly. 'Because if you don't, I'll tell Mr Boone you didn't even try to.'

'Bastard!' Florence said, *almost* under her breath.

The door of a run-down saloon opened, and a girl of about sixteen, carrying a jug of beer in her hand, stepped out on to the sidewalk.

'That's her!' Florence said.

'Are you sure?' Blackstone asked suspiciously.

'I'm sure,' Florence replied.

And the malicious glee with which she said the words was enough to convince Blackstone that this was indeed the girl he was looking for.

'What are you goin' to do with her?' Florence asked eagerly. 'Are you goin' to arrest her? Will she be sent to jail?'

'You can leave now,' Blackstone said, keeping his eyes firmly on the girl with the beer jug.

'What do yer mean? I can leave?'

'I mean that you've pointed out Nancy for me, and now I have no further use for you.'

'And how do yer think I'm supposed to get back to the house?' Florence demanded.

But Blackstone had already begun to walk rapidly towards the girl with the beer jug.

'I gave you seven dollars yesterday,' he said over his shoulder. 'Use it to take a bloody cab.'

He caught up with Nancy before she had gone two blocks, and when he said, 'Nancy Greene! I want to talk to you!' in a harsh authoritative voice, she froze, and slowly turned around to face him.

She was a pretty enough girl, he thought, and he himself could read in her features that same evidence of character that Mr Boone, the van Horne's butler had read.

But he could also see that she had a black eye.

'What do you want?' she asked, and though there was uncertainty in her voice, there was no sign of fear.

'I've already told you what I want, Nancy,' Blackstone replied. 'I want to talk to you.'

'Haven't got the time to talk,' the girl said. 'Eddie wants his beer, and if I keep him waiting for it too long . . .'

She left the rest unsaid, but there was no *need* to say it, when her black eye said it for her.

'If you won't talk to me voluntarily, then I'll have to arrest you,' Blackstone threatened.

Nancy nodded fatalistically.

She hadn't even asked on whose *authority* he would arrest her, or what she was supposed to have done wrong, he thought.

She simply assumed that he *did* have the right, and that she *had* done something wrong, even if she herself didn't know what it was – because that was what girls in her position *always* assumed.

'All right, I'll talk to you, mister – but can you make it quick?' Nancy pleaded.

Blackstone glanced up and down the sidewalk. Though the two of them had only been standing there for a minute, they had already begun to attract the attention of some of the boys who were loitering on the corner, as well as some of the men who were bent over their card game.

For the moment, these men and boys were showing nothing but mild curiosity at the encounter, but the longer he and Nancy stayed there, the more likely it was that someone would decide to take offence at a local girl being questioned by a stranger. And then things could turn extremely nasty.

'You live near here, don't you?' he asked.

'Yes,' Nancy replied.

He would not have believed her if she'd said she didn't, because the jug in her hand was evidence that she did not have far to go.

'We'll go back to your apartment,' he suggested.

'My apartment?' Nancy repeated incredulously. 'Who do you think I am, mister? I haven't got an *apartment* – I've got a room!'

'Then we'll go there.'

'We can't. Eddie's there, and he wouldn't like it if I brought anybody back with me who wasn't *paying* for the privilege.' Nancy paused. 'And that's not what you want, is it?'

'No, that's not what I want,' Blackstone said, without even bothering to ask what *that* was.

He quickly surveyed the street again. The card game had been temporarily suspended, and the boys on the street corner were looking first at the two of them, and then at each other.

Where could he take the girl? he wondered. In most other areas of New York, he would have headed immediately for the nearest tea room, but this was Five Points, and no such establishment existed.

It would just have to be the saloon, he decided.

'I'll buy you a drink,' he said.

'I don't want a drink,' Nancy said firmly.

'You might not *want* one, but, believe me, you're going to *need* one,' Blackstone assured her.

The tables in the saloon had a layer of filth on them that seemed to have been cultivated over generations. The glasses were chipped or cracked – or both – and to describe them as merely dirty would have been paying them a compliment. The floor was uneven, the windows were streaked with grime, and the barman – a fat brute of a man, who hadn't shaved for days – wore a stained apron over a stained shirt. All in all, it was far from the ideal place for this meeting – but it was the best that was on offer in Five Points.

Blackstone had ordered a beer for himself and a gin for the girl. He had already drunk half the beer, but the glass of gin sitting in front of Nancy remained untouched.

'Tell me about Jenny,' he said.

'Jenny?' Nancy repeated, as if she had never even heard the name before. 'Which Jenny would that be, then?'

Blackstone sighed. 'Jenny from the orphanage,' he said. 'Jenny, your best friend.'

'Oh, you mean *that* Jenny,' Nancy said. 'Why would you want to know anything about *her*?'

'Why wouldn't you want to *tell* me about her?' Blackstone countered.

'Because . . .'

'Yes?'

Nancy thought for a moment, then shrugged and said, 'No reason. Where do you want me to start?'

'At the beginning. In the orphanage.'

'I hated it,' Nancy said simply.

'Because they were cruel to you in there?'

'No. They weren't cruel to us. They were strict – but never cruel. I hated it because . . .' Nancy waved her hands helplessly in the air, '. . . just because of the place itself. You've no idea what it was like, living there.'

'That's where you're wrong,' Blackstone said. 'I have a very good idea – because I'm an orphan myself.'

'Then you'll know how very alone you can feel, even though

you're surrounded by other people. You'll know how you search for one thing, or one person, you can rely on – one thing or one person you can hold on to, that will convince you that everything's going to be all right.'

'Yes, I do know that,' Blackstone agreed, as he felt an involuntary shudder run though his body.

'Jenny found me,' Nancy said. 'She chose me as her big sister.'

And you exploited her, Blackstone thought. Not then. Not in the early days. But later.

He was trying to avoid getting angry – because, in many ways, Nancy was a victim, too – but it wasn't easy for him.

'Did you like being her big sister?' he asked.

'Yes, she's a sweet girl.'

It had been obvious from the start that Nancy didn't know Jenny was dead, Blackstone thought.

And in the terms of this interrogation, that was all to the good, because it meant he could hold the fact back – like a reserve cavalry unit – until he needed it to break down her defences.

'You continued to see her after you both left the orphanage, didn't you?' he asked.

'Yes. Jenny used to come and visit me on my half-day off.'

'Didn't *you* ever go and visit *her* on your half-day off?'

'No.'

'Why not?'

'Because . . .'

'Yes?'

'Because I didn't, that's all.'

'Surely it would have *better* for you to have visited her,' Blackstone persisted. 'When she came to see you, you both had to walk the streets – which must have been cold in winter. But if you'd gone to the O'Briens' apartment, I'm sure Mrs O'Brien would have allowed you to use one of the parlours.'

'I . . . didn't have as much time off as Jenny did,' Nancy said. 'If I'd had to travel across the city to see her, I'd have had to start back almost as soon as I'd arrived. That's why she came to me instead.'

It was a good lie – an intelligent lie, even – but it was still a lie.

'When did you meet Eddie Toscanini?' Blackstone asked.

Nancy gave him a hard stare. 'I never said Toscanini was Eddie's second name.'

'No, you didn't, did you?' Blackstone agreed. 'But I still want an answer to my question. When did you first meet him?'

'It was a few months ago now. When Jenny and me were out on one of our walks.'

'How did it happen?'

'He wasn't looking where he was going, and he accidentally bumped into us. He said he was very sorry for being so careless, and offered to buy us both a coffee to make up for it.'

But had that "bumping into them" been accidental at all, Blackstone wondered.

Or, because of who Jenny worked for, had they been carefully targeted?

'So he offered to buy you a coffee, and you said yes?'

'Of course we did. Neither of us had ever been into a real coffee house before. It was very exciting.'

'And you kept on seeing him?'

'Yes, every time we went out, Eddie joined us.'

'And you became his girlfriend?'

'Sort of. He couldn't *romance* me, 'cos Jenny was always with us, an' even if she hadn't been, you need a bit of privacy for romance.'

'Then in what way would you say that *you* – rather than Jenny – could have been called Eddie's girlfriend?'

'When we had drinks, he paid for both of us, and once he hired skates so we could both go ice skating in Central Park. But when he brought little presents, they were only for me.'

'And what did *you* do for *him* in return?'

'Nothing. Not then. But I'm paying for that now, because now he treats me worse than a slave.'

'So why don't you leave him?'

Nancy laughed bitterly. 'Leave him? And where would I go, if I did?'

'Mr Boone would find you a position if I asked him to,' Blackstone said. 'Not in the van Horne household, obviously, but somewhere very like it.'

'And would you do that for *me*?' Nancy asked, her voice suddenly thick with wonder and hope.

'That depends,' Blackstone said.

'On what?'

'Before I help you, you have to help me.'

'All right.'

'And you can start by telling me the truth.'

'I *have* been telling you the truth.'

'No, you haven't. When I asked you what you did for Eddie in the days when he used to buy you drinks and take you ice skating, you said that you did nothing at all.'

'And that was *true!*' Nancy protested. 'I was a scullery maid with no money of my own, so I couldn't buy him anything in return. I couldn't even let him have his way with me then, because we were always in public places. So what *could* I have done for him back then?'

'I'll tell you what you could have done,' Blackstone said. 'You could have persuaded Jenny to look through her master's private papers, and then passed the information on to Eddie. And not only is that what you *could* have done, it's what you *did* do.'

'You're mad,' Nancy said, with so much conviction that – but for the way the evidence was pointing – Blackstone would almost have believed her.

'So you deny you ever did that?' he asked.

'Course I deny it. I'd never have asked Jenny to do anything that might make her lose her job, and even if I had, she'd never have agreed.'

She was mounting a very good defence for herself, Blackstone thought, but the moment he released his cavalry, that defence would collapse in complete and utter confusion.

'Jenny's dead,' he said, making no effort to soften the blow. 'She's dead – and it's partly your fault.'

Nancy blanched.

'Oh my God,' she moaned.

And then she picked up the glass of gin from the table and knocked it back in a single gulp.

Blackstone waited patiently for her to speak again, because he was certain that when she did, she would tell him all he wanted to know.

But Nancy did *not* spout out a confession which would show that he'd been right all along.

Instead, she said, 'It was suicide, wasn't it?'

'Yes,' Blackstone agreed. 'But how did you—?'

'Then you're right in what you said,' Nancy interrupted him. 'It is partly my fault.'

'Why? Because it was you who persuaded her to betray her master to Eddie Toscanini?'

'No, I told you, I never did that.'

'Then why *is* it your fault?'

'Because I didn't push her enough. I should have tried harder to make her see . . .'

'Make her see what?'

'Nothing.'

'*Make her see what*?' Blackstone repeated.

'I'm not sayin' any more,' Nancy said firmly, crossing her arms. 'You can do what you like to me. You can arrest me. You can beat me up. But I'm not sayin' any more.

'Why?'

'Because poor little Jenny's dead, and now she should be allowed to rest in peace.'

'And how will your telling me the truth stop her doing that?'

'Are you arresting me?' Nancy asked, avoiding the question.

'No.'

'Then I'm going home.'

'It's still not too late to tell me the truth,' Blackstone said. 'And if you do, I promise that I'll rescue you from all this.'

'I want to go home,' Nancy repeated.

'Then I'll escort you to your door.'

'There's no need.'

'I think there is,' Blackstone said. 'You've had a shock, and that can do funny things to people.'

And besides that, he added silently to himself, I need to know where you live.

TWENTY-THREE

There were three policemen standing on the sidewalk outside Mrs de Courcey's establishment. Two of them were patrolmen in uniform – and they were looking very bored. The third was wearing a straw boater and white bow tie – and *he* was looking exhausted.

Blackstone walked over to the policeman who looked exhausted.

'You urgently need a couple of hours sleep, Alex,' he said.

'Can't leave now,' Meade said, slightly slurring his words.

'Don't trust that bastard O'Shaugnessy. If I go, he'll renege on the deal.'

'I'll take your place,' Blackstone told him.

'That'd . . . that'd be a waste of your time,' Meade replied, clearly having trouble keeping track of his argument. 'You're the senior detective . . . the experienced detective. You have more important things to do than keep watch on a brothel.'

But was that true? Blackstone wondered.

Did he *really* have more important things to do? And *if* he did, what *were* they?

He found himself starting to think about his conversation with Nancy, though perhaps 'starting to think' were the wrong words to use, because ever since he'd left her at the door of her hovel in Five Points, he'd been *continually* going over that conversation in his head.

This thinking process had brought him mixed results. Sometimes, when he'd worked his way through to the end of it, he was convinced that he had drawn a complete blank. But there were other times when he was almost convinced that (though she hadn't meant to) Nancy had told him almost everything he needed to know – and that all that was necessary to produce a solution was to look at what she'd said in just the right way.

Those words of hers kept bouncing around – echoing around – his now-tired brain.

'*I'd never have asked Jenny to do anything that might make her lose her job, and even if I had, she'd never have agreed.*'

That sounded so plausible, because Nancy clearly *had* cared for Jenny, and Jenny, from what he'd seen of her, *had* been a *good* girl.

And yet hadn't Jenny herself *admitted* to him on her deathbed that she'd betrayed O'Brien?

'*It was suicide, wasn't it?*'

There were so many other ways that Jenny could have died. She could have contracted a virulent and fatal disease. She could have been run over by a streetcar. She could have been struck by a bolt of lightning, shot in crossfire between the police and a gang of bank robbers, or eaten a poisoned mussel.

Yet the first thing Nancy had asked was if it was suicide. Why?

'*I didn't push her enough. I should have tried harder to make her see . . .*'

It was all so confusing. All so *bloody* confusing!

'Make her see what, for God's sake?' Blackstone said aloud – and rather loudly.

'Make *who* see what?' asked the puzzled Meade, who was still standing by his side, but seemed as if he might fall over at any moment.

'You need some rest, Alex,' Blackstone said. 'And don't worry about it being a waste of my time to take your place, because even a "brilliant" investigator like me needs to become involved in the routine work once in a while. It gives my "powerful" brain the opportunity it needs to sort the case out.'

'Quite right,' Meade said, so exhausted that he readily took what Blackstone had just said entirely at face value. 'But I'm still not sure that you should . . .'

'You'll feel a completely new man after two hours' sleep, Alex,' Blackstone said firmly.

Less than half an hour passed before the front door of the brothel opened and the doorman stepped out on to the sidewalk.

He looked worried, Blackstone thought. No, more than worried, he looked *distressed*.

The bouncer walked over to him.

'This ain't right, Mr Blackstone,' he said, in a strange melange of his native cockney and his mock Hungarian. 'It ain't fair at all. Mrs de Courcey's worked very hard to build up this business, an' you're destroyin' it overnight.'

'It's not my fault, Freddie,' Blackstone replied.

'It's Imre, Mr Blackstone,' the doorman said. '*Please!*'

'It's not my fault, *Imre*. If Mrs de Courcey wants the police to go away, she knows what she has to do.'

'Don't just think of her,' Imre pleaded. 'Think of the girls. She looks after them. She treats them better than their own mothers did.'

'Except for Trixie, of course,' Blackstone pointed out. '*She* was given a working over.'

'But only a gentle one,' Imre said.

'Gentle?'

The bouncer shrugged. 'She could walk the next day, couldn't she? And she wouldn't have had to have been touched at all if you an' that Sergeant Meade hadn't gone stickin' your oars in where they weren't wanted.'

'What's the message?' Blackstone asked.

'Message?'

'You're not here for a pleasant chat. You're here because the whore you work for *sent* you here.'

Imre stiffened, and the muscles under his jacket bulged alarmingly. 'There's no need to go talkin' about Mrs de Courcey like that,' he said angrily.

'The message,' Blackstone repeated.

'If it's at all convenient, Mrs de Courcey would very much like to see you.'

'It's convenient,' Blackstone told him.

Imre led Blackstone into the main salon, where Mrs de Courcey, wearing a highly respectable – almost modest – tea gown, was waiting.

'Inspector Blackstone, Madam,' Imre said, casting off the role of panderer's bouncer in favour of a new one as a gentle-woman's butler.

Mrs de Courcey smiled warmly at him. 'Thank you, Imre. That will be all for now.'

'Are you sure you wouldn't like me to stay with you, Ell . . . Madam?' Imre asked.

Her smile widened, and grew even warmer. 'It was very thoughtful of you to ask, but I think I can manage.'

Well, well, well, Blackstone thought.

Once Imre had left, the woman turned her attention to her visitor. There was still a smile on her face, but now it had lost most of its intensity and, even so, was only being held in place by an effort of will.

'I really must apologize for losing my temper the last time we met,' Mrs de Courcey said. 'I'm afraid we both said some things that we must have later regretted, didn't we?'

'Not that I can recall,' Blackstone said, determined not to give the madam an inch.

Mrs de Courcey's smile widened again, at just about the same rate as her eyes hardened.

'Well, that's all in the past,' she said. 'What I wanted to talk to you about was the situation I find myself in now.'

'Oh?' Blackstone said, non-committally.

'Because of those policemen you've posted outside, we have not had a single gentleman visit us all day.'

'And who knows where those gentlemen are *now*?' Blackstone pondered. 'Who knows if, having sampled the pleasures of other brothels, they'll ever come back to you?'

'You're ruining my business,' Mrs de Courcey said plaintively. 'A business I've worked so hard to build up.'

'Well, you know what to do about it, don't you?' Blackstone asked. 'Just give me the same address as you gave to Inspector O'Brien, and I'll call the patrolmen off immediately.'

'I was thinking of an alternative solution to the problem,' Mrs de Courcey said.

'Were you?'

'Yes. I was thinking of donating some money to your favourite charity, though, of course, while I would *provide* the money, *you* would make the actual donation.'

'Nice try,' Blackstone said, 'but I don't take bribes – not even in New York, where it seems almost bad manners to turn them down.'

'It would be quite a *substantial* donation I'd be offering,' Mrs de Courcey persisted.

'Why are you so concerned about giving me the address?' Blackstone asked. 'Is it because, by doing so, you'll actually be handing me evidence which would tie you in with some kind of criminal activity?'

'Of course not,' Mrs de Courcey replied.

But her eyes said, yes, that's *exactly* it.

'Because you need have no worries on that score,' Blackstone assured her. 'I have no interest at all in seeing you behind bars. The only thing I care about is catching a murderer, and whatever nasty little scheme you've been involved in, I promise you you'll hear no more about it from me.'

'I can't help you,' Mrs de Courcey said.

'And yet, after talking to Inspector O'Brien – in this very room – for only a few minutes, you were perfectly willing to hand the address over to *him*,' Blackstone said exasperatedly. 'Why was that? Because you were quite prepared to take *his* word that he'd grant you immunity from any prosecution, but you're not prepared to take *mine*?'

'It's not that simple,' Mrs de Courcey said. 'I knew it would be safe to give the address to Inspector O'Brien.'

'Safe? It what way?'

'I'm afraid I can't say.'

If she could hold out for two more days, it would be all over, Blackstone thought. And Mrs de Courcey showed every indication of doing just that – whatever it cost her.

But he still had one more card to play – a card he hadn't even known had existed until a few minutes earlier.

'Do you know what one of the most pathetic sights in the whole world is?' he asked – deliberately harsh, deliberately cruel. 'It's the sight of a clapped-out old whore mooning about over a younger man like a lovesick virgin.'

'You bastard!' Mrs de Courcey said, with feeling.

'His name's not Imre, you know,' Blackstone said. 'And he's not a Hungarian count. He's really called Horace Grubb, and he hails from some of the worst slums of Whitechapel.'

'Do you think I don't *know* that?' Mrs de Courcey asked. 'Do you think I even *care* about that?'

'If I can't arrest Inspector O'Brien's murderer, I'll arrest our Horace instead,' Blackstone said. 'I'll take him back to England with me, and you'll never see him again.'

'You . . . you wouldn't do that,' Mrs de Courcey gasped. 'You . . . you just *couldn't* do that!'

'Just *watch* me!' Blackstone told her.

For a moment, it looked as if Mrs de Courcey would crumple and faint quite away. But fainting away was not her style. She was a fighter, who had worked her way up from the gutter, and she did not give in so easily.

Blackstone watched, fascinated, as she pulled herself together again, and knew exactly what was going on in her mind.

She accepted defeat when it was inevitable, as it was inevitable here. But she was searching for a way to avoid it being a *total* defeat – looking around for what might be one minor victory of her own.

And, as a new smile – a *vindictive* one, this time – came to her face, he knew that she had found what she was searching for.

'You stand there in your shabby suit, thinking that you're so smart, when nothing could be further from the truth,' Mrs de Courcey said in a voice filled with the deepest contempt. 'You *call* yourself a detective, but you can detect *nothing*. In short, you really have no idea what is going on at all, and I truly despise you for that ignorance.'

'But you'll give me the address anyway, won't you?' Blackstone said, unmoved.

'But I'll give you the address anyway,' Mrs de Courcey agreed.

She crossed to the escritoire, took out a sheet of paper, and wrote something on it.

'What are you expecting me to give you, *Mr Detective*?' she taunted, as she walked back across the room towards him. 'The address of a corruptible congressman, perhaps?'

Yes, possibly something like that, Blackstone thought.

'Or maybe you think the address will lead you to the home of a rich and powerful businessman? Is *that* what you think?'

'Just hand it over,' Blackstone said wearily, and when she did, he looked down at what she had written and said, 'Dr Muller? A medical man?'

'No, not a medical man,' Mrs de Courcey said, savouring the small victory that his surprise had brought her. 'Not a medical man at all.'

'But this says . . .'

'Dr Muller is a medical *woman*.'

TWENTY-FOUR

Alex Meade looked much better for his short sleep, and as he and Blackstone climbed the stairs of the slightly seedy building in the very heart of Kleindeutschland, the inspector noticed that there was a distinct spring in the sergeant's step.

They reached the second floor, and came to a halt in front of a door which had a notice on it – in both English and German – stating that surgery hours were from 9 to 12 and 4 to 8.

'This is it,' Meade said, his enthusiasm once more bubbling over. 'Would you mind if *I* handled the interview?'

'Not at all,' Blackstone replied. 'After all that standing about outside Mrs de Courcey's, you deserve a bit of a treat.'

Meade grinned. 'And a treat is what it will be. We're on the brink of solving the case, Sam. I can *feel* it.'

Maybe we are, Blackstone thought. Or maybe this will be just one more dead end.

Meade's first knock on the door was no more than a gentle

inquiring tap with his knuckles. Then, remembering who he was – and why he was there – he made a fist and hammered so forcefully that the door frame shook.

A woman opened the door. She had a large, bony frame – although her hands, Blackstone noted, were surprisingly small and delicate. Her hair had been cut in a very masculine manner, and her eyes showed the natural concern of someone who was answering such an imperious summoning.

Meade held up his shield. 'Dr Helga Muller?'

'Yes,' the doctor replied.

And Blackstone saw that the look of concern in her eyes had developed into something akin to real fear.

'Do you mind if we come in?' Meade asked, before brushing past her and entering the office.

The office contained a desk, a filing cabinet, two chairs for visitors, and an examination table. Meade sat down on one of the visitors' chairs without waiting for an invitation, and gestured to Blackstone that he should sit in the other one. The doctor, meanwhile, hovered uncertainly by the still-open door.

'Close the door, can you?' Meade said casually, as if he were talking to a servant.

The doctor *did* close the door, but showed no signs of wanting to move any further away from it herself.

'So, why don't you tell us about this nice little practice of yours, doctor?' Meade suggested.

The fear was still there in her eyes, Blackstone thought. Muller was doing her best to hide it, but it was definitely still there.

'Why should you want to know about my practice?' the doctor asked, in a heavy accent.

Meade frowned. 'I don't know how things work over in Germany,' he said, 'but here in America, it's normally considered wise to answer a police officer when he asks you a question.'

'I practise general medicine,' the doctor said. 'Most of my patients are recent immigrants. The majority of them come from Germany.'

'Do they now?' Meade mused. 'And how's business, doc? Are you making a good living?'

'I do well enough,' Dr Muller replied stonily.

'Really?' Meade said, sounding surprised. He looked around the office. 'Well, if you "do well enough", there's certainly

not much evidence of it in this place. To tell you the truth, it
looks like a real dump to me.'

'If you are going to be rude about my office, then you
can—' Dr Muller began.

'If I'm going to be rude about your office, then I can *what*?'
Meade interrupted.

'I . . .'

'And before you answer that question, please remember
that your naturalization papers are still being processed,
and that it only requires one black mark against your name
for them to be rejected.' Meade paused for a second. 'Now
remind me, doctor, what were you going to do if I was rude?'

'Nothing,' Dr Muller said.

'That's good,' Meade told her. 'That's *very* good.' He stood
up and walked around the cramped room, stopping in front
of a framed medical certificate. 'The University of Berne,' he
said, admiringly. 'My, but ain't *you* a real powerhouse,
though?'

'It is an excellent school of medicine,' Doctor Muller said.

'I'm sure it is,' Meade agreed. 'Do you know what I would
do if I was in your place, doctor?'

The silence which followed lasted for perhaps twenty
seconds, and then Dr Muller reluctantly said, 'No. What would
you do?'

'I'd get myself a better practice in a classier neighbourhood. I mean, why should a woman with a medical degree
from the University of Berne work in a hole like this?'

'Why?' the doctor responded angrily. 'I will *tell* you why.
It is because this is not the land of the free. It is not the land
of opportunity. It is the land of *money*. And so it does not
matter how good a doctor you are – it matters only that you
can afford to buy yourself a nice office.'

Meade nodded. 'Very interesting,' he said. 'Well, it seems
to me, Dr Muller, that one way out of the trap that you've
found yourself in would be to work for some richer clients
who, for one reason or another, can't take their problems to
their regular doctor.'

'What do you mean?' Muller asked.

But Meade already seemed bored with the topic, and was
now focusing his attention on another certificate hanging on
the wall.

'I see you did additional studies in something called obstetrics,' he said. 'What does that mean, exactly?'

'It is the branch of medicine which is related to childbirth and women's problems.'

'Is that right?' Meade asked. He suddenly wheeled round to face the doctor. 'Well, that must have come in very useful when you started your little abortion business.'

'I . . . I don't know what you mean,' Muller said.

'Of course you do,' Meade said. 'If a girl working in a low-class brothel gets pregnant, she gets kicked out on to the street to fend for herself. But if she works for one of the better establishments – and especially if she's particularly popular with the clients – then her madam will come to you for help.'

'It's not true,' the doctor protested.

Meade slammed his hand down on the desk. 'Two things can happen,' he said. 'The first is that we can arrest you here and now. The second is that you can tell us what we want to know, and we'll leave you in peace. Which is it to be?'

'I'll tell you what you want to know,' the doctor said.

'That's good,' Meade told her. 'Now, on Tuesday a man called Patrick O'Brien came to see you. Do you remember that?'

'He did not give me his name. I only learned it when I read about his death in the newspaper.'

Meade tut-tutted. 'Now, you see, that's *not* good, because you've started lying to me *already*.'

'Lying? How have I been lying?'

'You said he didn't give you his name.'

'He didn't.'

'He was a police inspector, involved in an investigation in which you probably played no more than a small part. But even if your part *was* only small, he was bound to have identified himself before he started questioning you.'

'But . . . but he did not come here because of any investigation,' Muller protested.

'Then why *did* he come here?'

'To ask me to perform an abortion.'

Meade looked horrified. 'I . . . I . . .' he gasped.

'Who did he say he wanted this abortion for?' Blackstone asked.

'For his mistress.'

'I don't believe it,' Meade said, sounding as if he were almost choking.

But I do, Blackstone thought – because suddenly it was all starting to make sense.

O'Brien's mistress becomes pregnant and after some soul-searching he finally accepts that she must have an abortion. But because he sees himself as an honourable, decent man, he doesn't want to take her to some seedy backstreet establishment where she might well die in the process. He wants to give her the best that is available – *but he has no idea where to find it.*

He needs some kind of fixer, and arranges a meeting with that arch-fixer, Senator Plunkitt. But the moment the meeting begins, he realizes he has made a mistake. Because if he tells Plunkitt what his problem is, he will be giving the man power over him – and once Plunkitt has that power, his days as a reforming policeman will be over.

What was it Plunkitt had said?

'I spent half an hour with the man, and if he had a point to make, or a question he wanted to ask, he never got around to it.'

Of course he didn't – because once he had decided not to tell Plunkitt his problem, he had nothing to say to the man!

He has to come up with another solution, he realizes. He will ask a madam for advice. And the madam he asks is Mrs de Courcey.

'I knew it would be safe to give the address to Inspector O'Brien,' the madam had said.

And she'd been right – because, unlike Blackstone, he'd not been asking for the address as a *policeman*, he'd been asking for it as a man with a problem.

Meade had handled things perfectly up to that point, but now, what he had learned had knocked the wind quite out of his sails, and he was just standing there – slack-mouthed and staring at the wall.

'Did you agree to perform the abortion, Dr Muller?' Blackstone asked.

The doctor merely nodded.

'And what arrangements did you make with Inspector O'Brien? Were you going to do the abortion here?'

Muller shook her head. 'No, I told him that would be too dangerous for me, and he said that he would arrange for it to take place somewhere else.'

'Where?'

'I don't know. He didn't say. We were to meet in the Bayern Biergarten on the same night – the night he died – and he would take me there.'

'But you never turned up,' Blackstone said, remembering what the witness had said about O'Brien looking nervously at the door of the saloon, before finally stepping out through it to his death.

'No, I did not go there,' Dr Muller agreed.

'Why not?' demanded Meade, who had somewhat recovered himself. 'Was it because you were *paid* not to go there? Paid by the *assassin*?'

'No, no, of course not.'

'Then why? What other reason could there possibly have been?'

'I did not keep the appointment because *she* said there was no need to,' the doctor told Meade.

'She?' Blackstone said. 'Who is *she*?'

'The mistress, of course. The one who was to have the abortion.'

'Describe her to me.'

'She was a young woman with long red hair, probably in her middle twenties.' Dr Muller's lip curled in disgust. 'Much younger than him, and probably much younger than his wife. Men like him *always* choose mistresses who are younger than their wives.'

'And what did she say?'

'She said the abortion was no longer necessary, because she had miscarried. She said it had happened several days earlier.'

'Then why hadn't she told him that *before* he came to see you?'

'She said she had no way of contacting him – not without his wife finding out.' The lip curled again. 'I prefer to deal with whores. At least they do not pretend to be what they are not.'

'I've been drunk maybe four times in my entire life, and two of those times have been with you,' Alex Meade said, slurring his words. 'You want to tell me why that is, Sam?'

'You *know* why it is,' Blackstone said morosely.

'Deed I do,' Meade agreed, dipping his finger in his whiskey and drawing two sticky arcs on the table. 'Just need to join them up into a circle, and we've got it solved. Ain't that what you said?'

'It's what I said.'

'So lez . . . let's . . . take a look at the left one. You said

Nancy was using Jenny to get information for her boyfriend, Eddie, but Nancy says she wasn't. So who's right?'

'I don't know,' Blackstone admitted.

And he didn't. He *really* didn't.

'Then there's the right arc,' Meade continued drunkenly. 'Remind me what our theory was.'

'Inspector O'Brien was conducting an investigation into corruption, and Mrs de Courcey gave him an address which would further that investigation,' Blackstone said flatly.

'And once we'd got that address ourselves, we could probably figure out *who* he was investigating, and then, as a result of our brilliant deductive powers, we'd know who wanted him dead?'

'Yes.'

'Only it turns . . . it turns out that wasn't it at all. It turns out that he'd got some whore pregnant and wanted to arrange an abortion for her.' Meade paused. 'Why did he do that, Sam?'

'Why did he arrange the abortion?'

'Why did he betray that lovely wife of his? Why did he betray his beautiful children?'

'It happens,' Blackstone said, wishing he was as drunk as Meade, but knowing that getting drunk wasn't the answer.

'The man was a Catholic, Sam,' Meade said bitterly. 'And you know what that means, don't you?'

'Yes, I do know, so there's no need for you to . . .'

'It means that in the eyes of his church, he was getting himself involved in a murder.'

'The abortion never actually took place,' Blackstone reminded him. 'The woman—'

The mistress! The slut! The whore!'

'Told Dr Muller that she had miscarried naturally.'

'But it *could* have happened,' Meade protested. 'Patrick – the Catholic *saint* – was perfectly happy *for* it to happen.'

'We know that he was prepared to go through with it, but that's not the same as being *happy* about it,' Blackstone pointed out. 'In fact, though I never met the man, I'm sure he wasn't happy at all.'

'I used to look up to him, Sam,' Meade said drunkenly. 'He was my hero. Now, I'm not even sure I *want* to catch his killer any more.'

That was the trouble with hero-worship, Blackstone thought. You built your hero into such a colossus that he could never live up to your expectations for long. And when he failed to, it didn't just diminish his stature a little – it brought him crashing down to the ground.

'Whether or not you still like the victim, a crime has been committed, and it's your job to arrest the guilty man,' he said.

'Maybe . . . maybe you're right,' Meade agreed. 'But how do we go about arresting him when both your half circles are going nowhere?'

And there, Blackstone was forced to admit, Meade had a point.

TWENTY-FIVE

The sky above New York City that summer morning was perfect, Blackstone thought. Or at least, he corrected himself in the interest of accuracy, it was as perfect as any sky over a big city – which was constantly pushing poisonous fumes up into the air – ever could be.

And the sky was not the only thing which was working hard to show nature at its most benevolent. Flowers bloomed. Birds chirped happily in the trees. The softest of cooling breezes was blowing up the avenues. It was a day which celebrated life – a day which most people out on the street would feel promised fresh beginnings and new opportunities.

The promise wasn't working for Sergeant Alex Meade. As they drank their coffee together – in the same saloon where Meade had gotten smashed the night before – the sergeant grappled with a sense of failure and disillusionment which was even more powerful than his hangover.

'I was wrong – completely wrong – to have ever thought that Patrick O'Brien could be perfect,' he said.

'Yes, you were,' Blackstone agreed.

'But he worked hard for this city – he displayed a courage and determination that most men never come close to – and so I was *also* wrong to say that I didn't care whether or not his killer was caught.' Meade paused for a moment. 'I did *say* that, didn't I?'

'Among a lot of other things, yes,' Blackstone replied, with a smile. 'Consistency wasn't your strong point last night.'

'And neither was moderation,' Meade groaned.

A patrolman entered the saloon, carrying a buff envelope in his hand. He looked around briefly, before making for the table at which Blackstone and Meade were sitting.

'Is there something I can do for you, Officer Caldwell? Alex Meade asked, though his tone suggested that what he wanted most in the world was the patrolman to go away.

Caldwell studied the sergeant for a moment, then a broad grin spread across his face.

'You look rough, Sergeant,' he said. 'I think it must be quite a while since I've seen anybody look rougher.'

Meade groaned. 'Thank you, Caldwell,' he said. 'I really appreciate it that you've come all the way across the street just to tell me that.'

'Oh, it wasn't *just* for that,' Caldwell replied cheerily. 'They said at headquarters that you wanted to know when the girl's body would be released for burial. Well, it's ready now, and all the next-of-kin has to do is send the undertakers round to pick it up.'

'Good,' Meade said. 'Thank you, Caldwell. And sorry about snapping at you just now.'

'That's OK, Sarge, I've been hungover myself.' The patrolman turned to leave, then remembered the envelope he was holding. 'What do you want me to do with this?'

'What is it?'

'Post-mortem report on the girl.'

'I thought I'd asked them not to do a post-mortem,' Meade said, visibly pained by the process of having to use his brain. 'I thought I'd asked them as a special favour to me.'

'You probably did – but you know what they're like, they never listen,' Caldwell said, with a continuing cheerfulness that was even starting to irritate Blackstone. 'Anyway, they cut her up, and they did their report. The top copy's already been filed back at headquarters. This one's the spare. What do you want me to do with it?'

'Why should *I* want you to do anything with it?' Meade asked plaintively.

'Well, it is kind of connected with your case, ain't it? So what *should* I do with it?'

'I don't know,' Meade said, holding his head. 'Why don't you file it somewhere else?'

'Like where?'

'In somebody's desk drawer,' Meade suggested hopefully.

'Whose drawer?'

'Or you could simply throw it away,' Meade said. 'Hell, you can stick it up your ass, for all I care.' He grimaced. 'Sorry about that, Officer Caldwell. *Really* sorry! Making decisions just seems like very hard work at the moment.'

Blackstone held out his hand to the patrolman.

'I'll take it,' he said. 'I'll hold it until Sergeant Meade's eyes can read small print again, and then I'll give it to him.'

'The way he's looking now, that should be about next Tuesday,' Caldwell said. Then he handed the envelope to Blackstone, gave the two of them a parting grin, and left.

'Some night I'm going to get *him* drunk,' Meade said, with bitter sincerity. 'I'm going to get him so drunk he's legless. And then I'm going to stand over him, laughing – for hours!' He looked at the report in Blackstone's hand. 'Read it,' he suggested.

'Why?' Blackstone asked.

'Why not?' Meade countered. 'I'm going to be no good for anything until I've had at least *three* more cups of coffee, so you might as well entertain yourself in any way you can.'

Blackstone nodded. It wouldn't be a bad thing to do anyway, he thought. *Somebody* should show they cared enough about Jenny to at least *read* the report – and if not a fellow orphan like himself, then who?

He took the report out of the envelope and read about the organ failure which had resulted from the dramatic loss of blood.

But it was what was written at the bottom of the report – almost as an afterthought – which shook him.

'I have to go,' he said.

'What?'

'Stay here until I get back. Or, if you feel capable of moving, leave a message so I'll know where you've gone.'

'Is this . . .?' Meade asked, struggling for the words. 'Is this about something in the report?'

'Yes, it is,' Blackstone said, already heading for the door.

'But what . . .?'

'I'll tell you later,' Blackstone promised.

*   *   *

Nancy Greene and Eddie Toscanini lived on the first floor of a dilapidated house about halfway down Little Water Street, and when Blackstone hammered on the door, the whole building seemed to quake.

It was Nancy who opened the door, just wide enough for Blackstone to see the muscular young man with jet black hair who was lying lazily on the bed.

'You again!' Nancy said.

Her other eye had been blackened since the last time that he'd seen her, Blackstone saw.

And that was probably his fault. He had forced Nancy to stop and talk to him, which meant that Eddie had been kept waiting for his beer – and Eddie had punished her for that.

'What do you want?' Nancy asked.

'We need to go somewhere we can talk again. And this time, when it's over, I won't be bringing you back here,' Blackstone said.

'I don't understand,' Nancy said.

'I thought you were the one who'd got Jenny into trouble,' Blackstone explained. 'That's why I didn't care much about what happened to you. But *now* I know that you tried to help her as much as it was in your power to.'

'I did,' Nancy said, almost crying. 'I really did.'

'So I'm going to help *you*,' Blackstone promised. 'And I'm going to start by getting you out of this place.'

Eddie Toscanini had got off the bed and padded lithely across the room. Now he grabbed Nancy by the hair, jerked her roughly away, and took her place in the doorway.

'What's this all about?' he demanded.

He was a big man, Blackstone noted – a big man with a flat stomach and bulging biceps.

'Well?' Eddie said.

'I'm taking Nancy away,' Blackstone told him. 'And she won't be coming back.'

'She doesn't go anywhere without my say-so,' Eddie growled.

'She is this time,' Blackstone said firmly. 'And if I were you, I wouldn't try to stop her.'

Eddie glanced quickly up and down the corridor. 'You're on your own!' he said incredulously.

'That's right, I am,' Blackstone agreed.

'You're on your own, an' you're still *threatenin'* me?'

'No, I'm *warning* you,' Blackstone told him. 'This doesn't have to end in violence, you know.'

Eddie sneered. 'Oh, but it does,' he said. 'See, I like hurtin' people. It makes me feel good – even when the people I'm hurtin' are old men like you, with no real fight left in them.'

And as he spoke, he put his right hand into his pocket, where people like him always kept their brass knuckledusters.

Blackstone watched Eddie's pants' pocket bulge and undulate, as the young thug's fingers first located the holes in the knuckleduster, and then slipped quickly into them.

'I've got a pistol,' the inspector said.

'That won't do you no good at all,' Eddie said. 'If you was goin' to use your pistol, you should have drawn it while you had the chance. Now I'll have you on the ground before you even reach the holster.'

'You're missing the point,' Blackstone replied. 'I didn't draw it earlier because I didn't need to. I can handle you without it.'

The young bruiser chuckled. 'So you've got a bit of spirit after all,' he said. 'Oh, I am goin' to enjoy workin' *you* over. It's goin' to be a *real* pleasure.'

Eddie feinted with his left fist, and Blackstone side-stepped, putting himself in just the right spot for the real attack, which would come from the knuckleduster on Eddie's right hand.

Oh, this was really too easy, Eddie thought, in the split second before he realized that his knuckledustered right hand was travelling though empty air, and that his nose felt as if it was exploding.

'First law of street fighting, Eddie,' Blackstone said, as he grabbed the other man's arm and bent it right up around his back. 'If you don't get control in the first two seconds, you'll *never* get it.'

'You son-of-a-bitch!' Eddie mumbled, as he tried to breathe through his broken nose.

'Collect up anything you want, and we'll take it with us,' Blackstone told Nancy.

Eddie was starting to struggle again.

'If you keep doing that, I'll have to break your arm,' Blackstone warned the young thug.

'Break it anyway!' Nancy said.

'Anything to oblige,' Blackstone told her.

And he did just that.

Blackstone booked Nancy into a modest but pleasant boarding house near the Mulberry Street police headquarters, and then took her to the equally modest restaurant across the street for lunch.

'An' what happens to me now?' Nancy asked, after she had wolfed down her food.

'That's up to you,' Blackstone told her. 'As I told you before, you can't go back to the van Horne mansion, but I'm sure Mr Boone can find you a position in another house, if that's what you want.'

Nancy smiled. 'He's a nice man, that Mr Boone,' she said. 'A good, kind, helpful man. And so are you.'

'Could we talk about Jenny, now?' Blackstone asked.

Nancy nodded. 'Yes. What do you want to know?'

'Tell me about when you first began to suspect that something was wrong,' Blackstone suggested.

'It's hard to put a finger on it,' Nancy told him. 'A couple of months after she'd left the orphanage to work for the O'Briens, Jenny began to talk about a boyfriend. But she did it in a shy, teasing way – like she was proud of it, but worried about it all at the same time, if you know what I mean.'

'I know what you mean.'

'To be honest, I thought she was making him up at first. Some girls do that. But when she kept on about him, I started to believe he was real. And that's when she told me he wasn't a boy at all – he was a man.'

'Inspector O'Brien?'

'Yes.'

'And that's why you would never go to the O'Briens' house yourself? Because you knew what he was doing to her?'

'If I'd seen him in the flesh, I wouldn't have been able to stop myself scratching his eyes out.'

Blackstone laughed. 'I believe you'd have done just that,' he said admiringly. 'What advice did you give her?' he continued, more seriously.

'I told her to tell her mistress, Mrs O'Brien, that the master was interfering with her.'

'But she wouldn't do that?'

'No. She said that they were in love, and that soon they were going to run away together.'

'But you didn't believe that?'

'Of course I didn't believe it. I knew *exactly* what was going to happen to her.'

'And what was that?'

'Jenny was thirteen when she got the job with the O'Briens. The maid she took over from was sixteen, but she'd been working for the O'Briens since *she* was thirteen. I asked Jenny to see if she could find out about the maid *before* the one she replaced, and it turned out that she joined the household at thirteen and left at sixteen, as well. Do you see what I'm getting at?'

Blackstone nodded. 'When they reached a certain age, he no longer wanted them.'

'And that's just what would have happened to Jenny, too. I *told her* it was going to happen – but she didn't believe me. But it *did* happen, didn't it? Just like I knew it would. That's why I wasn't surprised when you told me that she'd killed herself.'

'When was the last time you saw her?' Blackstone asked softly.

'It was about a month ago, just before I ran away with that bastard Eddie Toscanini.'

'Why didn't you contact her after that?'

A single tear ran down Nancy's cheek and spattered on the table cloth. 'Eddie wouldn't let me,' she said.

'I see.'

Nancy shook her head, violently. 'I'm lying to you,' she said. 'And I'm lying to myself as well. If I'd really wanted to get in touch with her, I'd have found a way, whatever Eddie said.'

'But you didn't want to?'

'No.'

'Why not?'

'Eddie had promised me a grand life if I'd run away with him, but it didn't take me long to realize I'd made a big mistake.'

'No,' Blackstone agreed. 'I imagine it didn't.'

'And that's why I couldn't face Jenny, you see. I'd been a big sister to her. I'd tried to guide her. And then I'd gone and done something stupid like that myself. I was just so *ashamed*.'

She was a good kid, Blackstone thought tenderly. Better than that – she was a *lovely* kid.

'I'll be going back home to England soon,' he said. 'But I want you to write to me. You can write, can't you?

'Yes. They taught us to in the orphanage.'

'And when you write to me, I want you to tell me all about how you're getting on.'

'I'd like to do that,' Nancy said.

'And if you ever need anything, you've only got to tell me, and I'll do whatever I can to help.'

'You'd . . . you'd do that for me?'

'Yes, I would,' Blackstone said.

And also for Jenny, who would have wanted to see you happy after she'd gone, he thought.

There was one more thing he needed to say, and though he dreaded saying it, he knew there was no choice, because Nancy had the *right* to know.

'I'm going to tell you something that will shock you,' he said to the girl. 'Are you ready for it?'

Nancy swallowed, and then nodded her head. 'I'm ready.'

'When Jenny died, she was three months pregnant.'

'Oh God,' Nancy moaned. 'Is *that* why she killed herself?'

'No, that wasn't the reason at all,' Blackstone told her. 'She killed herself because she believed she'd betrayed her master.'

TWENTY-SIX

It was a late New York City afternoon, and the sun was beaming benevolently into the reception room of the O'Briens' modest apartment, where three people – Meade, Blackstone and Mary O'Brien herself – were taking afternoon tea.

It was a thoroughly pleasant – thoroughly civilized – event, and Mary insisted that Blackstone try one of the buttered scones that she had baked especially in his honour.

'I know how you English people like them,' Mary said.

'We *do* like them,' Blackstone agreed. 'We do more than that. We *crave* them.'

'And you simply can't buy them in any shop in New York. I know – because I've tried to.'

Blackstone tasted the scone, conscious of the other two watching him, waiting for his reaction.

'It's delicious,' he pronounced.

And so it was.

There was other confectionery on offer, too: dainty cakes and chocolate eclairs stuffed with cream.

'They're lethal for anyone who's watching their weight, but I just can't resist them,' Mary said. She sighed wistfully. 'But I suppose I shall have to *learn* to resist them in the future, because they'll be well beyond my budget.' A smile drove the wistful expression from her face. 'But I don't have any right to complain,' she continued. 'I have my children and I have my memories, and that's more than many women can say.'

'Yes, it is,' Blackstone agreed. 'Just think of poor Jenny, for example.'

Mary gave him a slightly odd expression – one which suggested that she considered the remark to be highly inappropriate, but was too much of a lady to actually say so.

'I know this is a painful subject for you,' said Meade, showing more sensitivity than his English colleague had done, 'but I've been informed that Jenny's body is now ready to be released for burial.'

'Thank you, Alex,' Mary said gratefully. 'I've spoken to her pastor, and most of the arrangements have already been made.'

'But I'm afraid I also have an apology to make,' Meade continued, sounding slightly uncomfortable.

'An apology?' Mary repeated.

'Yes. You said that the thought of Jenny being cut up – after all she'd been through – was painful to you. And you asked me – through Sam – to try and prevent the morgue from conducting a post-mortem.'

'Yes?'

'And I'm sorry, but by the time Sam told me of your wishes, it was already too late.'

'So there *was* a post-mortem?'

'Yes.'

Blackstone began to count silently to himself. One . . . two . . . three . . . four . . . five . . .

He had reached twenty when Mary O'Brien finally said, 'Have you read the post-mortem report yourself, Alex?'

'Yes,' Meade told her. 'And so has Sam.'

Blackstone started to count again, but this time he had only reached four when Mary said, 'So you both know that she was pregnant?'

'We're assuming that your husband was the father of the child,' Meade said. 'Is that right?'

Mary sighed again. 'My husband was a great man,' she said, 'and like so many great men, he had his tragic flaw. With Shakespeare's Othello it was jealousy, with Macbeth it was ambition—'

'And with your husband it was a fondness for little girls,' Blackstone interrupted.

Mary O'Brien shot him a look of sudden loathing.

'Not *girls*,' she said. 'Just *one* girl – and a girl who was *young* rather than *little*. In many ways, Jenny was old beyond her years, so much so that I believe it was *she* who initiated the relationship, and not Patrick.'

Blackstone felt an anger rising in the pit of his stomach. 'So you're blaming the child, rather than the man, are you?'

'And once he realized what a terrible mistake he'd made, Patrick did his best to put the situation right,' Mary continued, ignoring the comment. 'He could have kicked her out on the street, claiming someone else had gotten her pregnant, which is what men who've found themselves in his position have done from time immemorial. He could have taken her to an old crone with a knitting needle, who would probably have killed her. But he didn't do either of those things. Instead, he sought out the best medical care that was available in New York City.'

'You make him sound like a hero,' Blackstone said.

'He *was* a hero,' Mary responded sharply.

'So you knew, all along, that Patrick was looking for an abortionist?' Meade asked.

'I knew that he was looking for the most qualified person to carry out the medical procedure, yes,' Mary said, with a slight edge of disappointment in her voice at Meade's new-found crassness. 'When Patrick realized that Jenny was pregnant, he told me immediately. He confessed to me!'

'What a handy thing confession really is for you Catholics,' Blackstone said. 'Do something wrong, confess and say you're sorry, and it's all over. Of course, Jenny didn't go to confession, and neither did any of the girls who preceded her, because you got them from a *Protestant* orphanage.' He paused, as if he had just received a revelation.

'Do you think that's why your husband chose a Protestant orphanage over a Catholic one, Mrs O'Brien? Because there was no confession?'

'You have insulted my faith and you have insulted my husband, who – despite his weakness – was a good man,' Mary said angrily. 'And now I must ask you to leave.'

'She's right,' Meade said to Blackstone. 'You've insulted both Catholicism and Inspector O'Brien. And I think you should apologize.'

'I'm sorry,' Blackstone said contritely. 'I expressed myself very poorly – very insensitively.'

'Indeed you did,' Mary agreed, not even looking at him.

'I think we'd *both* better leave,' Meade said.

'Yes, I think that would be for the best,' Mary concurred.

Alex Meade stood up. 'But before we go, I must help you to clear away the tea things.'

'That won't be necessary,' Mary told him.

'Nonsense!' Alex Meade protested. 'You must be tired out, now that you no longer have a maid, and the least I can do is help you clean up the mess that *we're* responsible for.'

He brushed the crumbs from all the plates on to a single one, then stacked all the plates on the tray. That done, he collected up all the cups and saucers and lined them neatly along the other side of the tray.

'Would you like to show me where the kitchen is?' he asked, lifting the tray clear of the table.

'Really, Alex . . .'

'I've picked it all up now. I might as well carry it through to the kitchen.'

Mary sighed softly. 'It's this way,' she said.

Blackstone watched the two of them leave the room. Alex Meade's style was very different to his own, he thought, but the young man was shaping up into being a fine detective – and in a few years he would be quite formidable.

Mary and Meade returned to the reception room. The expression on Meade's face suggested he had quite forgotten the recent unpleasantness – and the expression on Mary's clearly indicating that she hadn't.

'So Patrick confessed to you about what he'd done,' Meade said, as if he were merely carrying on the earlier conversation.

'Yes, he did,' Mary replied. 'And I forgave him.'

'Just as I'm sure you've forgiven Sam for his stupid comments earlier,' Meade suggested.

There was a slight pause, then Mary said, 'Of course.'

'Is there any of that whiskey left?' Meade asked.

'Whiskey?'

'The whiskey that we used to drink a toast to Jenny. If memory serves me well, there was quite a lot still in the bottle when we'd finished.'

'Well, I certainly haven't touched it since then,' Mary said, sounding slightly sulky.

'Then why don't the three of us – three friends – drink a final toast to Patrick, who, for all his failings, was still a great man?' Meade said.

Mary walked over to the sideboard without a word. She poured three glasses of whiskey, and handed two of them – one for himself and one for Blackstone – to the sergeant.

Meade passed Blackstone his glass, and then took a sip of his own.

'Wonderful,' he pronounced, smacking his lips. 'Just the thing for a man with a hangover.' He paused for a moment to let the whiskey work its magic, then continued. 'Since you knew that Jenny was pregnant, Mary, did you also know that Patrick went to Senator Plunkitt for advice?'

'Yes,' Mary said. 'I thought that was a mistake from the start, and the moment Patrick began talking to Plunkitt, he realized for himself that I was right.'

'And you knew about Dr Muller?'

'Of course.'

'One thing that's been puzzling me is how his killer knew where to find your husband,' Blackstone said.

'Alex!' Mary said, looking warningly at Meade.

'It seems like a perfectly reasonable question to me,' Meade said. 'I can't see why anybody would object to Sam asking it.'

'You see, he'd probably never been to the Bayern Biergarten before in his entire life,' Blackstone continued. 'According to the witnesses we spoke to, he certainly acted as if the place was unfamiliar territory to him. And the *only* reason he went to it on the night he died was because he'd agreed to meet Dr Muller there. So I repeat, how did the killer know he would find him there?'

'The man could have followed him,' Mary said, her hostility to Blackstone reaching new heights.

'That's true, he could,' Blackstone agreed. 'But if he had done that, he would surely have had countless opportunities to shoot the inspector *before* he went inside. So why prolong things? Why not just get it over with?'

'I don't know,' Mary said.

'I'm more inclined to the theory that the killer *knew* he would be there, and waited in ambush for him to come out,' Blackstone continued. 'But who *did know* about the meeting? Well, there were only two people – your husband himself and the abortionist.'

'You must put a stop to this now, Alex,' Mary appealed to Meade. 'You must stop it, if not out of respect for me, then at least out of respect for my husband, to whom you owe so much.'

'You're forgetting the mistress, Sam,' Meade told Blackstone.

'Ah, yes, the mistress,' Blackstone agreed. 'When she went to see Dr Muller, to tell her that the abortion was no longer necessary, she must also have asked the doctor where she had been intending to meet Inspector O'Brien. But I have two problems with this whole "mistress" story.'

'Please, Alex!' Mary said.

'And what problems are those?' Meade asked.

'The first is that the "mistress" said she'd miscarried. But it wasn't the "mistress" who was pregnant at all.'

'No, it wasn't,' Meade agreed. 'It was Jenny!'

'And the second problem is that O'Brien didn't *like* women – his penchant was for young girls. So was there *ever* a woman in her twenties who went to see Dr Muller? Or was there, instead, a trained actress in her thirties, *pretending* to be a woman in her twenties?'

'Just what are you suggesting?' Mary demanded.

'And then there was the killer,' Blackstone continued. 'The witness we talked to said he was a boy of fourteen or fifteen, judging by his size. But say he wasn't a boy at all – say he was, in fact, a *woman*.'

'Are you accusing me of killing my own husband?' Mary asked.

'It would have been wiser to wait until after the abortion had been carried out before killing him,' Blackstone said. 'But you couldn't wait, could you? Your rage simply wouldn't let you.'

Mary laughed. 'This is ludicrous,' she said. 'Why should I have been in a rage with my husband?'

'We'd like you to confess now,' Meade said quietly. 'It will make things much easier all round.'

'I won't confess to something I didn't do,' Mary said. 'You can arrest me, if you like. You can even put me on trial –' her eyes blazed with anger and defiance – 'but I'll have the jury eating out of my hand before the trial's half over, and they'll *never* convict me.'

'That's probably true,' Meade agreed. 'That's why I said we need you to confess.'

'Why should I?' Mary asked.

'Because you're a mother,' Blackstone told her. 'Because it's your job to protect your brood. And you take that job seriously – or we wouldn't even be here now.'

'What in God's name are you talking about?'

'However much you might like to pretend that Jenny was your husband's first young girl, we all know she wasn't,' Blackstone said. 'There have been a succession of maids who have found their way into his bed, and, if necessary, we'll track them all down. I suspect you knew what was going on almost from the start, and that you were prepared to tolerate it, because you loved and admired your husband – and you wanted to keep him. And, when all's said and done, what did it matter if a few low-class girls – a few orphans – were made to suffer, as long as he stayed with you?'

'So I loved him so much that I was prepared to stand by while he did disgusting things to young girls?' Mary asked.

'Yes,' Blackstone agreed.

'But despite my love for him, I gunned him down as if he were no more than a mad dog?'

'By that stage, you'd decided that he *deserved* to be gunned down as if he were no more than a mad dog.'

'You're hateful!' Mary said. 'You're hateful and spiteful and mean, and I hope you burn in hell for all eternity.'

'If I do, I won't burn alone,' Blackstone countered. 'But to return to your husband – the problem was that when they reached a certain age, the girls ceased to be attractive to him, and they had to go. And even if she hadn't got pregnant, Jenny was reaching that age, wasn't she?'

'Enough!' Mary said.

'Are you prepared to confess now?' Blackstone asked.

'Of course not!'

'Then it's nowhere near enough. Do you know what Jenny said to me as she lay dying?'

Mary O'Brien clasped her hands over her ears. 'No, and I don't *want* to know.'

'She said, "He's dead because of me. He's dead because I betrayed him." I didn't understand that at all. *How* had she betrayed him? I wondered. By revealing some guilty secret, perhaps? And then there were other questions. *Why* had she betrayed him? And who had she betrayed him *to*? We know the answers to all those questions now, don't we?'

'I'm not listening!' Mary screamed.

But she was. She couldn't help herself.

'Jenny betrayed him to *you*, didn't she? And she did it because of jealousy – because he was moving on from her to his new love.'

'Please!' Mary O'Brien begged.

'I watched your children at his funeral,' Blackstone ploughed on relentlessly. 'Your son behaved with great dignity. Your younger daughter was in a daze, and hardly knew where she was. But your eldest daughter, Isobel – *who is just thirteen* – couldn't even look down at the coffin.'

'If there's a trial, we'll have to put Isobel on the witness stand,' Meade said, 'If there's a trial, she'll have to tell the whole world what her father did to her – and that will damage her even more than she's already been damaged. That's why you have to confess.'

Mary lowered her hands and bowed her head, defeated.

'Yes,' she agreed, in a flat, lifeless voice. 'That *is* why I have to confess.'

TWENTY-SEVEN

There was no sign of any paperwork on Captain O'Shaugnessy's desk, but then, Blackstone remembered, O'Shaugnessy had not got where he was by filling in forms but by wielding his nightstick. Besides, paperwork

would only have prevented the desk from fulfilling its proper
function.

It was fulfilling that function now. O'Shaugnessy had his
feet planted firmly in the middle of the desk and his hands
locked behind his head. Add to that general demeanour the
amused eyes and slightly sadistic curl of the mouth, and all-
in-all the captain had the appearance of a man who had been
looking forward to this meeting, and was determined to extract
the maximum amount of pleasure out of it.

'Take a seat, Inspector Blackstone,' he said jovially. 'Would
you like a cigar? 'Cos if you do, they're right there on the
corner of the desk.'

Blackstone sat – but ignored the cigars.

'Well, ain't you a hero?' O'Shaugnessy said. 'Only in New
York for a few days, and you've already gone an' caught yourself a murderer.'

'It was Sergeant Meade's case,' Blackstone said. 'I was no
more than his assistant.'

But he was thinking, why did O'Shaugnessy ask to see me?
And why is he looking so pleased with himself?

'Course, havin' set your heart on the killer bein' either a
dirty cop or a high muckety-muck politician, it must have
been a disappointment to you that it turned out to be St
Patrick's widow,' the captain said.

'It's never a disappointment to catch the *real* criminal. You
should try it yourself sometime,' Blackstone replied.

'Maybe I will at that,' O'Shaugnessy agreed, his good
humour unabated. He unclasped his hands, reached for one
his cigars, and lit it. 'I hate to rain on your parade,' he
continued, blowing smoke out of his mouth, 'but I'm afraid
to say I've got some bad news for you.'

He didn't look *afraid* to say it at all, Blackstone thought.
In fact, he looked positively delighted at the prospect.

'What kind of bad news?' the inspector asked.

'You remember that prisoner you came over here for? Now,
what the hell was his name?'

'James Duffy.'

'That's right, James Duffy. Well, Inspector, it would appear
that he's escaped.'

'How in God's name did that happen?'

'He was bein' transferred from Mulberry Street to my precinct, an' he seems to have gone missin' along the way.' O'Shaugnessy smiled. 'Which, when you think about it, is all your fault.'

'All *my* fault!' Blackstone exploded.

'Well, not *all* your fault – your little friend Sergeant Alex Meade's gotta take some of the blame as well.'

'How could it possibly be *our* fault?' Blackstone wondered.

'Ain't it obvious,' O'Shaugnessy said. 'Duffy was safe as houses in Mulberry Street. It was only when he was bein' moved he got the chance to escape.'

'But we had nothing to do with him being moved.'

'See, that's where you're wrong. Remember that poster – the one with Inspector O'Brien's face on it – that you had plastered all over the Lower East Side?'

'Yes?'

'Well, that brought a crowd of bums floodin' into Mulberry Street, didn't it? An' where did the desk sergeant put 'em?'

'In the cells,' Blackstone said, with a sinking feeling.

'In the cells,' O'Shaugnessy agreed. 'Which was the only place he *could* put 'em. Which meant that Duffy had to be moved someplace else. Which gave him his opportunity to run. So if you'd never put them posters up, Duffy would still be in custody. That's the simple truth, an' that's what I said in my *long* telegram to your boss in Scotland Yard.'

'Did he *really* escape?' Blackstone asked.

O'Shaugnessy made a great show of looking around him. 'Well, he sure ain't here.'

'When I spoke to Duffy, he offered me a large bribe to pretend he wasn't the man I was looking for,' Blackstone said. '*I* didn't take it. Did *you*?'

'Well, see here, I had this accountin' problem,' O'Shaugnessy said. 'An' the reason I had the problem was 'cos of what you talked me into doin' to that nice Mrs de Courcey. Remember you said that it would be good for discipline to starve her out for a few days?'

'Yes?'

'Turns out you were wrong. Didn't work out that way *at all*. From what I've heard, there's some gentlemen that go to *her* for discipline, an' she's quite happy to administer it, if the money's right. But she ain't too keen on bein' on the receivin' end herself.'

'Get to the point!' Blackstone said.

But O'Shaugnessy was enjoying himself too much to rush things.

'So she started to think about how she could get back at me, an' she come with a jim-dandy of an idea. See, when you've been in the game as long as she has, you've had half the politicians in this city ruttin' away between your legs. An' she decided to give a few of them politicians a call, and ask if they'd do her a little favour for old times' sake.'

'And that favour she wanted was for them to serve her your head on a platter?' Blackstone asked.

'More like my balls on a platter,' O'Shaugnessy said. 'So I went to see the lady, an' asked if there was anythin' I could do to make it up to her. An' sure enough, there was. She said that if I didn't ask her for any money for a whole year, we'd go back to bein' the same good friends we'd always been.'

'And you said yes?'

'Didn't see I had any choice in the matter. But see, that left me with what the bookkeepers call an imbalance in my accounts. An' I got expenses to meet every month, same as everybody else.'

'So Duffy seemed like manna from heaven,' Blackstone said. 'But he didn't escape en route to this precinct, did he? You let him go once he was in your custody – and after you'd seen the colour of his money.'

'The records show he escaped on the way here, so that must be what happened,' O'Shaugnessy said, not even trying to sound convincing. 'Cheer up, Inspector,' he continued. 'It's only like he's out on bail.'

'Is that right?'

'Sure. Guys like Duffy are too stupid to put themselves out of harm's way for long. He'll stay in the city, an' sooner or later we'll pick him up again. An' next time, he *won't* escape.'

'No?'

'No! Because to escape, he'll need money – and as of today, the man's flat broke.'

Blackstone had suddenly had enough of the New York Police Department in general, and of Captain O'Shaugnessy in particular.

'Oh, to hell with you,' he said, standing up. 'And to hell

with Duffy, as well. Re-capture him or *don't* recapture him.
It's not my problem.'
   'Ain't it?'
   'No, it isn't – because in a few days I'll be back in England.'
   'Is that right?' O'Shaugnessy asked. 'Remember I cabled
your boss to tell him how Duffy escaped?'
   'Or rather, how Duffy was *supposed* to have escaped,'
Blackstone corrected him.
   'Exactly. Well, this Sir Todd guy sent two cables back, one
for me, an' one for you. An' this is yours.'
   O'Shaugnessy took a telegram envelope out of his jacket
pocket and handed it to Blackstone.
   'You've opened it,' Blackstone said.
   'Sure,' O'Shaugnessy agreed easily. 'See, I wanted to know
if I was right in my suspicions about what he was gonna say.
An' guess what – I was spot on the money.' He paused. 'You
gonna read it now?'
   'Why should you care *when* I read it, if you already know
what it says?' Blackstone asked.
   'I just want to see the look on your face when you *do* read
it,' O'Shaugnessy said.
   Well, why not? Blackstone asked himself.
   And then he took the telegram out of the envelope, read it,
and realized why O'Shaugnessy had been so amused.

   +++Completely+incompetent+as+usual+stop+Do+not+d
   are+return+England+without+prisoner+stop+Todd+
   stop+++

It could be weeks before they catch Duffy again,' Blackstone
said morosely, after taking a deep swig of the beer that
Meade had just bought him. 'Bloody hell, it could be
months!'
   'Cheer up, Sam, it ain't that bad,' Alex Meade replied. 'The
commissioner's agreed to pay your wages for as long as you're
here on American soil – and being here a while longer will
give you a chance to see New York.'
   'I've *already* seen New York,' Blackstone told him.
   'You've seen the Lower East Side, Central Park and Fifth
Avenue,' Meade pointed out.
   'That's what I said.'

'Why, that's only scratching the surface of a place like New York City. What about the wonders of Chinatown and Harlem?'

'*What* about them?'

'And have you ever met even a *single* Dodger?' Meade asked. 'I don't think so!'

'A Dodger?' Blackstone repeated.

'It's what we've been calling the folks from Brooklyn ever since all their streetcars went electric.'

'Go on,' Blackstone said, knowing he shouldn't.

'A horsecar can go at maybe six miles an hour, but an electric car can reach up to *thirty* miles an hour. Problem is, you see, that though the electric cars have got the weight and power of a locomotive, they've still got the *braking system* of the old horsecar.'

'So they find it hard to stop in an emergency?'

'They find it *impossible* to stop in an emergency. In 1895 there were a hundred and five people killed and four hundred and seven maimed in streetcar accidents. And that's when the folks across the river started to wise up. That's when they got to develop the habit of always keeping one eye open for approaching streetcars, so they could jump out of the way if they had to. And that's when we got to calling them—'

'Brooklyn Dodgers,' Blackstone interrupted. 'Have you got any more fascinating stories about New York City, Alex?'

Alex Meade grinned. 'Well, yes, Sam, now you mention it, I think I must have hundreds of them.'

Blackstone nodded gravely. 'That's what I was afraid of,' he said.